"A MARVELOUS TALE."
*Los Angeles Times*

"TV's Colombo would have had some pretty stiff competition from this wily detective if he had lived in the Middle Ages. . . .Peters mixes powerful emotions and murder to produce a mystery equal to Agatha Christie's best and just as difficult for the reader to solve. Her characters have a liveliness that makes her readers care what happens to them. . . .a fine murder mystery in an unusual setting."
*Sacramento Bee*

"THE PLOT IS TAUT AND SUSPENSEFUL, AND THE SCENERY SIMPLY MARVELOUS . . . .Ellis Peters possesses a highly polished style and one can easily become lost midst the freshness and beauty of her strongly descriptive writing. . . .a pleasurable story."
*Best Sellers*

# THE SANCTUARY SPARROW

*The Seventh Chronicle of Brother Cadfael*

Ellis Peters

FAWCETT CREST • NEW YORK

A Fawcett Crest Book
Published by Ballantine Books

Library of Congress Catalog Card Number: 83-5389

ISBN 0-449-20613-0

This edition published by arrangement with William Morrow and Company, Inc.

Manufactured in the United States of America

First Ballantine Books Edition: December 1984
Second Printing: March 1985

# One

IT BEGAN, AS THE GREATEST OF STORMS DO BEGIN, AS A mere tremor in the air, a thread of sound so distant and faint, yet so ominous, that the ear that was sharp enough to catch it instantly pricked and shut out present sounds to strain after it again, and interpret the warning. Brother Cadfael had a hare's hearing, readily alerted and sharply focused. He caught the quiver and bay, at this point surely still on the far side of the bridge that crossed Severn from the town, and stiffened into responsive stillness, braced to listen.

It could have been an innocent sound enough, or if not innocent of murderous intent, at any rate natural, the distant voices of hunting owls, and the predatory bark of a dog-fox prowling his nocturnal barony. Certainly the ferocious note of the hunt sounded clearly in it to Cadfael's ear. And even Brother Anselm the precentor, wholly absorbed into his chanting of the office, wavered and slipped off-key for an instant, and took up the cadence jealously, composing his mind sternly to duty.

For there could not be anything in it to trouble the midnight rite of Matins, here in this kindly spring, barely four

1

weeks past Easter of the year of Our Lord 1140, with Shrewsbury and all this region secure within the king's peace, whatever contentions raged farther south between king and empress, cousins at odds for the throne. The winter had been hard indeed, but was blessedly over, the sun had shone on Easter Day, and continued shining ever since, with only light, scattered showers to confirm the blessing. Only westward in Wales had there been heavy spring rains, swelling the river level. The season promised well, the town enjoyed fair rule under a dour but just sheriff, and defended stoutly by a sensible provost and council. In a time of civil war, Shrewsbury and its shire had good cause to thank God and King Stephen for relative order. Not here, surely, should the conventual peace of Matins fear any disruption. And yet Brother Anselm, for one instant, had faltered.

In the dim space of the choir, partially shut off from the nave of the church by the parish altar and lit only by the constant lamp and the candles on the high altar, the brothers in their stalls showed like carven copies, in this twilight without age or youth, comeliness or homeliness, so many matched shadows. The height of the vault, the solid stone of the pillars and walls, took up the sound of Brother Anselm's voice, and made of it a disembodied magic, high in air. Beyond where the candle-light reached and shadows ended, there was darkness, the night within, the night without. A benign night, mild, still and silent.

Not quite silent. The tremor on the air became a faint, persistent murmur. In the dimness under the rood loft, to the right of the entrance to the choir, Abbot Radulfus stirred in his stall. To the left, Prior Robert's habit rustled briefly, with an effect of displeasure and reproof rather than uneasiness. The merest ripple of disquiet shivered along the ranks of the brothers, and again subsided.

But the sound was drawing nearer. Even before it grew so loud as to compel notice there was no mistaking the anger in it, the menace and the dangerous excitement, all the marks of the hunt. It sounded as if the pursuit had reached the point where the van chasseours had run the quarry to exhaustion, and the parfytours were closing in for the kill. Even at this distance it was clear that some creature's life was in peril.

The sound drew nearer now very rapidly, hard to ignore, though the precentor continued valiantly leading his flock in the office, and raised his voice and quickened his tempo to ride over the challenge. The younger brothers and novices were shifting uneasily, even whispering, half stimulated, half affrighted. The murmur had become a ferocious, muted howl, as if gigantic bees were in swarm after an intruder. Even abbot and prior had leaned forward ready to rise from their stalls, and were exchanging questioning looks in the dimness.

With obstinate devotion Brother Anselm lifted the first phrase of Lauds. He got no farther. At the west end of the church the unlatched leaf of the great parish door was suddenly hurled open to crash against the wall, and something unseen came hurtling and scrabbling and gasping down the length of the nave, reeling and fumbling and fending itself off from wall and pillar, heaving at breath as though run to death already.

They were on their feet, every man. The younger ones broke out in frightened exclamation and wonder, nudging and wavering in doubt what to do. Abbot Radulfus in his own domain was hampered by no such hesitation. He moved with speed and force, plucked a candle from the nearest sconce, and went striding out round the parish altar in great, loping strides that sent his gown billowing out behind him. After him went Prior Robert, more tender of his dignity, and therefore slower to reach the scene of need, and after Robert all the brothers in jostling agitation. Before they reached the nave they were met by a great, exultant bellow of triumph, and a rushing and scrambling of dozens of frenzied bodies, as the hunt burst in at the west door after its prey.

Brother Cadfael, once well accustomed to night alarms by land and by sea, had surged out of his stall as soon as the abbot moved, but took time to grasp a double candelabrum to light his way. Prior Robert in full sail was already blocking the right-hand way round the parish altar, too patrician to make enough haste to ruffle his silvery beauty. Cadfael doubled round to the left and emerged into the nave before him, with his light thrust out ahead, as much weapon as illumination.

The hounds were streaming in by then, a quarter of the town, and not the best quarter, though not necessarily the worst either; decent craftsmen, merchants, traders, jostled with the riff-raff always ready for any brawl, and all of them beyond themselves either with drink or excitement or both together, howling for blood. And blood there was, slippery on the tiles of the floor. On the three steps to the parish altar lay sprawled some poor wretch flattened beneath a surge of trampling, battering foes, all hacking away with fist and boot, happily in such a tangle that comparatively few of their kicks and blows got home. All Cadfael could see of the quarry was a thin arm and a fist hardly bigger than a child's, that reached out of the chaos to grip the edge of the altarcloth with life-and-death desperation.

Abbot Radulfus, all the long, lean, muscular length of him, with his gaunt, authoritative lantern head blazing atop, sailed round the altar, smoky candle in hand, slashed the skirts of his habit like a whip across the stooping beast-faces of the foremost attackers, and with a long bony leg bestrode the fallen creature that clawed at the fringes of the altar.

'Rabble, stand off! Blasphemers, quit this holy place, and be ashamed. Back, before I blast your souls eternally!'

He had no need to raise his voice to a shout, he had only to unsheathe it like a knife, and it sliced through the babble as through cheese. They recoiled as though his nearness seared, but they did not go far, only out of range of the burning. They hopped and hovered and clamoured, indignant, aggrieved, but wary of tempting Heaven. They drew off from a miserable fragment of a man, flat on his face up the altar steps, soiled and crumpled and bloodied, and no bigger than a boy fifteen years old. In the brief, daunted silence before they screamed their charge against him, every soul present could hear how his breath heaved and laboured and clapped in his ribs, toiling for dear life, threatening to break his meagre frame apart. Flaxen hair dabbled with dust and blood spilled against the fringes of the altar-cloth he gripped so frantically. Skinny arms and legs hugged the stone as if his life depended upon the contact. If he could speak, or lift his head, he had too much sense left in him to venture the attempt.

'How dare you so affront the house of God?' demanded the abbot, darkly smouldering. He had not missed the steely flash of reflected light in the hand of one squat fellow who was sliding roundabout to get at his victim privily. 'Put up that knife or court your soul's damnation!'

The hunters recovered breath and rage together. A dozen at least gave tongue, crying their own justification and the hunted man's offences, so variously that barely a word conveyed any meaning. Radulfus brandished a daunting arm, and their clamour subsided into muttering. Cadfael, observing that the armed man had done no more than slide his weapon out of sight, took his stand firmly between, and advanced his candles with a flourish in the direction of a fine bushy beard.

'Speak one, if you have anything of worth to say,' ordered the abbot. 'The rest be silent. You, young man, you would seem to put yourself forward . . .'

The young man who had taken a pace ahead of his supporters, and whose prior right they seemed to acknowledge, stood forth flushed and important, an unexpected figure enough to be out man-hunting at midnight. He was tall and well-made and assured of manner, a little too well aware of a handsome face, and he was very elegant in festival finery, even if his best cotte was now somewhat crumpled and disordered from the turmoil of pursuit, and his countenance red and slack from the effects of a good deal of wine drunk. Without that induced courage, he would not have faced the lord abbot with quite so much impudence.

'My lord, I will speak for all, I have the right. We mean no disrespect to the abbey or your lordship, but we want that man for murder and robbery done tonight. I accuse him! All

5

here will bear me out. He has struck down my father and plundered his strong-box, and we are come to take him. So if your lordship will allow, we'll rid you of him.'

So they would, never a doubt of it. Radulfus kept his place, the brothers crowding close to complete the barrier.

'I had thought to hear you make some amend,' said the abbot sharply, 'for this intrusion. Whatever this fellow may or may not have done, it is not he who has shed blood and drawn steel here within the church on the very steps of the altar. Violence he may have done elsewhere, but here none, he does but suffer it. The crime of sacrilege is yours, all of you here breaking our peace. You had best be considering on the health of your own souls. And if you have a lawful complaint against this person, where is the law? I see no sergeant here among you. I see no provost, who could at least make a case for the town. I see a rabble, as far at fault in law as robber and murderer can be. Now get hence, and pray that your offence may be pardoned. Whatever charges you have to make, take them to the law.'

Some among them were drawing back stealthily by then, sobering and thinking better of their invasion, and only too anxious to sneak away to their homes and beds. But the vagabonds, always ready for mischief, stood their ground with sullen, sly faces, and had no intention of going far, and the more respectable, if they abated their noisy ardour, kept their bitter indignation. Cadfael knew most of them. Perhaps Radulfus himself, though no Shrewsbury man by birth, was better-read in them than they supposed. He kept his place, and bent his steady, menacing brow against them, forbidding action.

'My lord abbot,' ventured the fine young man, 'if you will let us take him hence we will deliver him up to the law.'

To the nearest tree, thought Cadfael. And there were trees in plenty between here and the river. He snipped at the wicks of his candles and let them flare afresh. The beard was still hovering in the shadows.

'That I cannot do,' said the abbot crisply. 'If the law itself were here, there is no power can now take away this man from the sanctuary he has sought. You should know the right of it as well as I, and the peril, body and soul, to any who dares to breach that sanctuary. Go, take the pollution of your violence out of this holy place. We have duties here which your presence in hatred defiles. Go! Out!'

'But my lord,' bleated the angry young man, tossing his curled head but keeping his distance, 'you have not heard us as to the crime . . .'

'I will hear you,' said Radulfus with a snap, 'by daylight, when you come with sheriff or sergeant to discuss this matter calmly, and in proper form. But I warn you, this man has claimed sanctuary, and the rights of sanctuary are his, according to custom, and neither you nor any other shall force him away out of these walls until the time of his respite is over.'

'And I warn you, my lord,' flared the youth, blazing red, 'that should he venture a step outside, we shall be waiting for him, and what falls out of your lordship's lordship will be no concern of yours, or the church's.' Yes, unquestionably he was moderately drunk, or he would never have gone so far, an ordinary young burgess of the town, if a wealthy one. Even with an evening's wine in him, he blenched at his own daring, and shuffled back a pace or two.

'Or God's?' said the abbot coldly. 'Go hence in peace, before his bolt strike you.'

They went, shadows edging backwards into shadow, through the open west door and out into the night, but always with their faces turned towards the miserable bundle prostrate clutching the altar-cloth. Mob madness is not so easily subdued, and even if their grievance proved less than justified, it was real enough to them. Murder and robbery were mortal crimes. No, they would not all go away. They would set a watch on the parish door and the gatehouse, with a rope ready.

'Brother Prior,' said Radulfus, running an eye over his shaken flock, 'and Brother Precentor, will you again begin Lauds? Let the office proceed, and the brothers return to their beds according to the order. The affairs of men require our attention, but the affairs of God may not be subordinated.' He looked down at the motionless fugitive, too tensely still not to be aware of everything that passed above him, and again looked up to catch Brother Cadfael's concerned and thoughtful eye. 'We two, I think, are enough to take what confession this guest of ours wills to make, and tend his needs. They are gone,' said the abbot dispassionately to the prone figure at his feet. 'You may get up.'

The thin body stirred uneasily, keeping one hand firmly on the fringe of the altar-cloth. He moved as if every flinching movement hurt, as well it might, but it seemed that he had at least escaped broken bones, for he used his free arm to help him up to his knees on the steps, and raised to the light a gaunt, bruised face smeared with blood and sweat and the slime of a running nose. Before their eyes he seemed to dwindle both in years and size. They might have been gazing at some unlucky urchin of the Foregate who had been set upon by a dozen or more of his capricious fellows for some trivial offence, and left howling in a ditch, but for the desperation of fear that emanated from him, and the memory of the pack that had been beaten off from his heels just in time.

A poor little wretch enough to be credited with murder and robbery. On his feet he might perhaps be about as tall as Cadfael, who was below the middle height, but widthways Cadfael would have made three of him. His cotte and hose were ragged and threadbare, and had several new rents in them now from clawing hands and trampling feet, besides the dust and stains of long use, but originally they had been brightly-coloured in crude red and blue. He had a decent width of shoulder, better feeding might have made a well-proportioned man of him, but as he moved stiffly to look up at them he seemed all gangling limbs, large of elbow and knee, and very low in flesh to cover them. Seventeen or eighteen years old, Cadfael guessed. The eyes raised to them in such desolate entreaty were hollow and evasive, and one of them half-closed and swelling, but in the light of the candles they flared darkly and brilliantly blue as periwinkle flowers.

'Son,' said Radulfus, with chill detachment, for murderers come in all shapes, ages and kinds, 'you heard what is charged against you by those who surely sought your life. Here you have committed body and soul to the care of the church, and I and all here are bound to keep and succour you. On that you may rely. As at this moment, I offer you only one channel to grace, and ask of you but one question. Whatever the answer, here you are safe as long as the right of sanctuary lasts. I promise it.'

The wretch crouched on his knees, watching the abbot's face as though he numbered him among his enemies, and said no word.

'How do you answer to this charge?' asked Radulfus. 'Have you this day murdered and robbed?'

Distorted lips parted painfully to loose a light, high, wary voice like a frightened child's. 'No, Father Abbot, I swear it!'

'Get up,' said the abbot, neither trusting nor judging. 'Stand close, and lay your hand upon this casket on the altar. Do you know what it contains? Here within are the bones of the blessed Saint Elerius, the friend and director of Saint Winifred. On these holy relics, consider and answer me once again, as God hears you: are you guilty of that which they charge you?'

With all the obstinate, despairing fervour so slight a body could contain, and without hesitation, the light voice shrilled: 'As God sees me, I am not! I have done no wrong.'

Radulfus considered in weighty silence an unnerving while. Just so would a man answer who had nothing to hide and nothing to fear from being heard in Heaven. But no less, so would a godless vagabond answer for his hide's sake, having no faith in Heaven, and no fear of anything beyond the terrors of this world. Hard to decide between the two. The abbot suspended judgment.

'Well, you have given a solemn word, and whether it be true or no, you have the protection of this house, according to law, and time to think on your soul, if there is need.' He looked at Cadfael, and eye to eye they considered the needs that came before all. 'He had best keep to the church itself, I think, until we have spoken with the officers of law, and agreed on terms.'

'So I think, also,' said Cadfael.

'Should he be left alone?' They were both thinking of the pack recently expelled from this place, still hungry and ripe for mischief, and surely not gone far.

The brothers had withdrawn, led back to the dortoir by Prior Robert, very erect and deeply displeased. The choir had grown silent and dark. Whether the brethren, particularly the younger and more restless, would sleep, was another matter. The smell of the dangerous outer world was in their nostrils, and the tremor of excitement quivering like an itch along their skins.

'I shall have work with him a while,' said Cadfael, eyeing the smears of blood that marked brow and cheek, and the painful list with which the man stood. A young, willowy body, accustomed to going lightly and lissomely. 'If you permit, Father, I will stay here with him, and take his care upon me. Should there be need, I can call.'

'Very well, do so, brother. You may take whatever is necessary for his provision.' The weather was mild enough, but the hours of the night would be cold, in this sanctified but stony place. 'Do you need a helper to fetch and carry for you? Our guest should not be left unfellowed.'

'If I may borrow Brother Oswin, he knows where to find all the things I may need,' said Cadfael.

'I will send him to you. And should this man wish to tell his own side of this unhappy story, mark it well. Tomorrow, no doubt, we shall have his accusers here in proper form, with one of the sheriff's officers, and both parties will have to render account.'

Cadfael understood the force of that. A small discrepancy in the accused youth's story between midnight and morning could be revealing indeed. But by morning the voluble accusers might also have cooled their heads, and come with a slightly modified tale, for Cadfael, who knew most of the inhabitants of the town, had by this time recalled the reason for their being up so late in their best clothes, and well gone in drink. The young cockerel in the festival finery should by rights have been bedding a bride rather than pursuing a wretched wisp of manhood over the bridge with hunting cries of murder and robbery. Nothing less than the marriage of the heir could have unloosed the purse-strings of the Aurifaber household enough to provide such a supply of wine.

'I leave the watch to you,' said Radulfus, and departed to hale out Brother Oswin from his cell, and send him down to join the vigil. He came so blithely that it was plain he had been hoping for just such a recall. Who but Brother Cadfael's apprentice should be admitted to his nocturnal ministrations? Oswin came all wide eyes and eager curiosity, as excited as a truant schoolboy at being footloose at midnight, and attendant on the fringes of a sensational villainy. He hung over the shivering stranger, between fascinated horror at viewing a murderer close, and surprised pity at seeing so miserable a human being, where a brutal monster should have been.

Cadfael gave him no time to marvel. 'I want water, clean linen, the ointment of centaury and cleavers, and a good measure of wine. Hop to it, sharp! Better light the lamp in the workshop, we may need more things yet.'

Brother Oswin plucked out a candle from its socket, and departed in such a gust of dutiful enthusiasm that it was a marvel his light was not blown out in the doorway. But the night was still, and the flame recovered, streaming smokily across the great court towards the gardens.

'Light the brazier!' called Cadfael after him, hearing his wretched charge's teeth begin to chatter. A close brush with death is apt to leave a man collapsing like a pricced bladder, and this one had little flesh or strength about him to withstand the shock. Cadfael got an arm about him before he folded like an empty coat, and slid to the stones.

'Here, come . . . Let's get you into a stall.' The weight was slight as a child's, he hoisted it bodily, and made to withdraw round the parish altar to the somewhat less draughty confines of the choir, but the skinny fist that had all this time held fast to the altar-cloth would not let go. The thin body jerked in his arms.

'If I loose, they'll kill me . . .'

'Not while I have hands or voice,' said Cadfael. 'Our abbot has held his hand over you, they'll make no further move tonight. Leave go of the cloth and come within. There are relics enough there, trust me, holier even than this.'

The grubby fingers, with black and bitten nails, released the cloth reluctantly, the flaxen head drooped resignedly on Cadfael's shoulder. Cadfael bore him round into the choir and laid him in the nearest and most commodious stall, which was that of Prior Robert. The usurpation was not unpleasing. The young man was shivering violently from head to toe, but relaxed into the stall with a huge sigh, and was still.

'They've hunted you into the ground,' Cadfael allowed, settling him into shelter, 'but at least into the right earth. Abbot Radulfus won't give you up, never think it. You can draw breath, you have a home here for some days to come. Take heart! Nor are that pack out there so bad as you suppose, once the drink's out of them they'll cool. I know them.'

'They meant to kill me,' said the youth, trembling.

No denying that. So they would have done, had they got their hands on him out of this enclave. And there was a note of simple bewilderment in the high voice, of terror utterly at a loss, that caught Cadfael's leaning ear. The lad was far gone in weakness, and relief from fear, and truly it sounded as if he did not know why he had ever been threatened. So the fox must feel, acting innocently after his kind, and hearing the hounds give tongue.

Brother Oswin came, burdened with a scrip full of wineflask and unguent-jar, a roll of clean linen under one arm, and a bowl of water in both hands. His lighted candle he must have stuck to the bench in the porch, where a tiny, flickering light played. He arrived abrupt, urgent and glowing, the light-brown curls round his tonsure erected like a thorn-hedge. He laid down his bowl, laid out his linen, and leaned eagerly to support the patient as Cadfael drew him to the light.

'Be thankful for small mercies, I see no sign of broken bones in you. You've been trampled and hacked, and I make no doubt you're a lump of bruises, but that we can deal with. Lean here your head — so! That's a nasty welt across your temple and cheek. A cudgel did that. Hold still, now!'

The fair head leaned submissively into his hands. The weal grazed the crest of the left cheekbone, and broke the skin along the left side of his head, oozing blood into the pale hair. As Cadfael bathed it, stroking back the tangled locks, the skin quivered under the cold water, and the muck of dust and drying blood drained away. This was not the newest of his injuries. The smoothing of the linen over brow, cheek and chin uncovered a thin, pure, youthful face.

'What's your name, child?' said Cadfael.

'Liliwin,' said the young man, still eyeing him warily.

'Saxon. So are your eyes, and your hair. Where born? Not here along the borders.'

'How should I know?' said the youth, listless. 'In a ditch, and left there. The first I know is being taught to tumble, as soon as I walked.'

He was past fending for himself; perhaps he was even past lying. As well to get out of him whatever he was willing to tell, now, while he was forced to surrender himself to the hands of others, with his own helplessness like a weight of black despair on him.

'Is that how you've lived? Travelling the road, cutting capers at fairs, doing a little juggling and singing for your supper? It's a hard life, with more kicks than kindnesses, I dare say. And from a child?' He could guess at the manner of training that went to school a childish body to the sort of contortions a fairground crowd would gape at. There were ways of hurting, by way of punishment, without spoiling the agility of growing limbs. 'And solitary now? They're gone,

13

are they, that picked you out of your ditch and bent you to their uses?'

'I ran from them as soon as I was half-grown,' said the soft, weary voice. 'Three mummers padding the road, a lad come by for nothing was a gift to them, they had their worth out of me. All I owed them was kicks and blows. I work for myself now.'

'At the same craft?'

'It's all I know. But that I know well,' said Liliwin, suddenly raising his head proudly, and not wincing from the sting of the lotion bathing his grazed cheek.

'And that's what brought you to Walter Aurifaber's house last night,' said Cadfael mildly, stripping back a torn sleeve from a thin, sinewy forearm marked by a long slash from a knife. 'To play at his son's wedding-feast.'

One dark-blue eye peered up at him sidelong. 'You know them?'

'There are few people in the town that I don't know. I tend many folk within the walls, the old Aurifaber dame among them. Yes, I know that household. But it had slipped my mind that the goldsmith was marrying his son yesterday.' Knowing them as well as he did, he was sure that for all their wish to make an impressive show, they would not pay out money enough to attract the better sort of musicians, such as the nobility welcomed as guests. But a poor vagrant jongleur trying his unpromising luck in the town, that they might consider. All the more if his performance outdid his appearance, and genuine music could be had dead cheap. 'So you heard of the celebration, and got yourself hired to entertain the guests. Then what befell, to bring the jollity to such a grim ending? Reach me here a pad of cloth, Oswin, and hold the candle nearer.'

'They promised me three pence for the evening,' said Liliwin, trembling now as much with indignation as fear and cold, 'and they cheated me. It was none of my fault! I played and sang my best, did all my tricks . . . The house was full of people, they crowded me, and the young fellows, they were drunk and lungeous, they hustled me! A juggler needs room! It was not my fault the pitcher was broken. One of the youngsters jumped to catch the balls I was spinning, he knocked me flying, and the pitcher went over from the table, and smashed. She said it was her best . . . the old beldame . . . she screeched at me, and hit out with her stick . . .''

'She did this?' questioned Cadfael gently, touching the swathed wound on the jongleur's temple.

'She did! Lashed out like a fury, and swore the thing was worth more than I'd earned, and I must pay for it. And when I complained, she threw me a penny, and told them to put me out!'

So she would, thought Cadfael ruefully, seeing her life-blood spilled if a prized possession was broken, she who hoarded every groat that was not spent on her perverse tenderness for her soul, which brought alms flowing to the abbey altars, and rendered Prior Robert her cautious friend.

'And they did it?' It would not have been a gentle ejection, they would all have been inflamed and boisterous by then. 'How late was that? An hour before midnight?'

'More. None of them had left, then. They tossed me out of door, and wouldn't let me in again.' He had long experience of his own helplessness in similar circumstances, his voice sagged despondently. 'I couldn't even pick up my juggling balls, I've lost them all.'

'And you were left chill in the night, thrown out of the burgage. Then how came this hunt after you?' Cadfael smoothed a turn of his linen roll round the thin arm that jerked in his hands with frustrated rage. 'Hold still, child, that's right! I want this slit well closed, it will knit clean if you take ease. What did you do?'

'Crept away,' said Liliwin bitterly. 'What else could I do? The watch let me out of the wicket in the town gate, and I crossed the bridge and slipped into the bushes this side, meaning to make off from this town in the morning, and make for Lichfield. There's a decent grove above the path down to the river, the other side the highroad from the abbey here, I went in there and found me a good place in the grass to sleep the night out.' But with his grievance boiling and festering in him, and his helplessness over and above, if what he told was truth. And long acquaintance with injustice and despite does not reconcile the heart.

'Then how comes it the whole pack of them should be hunting you an hour or so later, and crying murder and theft on you?'

'As God sees me,' blurted the youth, quaking, 'I know no more than you! I was near to sleeping when I heard them come howling across the bridge. I'd no call to suppose it was ought to do with me, not until they were streaming down into the Foregate, but it was a noise to make any man afraid, whether he'd anything on his conscience or no. And then I could hear them yelling murder and vengeance, and crying it was the mummer who did it, and baying for my blood. They spread out and began to beat the bushes, and I ran for my life, being sure they'd find me. And all the pack of them came roaring after. They were all but plucking at my hair when I stumbled in here at the door. But God strike me blind if I know what I'm held to have done — and dead if I'm lying to you now!'

Cadfael completed his bandage, and drew the tattered sleeve down over it. 'According to young Daniel, it seems his father's been struck down and his strong-box emptied. A poor way of rounding off a wedding night! Do you tell me all this can have happened after you were put out without your pay? On the face of it, that might turn their minds to you and your grievance, if they were casting about for a likely felon.'

'I swear to you,' insisted the young man vehemently, 'the goldsmith was hale and well the last time I set eyes on him. There was no quarrelling, no violence but what they used on me, they were laughing and drinking and singing still. What's happened since I know no more than you. I left the place — what use was there in staying? Brother, for God's sake believe me! I've touched neither the man nor his money.'

'Then so it will be found,' said Cadfael sturdily. 'Here you're safe enough in the meantime, and you must needs put your trust in justice and Abbot Radulfus, and tell your tale as you've told it to me when they question you. We have time, and given time, truth will out. You heard Father Abbot — stay here within the church tonight, but if they come to a decent agreement tomorrow you may have the run of the household.' Liliwin was very cold to the touch, with fear and shock, and still trembling. 'Oswin,' said Cadfael briskly, 'go and fetch me a couple of brychans from the store, and then warm me up another good measure of wine on the brazier, and spice it well. Let's get some warmth into him.'

Oswin, who had held his tongue admirably while his eyes devoured the stranger, departed in a flurry of zeal to do his errands. Liliwin watched him go, and then turned to watch Cadfael no less warily. Small wonder if he felt little trust in anyone just now.

'You won't leave me? They'll be peering in at the door again before the night's out.'

'I won't leave you. Be easy!'

Advice difficult to follow, he admitted wryly, in Liliwin's situation. But with enough mulled wine in him he might sleep. Oswin came again glowing with haste and the flush of bending over the brazier, and brought two thick, rough blankets, in which Liliwin thankfully wound himself. The spiced draught went down gratefully. A little colour came back to the gaunt, bruised face.

'You go to your bed, lad,' said Cadfael, leading Oswin towards the night stairs. 'You can, now, he'll do till morning. Then we shall see.'

Brother Oswin looked back in some wonder at the swaddled body almost swallowed up in Prior Robert's capacious stall, and asked in a whisper: 'Do you think he can really be a murderer, though?'

'Child,' said Cadfael, sighing, 'until we get some sensible account of what's happened in Walter Aurifaber's burgage tonight, I doubt if there's been murder done at all. With enough drink in them, the fists may well have started flying, and a few noses been bloodied, and some fool may very well have started a panic, with other fools ready enough to take up the cry. You go to your bed, and wait and see.'

And so must I wait and see, he thought, watching Oswin obediently climb the stair. It was all very well distrusting the alarms of the moment, but for all that, not all those voluble accusers had been drunk. And something unforeseen had certainly happened in the goldsmith's house, to put a violent end to the celebrations of young Daniel's marriage. How if Walter Aurifaber had really been struck dead? And his treasury robbed? By that woebegone scrap of humanity huddled in his brychans, half-drunk with the wine they had poured into him, half asleep but held alert by terror? Would he dare, even with a bitter grievance? Could he have managed the affair, even if he had dared? One thing was certain, if he had robbed he must have disposed of his gains in short order in the dark, in a town surely none too well known to him. In those scanty garments of his, that threadbare motley, there was barely room to conceal the single penny the old dame had thrown at him, much less the contents of a goldsmith's coffer.

When he approached the stall, however quietly, the bruised eyelids rolled wide from the dark blue eyes, and they fixed on him in instant dread.

'Never shrink, it's I. No one else will trouble you this night. And my name, if you need it, is Cadfael. And yours is Liliwin.' A name strangely right for a vagabond player, very young and solitary and poor, and yet proud of his proficiency in his craft, tumbler, contortionist, singer, juggler, dancer, purveying merriment for others while he found little cause to be merry himself. 'How old are you, Liliwin?'

Half asleep and afraid to give way and sleep in earnest, he looked ever younger, dwindling into a swaddled child, reassuringly flushed now as the chill ebbed out of him. But he himself did not know the answer. He could only knit his fair brows and hazard doubtfully: 'I think I may be turned twenty. It could be more. The mummers may have said I was less than I was — children draw more alms.'

So they would, and the boy was lightly built, spare and

small. He might be as much as two and twenty, perhaps, surely no more.

'Well, Liliwin, if you can sleep do so, it will be aid and comfort, and you have need of it. You need not watch, I shall be doing that.'

Cadfael sat down in the abbot's stall, and trimmed the attendant candles, so that he might have a fair view of his charge. The quiet came in, on the heels of their silence, very consolingly. The night without might well have its disquiets, but here the vault of the choir was like linked hands sheltering their threatened and precarious peace. It was strange to Cadfael to see, after prolonged calm, two great tears welling from beneath Liliwin's closed eyelids, and rolling slowly over the jut of his gaunt cheek-bone, to fall into the brychan.

'What is it? What troubles you?' For himself he had shivered, argued, burned, but not wept.

'My rebec — I had it with me in the bushes, in a linen bag for my shoulder. When they flushed me out — I don't know how, a branch caught in the string, and plucked it away. And I dared not stop to grope for it in the dark . . . And now I can't go forth! I've lost it!'

'In the bushes, this side the bridge — across the highway from here?' It was a grief Cadfael could comprehend. 'You cannot go forth lad, no, not yet, true enough. But *I* can. I'll look for it. Those who hunted you would not go aside once they had you in view. Your rebec may be lying safe enough among the bushes. Go to sleep and leave grieving,' said Cadfael. 'It's too early to despair. For despair,' he said vigorously, 'it is always too early. Remember that, and keep up your heart.'

One startled blue eye opened at him, he caught the gleam of the candles in it before it closed again. There was silence. Cadfael lay back in the abbot's stall, and resigned himself to a long watch. Before Prime he must rouse himself to remove the interloper to a less privileged place, or Prior Robert would be rigid with offence. Until then, let God and his saints take charge, there was nothing more mere man could do.

As soon as the first light of dawn began to pluck colours out of the dark, on this clear May morning, Griffin, the locksmith's boy who slept in the shop as a watchman, got up from his pallet and went to draw water from the well in the rear yard. Griffin was always the first up, from either household of the two that shared the yard, and had usually kindled the fire and made all ready for the day's work before his master's journeyman came in from his home two streets away. On this day in particular Griffin took it for granted that all those who had kept it up late at the wedding would be in no condition to rise early about their work. Griffin himself had not been invited to the feast, though Mistress Susanna had sent Rannilt across to bring him a platter of meats and bread, a morsel of cake and a draught of small ale, and he had eaten his fill, and slept innocently through whatever uproar had followed at midnight.

Griffin was thirteen years old, offspring of a maidservant and a passing tinker. He was well-grown, comely, of contented nature and good with his hands, but he was a simpleton. Baldwin Peche the locksmith preened himself on his goodness in giving house-room to such an innocent, but the truth was that Griffin, for all his dimness of wit, had a gift for picking up practical skills, and far more than earned his keep.

The great wooden bucket, its old boards worn and fretted within and without from long use, came up out of the depths sparkling in the first slanting ray of the rising sun. Griffin filled his two pails, and was slinging the bucket back over the shaft when the gleam caught a flash of silver between two of the boards, lodged edgeways in the crevice. He balanced the bucket on the stone rim of the well, and leaned and fished out the shining thing, tugging it free between finger and thumb, and shaking off a frayed shred of blue cloth that came away with it. It lay in his palm shining, a round disc of silver prettily engraved with a head, and some strange signs he did not know for letters. On the reverse side there was a round border and a short cross within it, and more of the mysterious signs. Griffin was charmed. He took his prize back with him to the workshop, and when Baldwin Peche finally arose from his bed and came forth blear-eyed and cross-grained, the boy presented him proudly with what he had found. Whatever belonged here belonged to his master.

The locksmith clapped eyes on it and kindled like a lighted lamp, head and eyes clearing marvellously. He turned it in his fingers, examining both sides closely, and looked up with a curious, private grin and a cautious question:

'Where did you find this, boy? Have you shown it to anyone else?'

'No, master, I brought it straight in for you. It was in the bucket of the well,' said Griffin, and told him how it had lodged between the boards.

'Good, good! No need to let others know I have such. Stuck fast in the boards, was it?' mused Baldwin, brooding gleefully over his treasure. 'You're a good lad! A good lad! You did right to bring it straight to me, I set a great value on this! A great value!' He was grinning to himself with immense satisfaction, and Griffin reflected his content proudly. 'I'll give you some sweetmeats to your dinner I got from last night's feast. You shall see I can be grateful to a dutiful boy.'

# Two

BROTHER CADFAEL HAD LILIWIN AWAKE AND MADE AS PRE-
sentable as possible before the brothers came down to
Prime. He had risked helping him out at first light to the necessary offices, where he might at least wash his battered face
and relieve himself, and return to stand up before the assembled convent at Prime with some sad dignity. Not to speak
of the urgent need to have Prior Robert's stall vacant and
ready for him, for Robert's rigid disapproval of the intrusion
and the intruder was already sufficiently clear, and there was
no need to aggravate his hostility. The accused had enough
enemies already.

And in they came at the gatehouse, just as the brothers
emerged from Prime, a solid phalanx of citizens intent on
lodging their accusations this time in due and irreproach-
able form. Sheriff Prestcote had deputed the enquiry and
negotiations to his own sergeant, having more important
items of the king's business on his hands than a passing
assault and robbery in a town dwelling. He was newly
back from his Easter attendance at King Stephen's court
and the delivery of the shire accounts and revenues, and

22

his early summer survey of the county's royal defences was about to begin. Already Hugh Beringar, his deputy, was in the north of the shire about the same necessary business, though Cadfael, who relied on Hugh's good sense in all matters of poor souls fetched up hard against the law, hoped fervently that he would soon be back in Shrewsbury to lend a shrewd eye and willing ear to both sides in the dispute. The accusers had always the advantage without a healthy sceptic in attendance.

Meantime, here was the sergeant, large, experienced and sharp enough, but disposed to the accusers rather than the accused, and with a formidable array of townsmen behind him, led by the provost, Geoffrey Corviser. A decent, stout, patient man, and in no hurry to condemn without conscientious probing, but already primed with the complaints of several equally solid citizens, in addition to the aggrieved family. A wedding party provides at once large numbers of witnesses, and a powerful argument for doubting the half of their evidence.

Behind the authorities of shire and town came young Daniel Aurifaber, slightly the worse for wear after his hectic and unorthodox wedding night, and in his working clothes this time, but still belligerent. Surely, however, not so disturbed as a young man should be at his father's untimely slaying? Even slightly sheepish, and all the surlier because of it.

Cadfael withdrew to the rear of the brothers, between the citizen army and the church, and prepared to block the doorway if any of the witnesses should again lose his head and dare the abbot's thunder. It did not seem likely, with the sergeant there in control, and well aware of the necessity of dealing civilly and amicably with a mitred abbot. But in any dozen men there may well be one incorrigible idiot capable of any folly. Cadfael cast a glance over his shoulder, and glimpsed a pallid, scared face, but a body still, silent and intent, whether trusting in his ecclesiastical shelter, or simply resigned, there was no knowing.

'Keep within, out of sight, lad,' said Cadfael over his

shoulder, 'unless you're called for. Leave all to the lord abbot.'

Radulfus greeted the sergeant composedly, and after him the provost.

'I expected your visit, after the night's alarm. I am acquainted with the charges then made against a man who has appealed to sanctuary within our church, and been received according to our duty. But the charges have no force until made in due form, through the sheriff's authority. You are very welcome, sergeant, I look to you to inform me truly how this matter stands.'

He had no intention, Cadfael thought, watching, of inviting them withindoors into chapterhouse or hall. The morning was fine and sunny, and the matter might be agreed more briskly here, standing. And the sergeant had already recognised that he had no power to take the fugitive out of the hands of the church, and was intent only on agreeing terms, and hunting his proofs elsewhere.

'There is a charge lodged with me,' he said practically, 'that the jongleur Liliwin, who was employed last night to play at a wedding in the house of Master Walter Aurifaber, struck down the said Walter in his workshop, where he was then laying away certain valuable wedding gifts in his strong-box, and robbed the strong-box of a treasure in coins and goldsmith's work to a great value. This is sworn to by the goldsmith's son, here present, and by ten of the guests who were at the feast.'

Daniel braced his feet, stiffened his neck, and nodded emphatic confirmation. Several of the neighbours at his back murmured and nodded with him.

'And you have satisfied yourself,' said Radulfus briskly, 'that the charges are justified? At least, whoever did them, that these deeds were done?'

'I have viewed the workshop and the strong-box. The box is emptied of all but heavy items of silverware that would be ill to carry undetected. I have taken sworn witness that it held a great sum in silver pence and small, fine works of jewellery. All are gone. And as to the act of violence against

24

Master Aurifaber, I have seen the marks of his blood close to the coffer, where he was found, and I have seen how he lies still out of his senses.'

'But *not* dead?' said Radulfus sharply. 'It was murder was cried here at midnight.'

'Dead?' The sergeant, an honest man, gaped at the suggestion. 'Not he! He's knocked clean out of his wits, but it was not so desperate a blow as all that. If he hadn't had a fair wash of drink in him he might have been fit to speak up for himself by now, but he's still addled. It was a fair dunt someone gave him, but with a good hard head . . . No, he's well alive, and will live his proper span if I'm a judge.'

The witnesses, solid and sullen at his back, shifted their feet and looked elsewhere, but covertly came back to eyeing the abbot and the church door, and if they were discomfited at having their largest claims refuted, nonetheless held fast to their mortal grievance, and wanted a neck stretched for it.

'It seems, then,' said the abbot composedly, 'that the man we have in sanctuary is accused of wounding and robbing, but not of murder.'

'So it stands. The evidence is that he was docked of his full fee because he broke a pitcher in his juggling, and complained bitterly when he was put out. And some time after that, this assault upon Master Aurifaber was made, while most of those invited were still there in the house, and vouched for.'

'I well understand,' said the abbot, 'that on such a charge you must enquire, and may justice be done. But I think you also know well the sacredness of sanctuary. It is not shelter against sin, it is the provision of a time of calm, when the guilty may examine his soul, and the innocent confide in his salvation. But it may not be violated. It has a period, but until that time is spent it is holy. For forty days the man you seek on this charge is ours — no, he belongs to God! — and he may not be haled forth, nor persuaded forth, nor any way removed against his will from these premises. He is ours to feed, to care for and to shelter, for those forty days.'

'That I grant,' said the sergeant. 'But there are conditions. He came of his own will within, he may enjoy only the allowance of food those within here enjoy.' Less than he did, by his lusty bulk, but surely more than Liliwin had ever enjoyed as his regular provision. 'And when the respite is over, he may not again be supplied with food, but must come forth and submit himself to trial.'

He was as iron-sure of his case here as was Radulfus in the days of grace, he voiced his mandate coldly. There would be no extension of the time allowed, after that they would make sure he starved until he came forth. It was fair. Forty days is consideration enough.

'Then during that time,' said the abbot, 'you agree that the man may rest here and study on his soul. My concern for justice is no less than yours, you know I will keep to terms, and neither make nor allow others to make any offer to help the man away out of hold and out of your reach. But it would be seemly to agree that he need not confine himself to the church, but have the freedom of the whole enclosure here, so that he may make use of the lavatorium and necessarium, take some exercise in the open air, and keep himself decent among us.'

To that the sergeant agreed without demur. 'Inside your pale, my lord, he may make free. But if he step one pace outside, my men will be ready and waiting for him.'

'That is understood. Now, if you so wish, you may speak with the accused youth, in my presence, but without these witnesses. Those who charge him have told their story, it is fair that he should also tell his just as freely. After that, the matter must wait for trial and judgement hereafter.'

Daniel opened his mouth as if to make furious protest, caught the abbot's cold eye, and thought better of it. The henchmen at his back shuffled and muttered, but did not venture to be clearly heard. Only the provost spoke up, in the interests of the town in general.

'My lord, I was not a guest at yesterday's marriage, I have no direct knowledge of what befell. I stand here for the fair mind of Shrewsbury, and with your leave I would wish to hear what the young man may say for himself.'

The abbot agreed to that willingly. 'Come, then, into the church. And you, good people, may disperse in peace.' So they did, still with some reluctance at not getting their hands immediately on their prey. Only Daniel, instead of withdrawing, stepped forward hastily to arrest the abbot's attention, his manner now anxious and ingratiating, his grievance put away in favour of a different errand.

'Father Abbot, if you please! It's true we all ran wild last night, finding my poor father laid flat as he was, and bleeding. Truly we did believe him murdered, and cried it too soon, but even now there's no knowing how badly he's hurt. And my old grandmother, when she heard it, fell in a seizure, as she has once before, and though she's better of it now, she's none too well. And from the last fit she had, she puts more faith in Brother Cadfael's remedies than in all the physicians. And she bid me ask if he may come back with me and medicine her, for he knows what's needed when this breathlessness takes her, and the pains in her breast.'

The abbot looked round for Cadfael, who had come forth from the shadow of the cloister at hearing this plea. There was no denying he felt a distinct quiver of anticipation. After the night he had spent beside Liliwin, he could not help being consumed with curiosity as to what had really happened at Daniel Aurifaber's wedding supper.

'You may go with him, Brother Cadfael, and do what you can for the woman. Take whatever time you need.'

'I will, Father,' said Cadfael heartily, and went off briskly into the garden, to fetch what he thought might be required from his workshop.

The goldsmith's burgage was situated on the street leading to the gateway of the castle, where the neck of land narrowed, so that the rear plots of the houses on either side the street ran down to the town wall, while the great rondel of Shrewsbury lay snug to the south-west in the loop of the Severn. It was one of the largest plots in the town, as its owner was thought to be one of the wealthiest men; a right-angled house with a wing on the street, and the hall and main dwelling running lengthwise behind. Aurifaber, ever on the lookout for another means of making money, had divided off the wing and let it as a shop and dwelling to the lock-smith Baldwin Peche, a middle-aged widower without children, who found it convenient and adequate to his needs. A narrow passage led through between the two shops to the open yard behind, with its well, and the separate kitchens, byres and privies. Rumour said of Walter Aurifaber that he even had his cesspit stone-lined, which many considered to be arrogating to himself the privileges of minor nobility. Beyond the yard the ground fell away gradually in a long vegetable-garden and fowl-run to the town wall, and the family holding extended even beyond, through an arched doorway to an open stretch of smooth grass going down to the riverside.

Cadfael had paid several visits to the house at the old woman's insistence, for she was now turned eighty years old, and held that her gifts to the abbey entitled her to medical care in this world, as well as purchasing sanctity for the next. At eighty there is always something ailing the body, and Dame Juliana was given to ulcers of the leg if she suffered any slight wound or scratch, and stirred very little from her own chamber, which was one of the two over the hall. If she had presided at Daniel's wedding supper, as clearly she had, it must have been with her walking-stick ready to hand — unluckily for Liliwin! She was known to be willing to lash out with it readily if anything displeased her.

The only person on whom she doted, people said, was this young sprig of a grandson of hers, and even he had never yet found a way to get her to loose her purse-strings. Her son Walter was made in her own image, as parsimonious as the dame, but either surer of his own virtue as admitting him by right to salvation, or else not yet so old as to be worrying about the after-life, for the abbey altars owed no great benefits to him. There would have been an impressive show for the heir's wedding, but the pence that paid for it would be screwed out of the housekeeping for the next few months. It was a sour joke among those who did not like the goldsmith that his wife had died of starvation as soon as she had borne him a son, spending on her keep being no longer necessary.

Cadfael followed a glum and taciturn Daniel through the passage between the shops. The hall door stood wide open on the yard, at this hour in long shadow, but with a pale blue sky radiant overhead. Within, timber-scented gloom closed on them. There was a chamber door on the right, the daughter's room, and beyond that the household stores over which she presided. Beyond that doorway the stairs went up to the upper floor. Cadfael climbed the broad, unguarded wooden steps, needing no guidance here. Juliana's chamber was the first door off the narrow gallery that ran along the side wall. Daniel, without a word, had slouched back out of the hall below, and made for the shop. For a few days, at least, he was the goldsmith. A good workman, too, they said, when he chose, or when his elders could hold him to it.

A woman came out of the room as Cadfael approached it. Tall, like her young brother, of the same rich brown colouring, past thirty years old and mistress of this household for the last fifteen of those years, Walter's daughter Susanna had a cool dignity about her that went very ill with violence and crime. She had stepped into the shoes of her mother, whom she was said to resemble, as soon as Dame Juliana began to ail. The keys were hers, the stores were hers, the pillars and the roof of the house were held up by her, calmly and competently. A good girl, people said. Except that her girlhood was gone.

She smiled at Brother Cadfael, though even her smile was distant and cool. She had a pale, clear oval face with wide-set grey eyes, that went very strangely with her wealth of russet hair, braided and bound austerely on her head. Her housewifely gown was neat, dark and plain. The keys at her waist were her only jewellery.

They were old acquaintances. Cadfael could not claim more or better than that.

'No call to fret,' said the girl briskly. 'She's over it already, though frightened. In good case to take advice, I hope. Margery is in there with her.'

Margery? Of course, the bride! Strange office for a bride, the day after the wedding, to be nursing her bridegroom's grandam. Margery Bele, Cadfael recalled, daughter to the cloth-merchant Edred Bele, had a very nice little fortune in line for her some day, since she had no brother, and brought with her a very proper dowry even now. Well worth a miserly family's purchase for their heir. But was she, then, so bereft of suitors that this one offer must buy her? Or had she already seen and wanted that curly-haired, spoiled, handsome brat now no doubt frowning and fretting over his losses in the shop here?

'I must leave her to you and God,' said Susanna. 'She takes no notice of anyone else. And I have the dinner to prepare.'

'And what of your father?'

'He'll do well enough,' she said practically. 'He was very mellow, it did him good service, he fell soft as a cushion. Go along and see him, when *she's* done with you.' She gave him her wry smile, and slipped away silently down the stairs.

If Dame Juliana's attack had affected her speech at all on this occasion, she had made a remarkable recovery. Flat on her pillows she might be, and indeed had better remain for a day or so, but her tongue wagged remorselessly all the time Cadfael was feeling her forehead and the beat of her heart, and drawing back an eyelid from a fierce grey eye to look closely at the pupil. He let her run on without response or encouragement, though he missed nothing of what she had to say.

'And I expected better of the lord abbot,' she said, curling thin, bluish lips, 'than to take the part of a vagabond foot-pad, murderer and thief as he is, against honest craftsmen who pay their dues and their devotions like Christians. It's great shame to you all to shelter such a rogue.'

'Your son, I'm told,' said Cadfael mildly, rummaging in his script for the little flask of powder dried from oak mistletoe, 'is not dead, nor like to be yet, though the pack of your guests went baying off through the night yelling murder.'

'He well might have been a corpse,' she snapped. 'And dead or no, either way this is a hanging matter, as well you know. And how if I had died, eh? Whose fault would that have been? There could have been two of us to bury, and the family left ruined into the bargain. Mischief enough for one wretched little minstrel to wreak in one night. But he'll pay for it! Forty days or no, we shall be waiting for him, he won't escape us.'

'If he ran from here loaded with your goods,' said Cadfael, shaking out a little powder into his palm, 'he certainly brought none of them into the church with him. If he has your one miserly penny on him, that's all.' He turned to the young woman who stood anxiously beside the head of the bed. 'Have you wine there, or milk? Either does. Stir this into a cup of it.'

She was a small, round, homely girl, this Margery, perhaps twenty years old, with fresh, rosy colouring and a great untidy mass of yellow hair. Her eyes were round and wary. No wonder if she felt lost in this unfamiliar and disrupted household, but she moved quietly and sensibly, and her hands were steady on pitcher and cup.

'He had time to hide his plunder somewhere,' the old woman insisted grimly. 'Walter was gone above half an hour before Susanna began to wonder, and went to look for him. The wretch could have been over the bridge and into the bushes by then.'

She accepted the drink that was presented to her lips, and swallowed it down readily. Whatever her dissatisfaction with abbot and abbey, she trusted Cadfael's remedies. The two of them were unlikely to agree on any subject under the sun, but for all that they respected each other. Even this avaricious, formidable old woman, tyrant of her family and terror of her servants, had certain virtues of courage, spirit and honesty that were not to be despised.

'He swears he never touched your son or your gold,' said Cadfael. 'As I grant he may be lying, so you had better grant that you and yours may be mistaken.'

She was contemptuous. She pushed away from under her wrinkled neck the skimpy braid of brittle grey hair that irritated her skin. 'Who else could it have been? The only stranger, and with a grudge because I docked him the value of what he broke . . .'

'Of what he says some boisterous young fellow hustled him and caused him to break.'

'He must take a company as he finds it, wherever he hires himself out. And now I recall,' she said, 'we put him out without those painted toys of his, wooden rings and balls. I want nothing of his, and what he's taken of mine I'll have back before the end. Susanna will give you the playthings for him, and welcome. He shall not be able to say we've matched his thievery.'

She would give him, scrupulously, what was his, but she would see his neck wrung without a qualm.

'Be content, you've already broken his head for him. One more blow like that, and you might have had the law crying murder on *you*. And you'd best listen to me soberly now! One more rage like that, and you'll be your own death. Learn to take life gently and keep your temper, or there'll be a third and worse seizure, and it may well be the last.'

She looked, for once, seriously thoughtful. Perhaps she had been saying as much to herself, even without his warning. 'I am as I am,' she said, rather admitting than boasting.

'Be so as long as you may, and leave it to the young to fly into frenzies over upsets that will all pass, given time. Now here I'm leaving you this flask — it's the decoction of heart trefoil, the best thing I know to strengthen the heart. Take it as I taught you before, and keep your bed today, and I'll take another look at you tomorrow. And now,' said Cadfael, 'I'm going along to see how Master Walter fares.'

The goldsmith, his balding head swathed and his long, suspicious face fallen slack in sleep, was snoring heavily, and it seemed the best treatment to let him continue sleeping. Cadfael went down thoughtfully to find Susanna, who was out in the kitchen at the rear of the house. A skinny little girl laboured at feeding a sluggish fire and heaving a great pot to the hook over it. Cadfael had caught a glimpse of the child once before, all great dark eyes in a pale, grubby face, and a tangle of dark hair. Some poor maidservant's by-blow by her master, or her master's son, or a passing guest. For all the parsimony in this household, the girl could have fallen into worse hands. She was at least fed, and handed down cast-off clothing, and if the old matriarch was grim and frightening, Susanna was quiet and calm, no scold and no tyrant.

Cadfael reported on his patient, and Susanna watched his face steadily, nodded comprehension, and asked no questions.

'And your father is asleep. I left him so. What better could anyone do for him?'

'I fetched his own physician to him last night,' she said, 'when we found him. She'll have none but you now, but father relies on Master Arnald, and he's close. He says the blow is not dangerous, though it was enough to lay him senseless some hours. Though it may be the drink had something to do with that, too.'

'He hasn't yet been able to tell you what happened? Whether he saw who the man was who struck him?'

'Not a word. When he comes to, his head aches so he can remember nothing. It may come back to him later.'

For the saving or the damning of Liliwin! But whichever way that went, and whatever else he might be, Walter Aurifaber was not a liar. Meantime, there was nothing to be learned from him, but from the rest of the household there might be, and this girl was the gravest and most reasonable of the tribe.

'I've heard the general cry against this young fellow, but not the way the thing happened. I know there was some horse-play with the lads, nothing surprising at a wedding feast, and the pitcher got broken. I know your grandmother lashed out at him with her stick, and had him cast out with only one penny of his fee. His story is that he made off then, knowing it was hopeless to protest further, and he knew nothing of what followed until he heard the hunters baying after him, and ran to us for shelter.'

'He would say so,' she agreed reasonably.

'Every man's saying may as well be true as untrue,' said Cadfael sententiously. 'How long after his going was it when Master Walter went to his workshop?'

'Nearly an hour it must have been. Some of the guests were leaving then, but the more lively lads would stay to see Margery bedded, a good dozen of them were up the stair to the chamber. The wedding gifts were on the table to be admired, but seeing the night was ending, father took them and went to lock them away safely in his strong-box in the workshop. And it must have been about half an hour later, with all the merriment above, that I began to wonder that he hadn't come back. There was a gold chain and rings that Margery's father gave her, and a purse of silver links, and a breast ornament of silver and enamel — fine things. I went out by the hall door and round to the shop, and there he was, lying on his face by the coffer, and the lid open, and all but the heavy pieces of plate gone.'

'So the singing lad had been gone a full hour before this happened. Did anyone see him lurking after he was put out?'

She smiled, shaking a rueful head. 'There was darkness enough to hide a hundred loiterers. And he did not go so tamely as you suppose. He knows how to curse, too, he cried us names I'd never heard before, I promise you, and howled that he'd have his own back for the wrong we did him. And I won't say but he was hard done by, for that matter. But who else should it be? People we've known life-long, neighbours here in the street? No, you may be sure he hung about the yard in the dark until he saw my father go alone to the shop, and he stole in there, and saw what wealth there was in the open coffer. Enough to tempt a poor man, I grant you. But even poor men must needs resist temptation.'

'You are very sure,' said Cadfael.

'I am sure. He owes a life for it.'

The little maidservant turned her head sharply, gazing with lips parted. Such eyes, huge and grieved. She made a very small sound like a kitten's whimper.

'Rannilt is daft about the boy,' said Susanna simply, scornfully tolerant of folly. 'He ate with her in the kitchen, and played and sang for her. She's sorry for him. But what's done is done.'

'And when you found your father lying so, of course you ran back here to call help for him?'

'I couldn't lift him alone. I cried out what had happened, and those guests who were still here came running, and Iestyn, our journeyman, came rushing up the stairs from the undercroft where he sleeps — he'd gone to bed an hour or more earlier, knowing he'd have to man the shop alone this morning . . .' Of course, in expectation of the goldsmith's thick head and his son's late tarrying with his bride. 'We carried father up to his bed, and someone — I don't know who was the first — cried out that this was the jongleur's doing, and that he couldn't be far, and out they all went streaming, every man, to hunt for him. And I left Margery to watch by father, while I ran off to fetch Master Arnald.'

'You did what was possible,' Cadfael allowed. 'Then when was it Dame Juliana took her fit?'

'While I was gone. She'd gone to her chamber, she may even have been asleep, though with the larking and laughing in the gallery I should doubt it. But I was hardly out of the door when she hobbled along to father's room, and saw him lying, with his bloody head, and senseless. She clutched at her heart, Margery says, and fell down. But it was not such a bad fit this time. She was already wake and talking,' said Susanna, 'when I came back with the physician. We had help then for both of them.'

'Well, they've both escaped the worst,' said Cadfael, brooding, 'for this time. Your father is a strong, hale man, and should live his time out without harm. But for the dame, more shocks of the kind could be the death of her, and so I've told her.'

'The loss of her treasury,' said Susanna drily, 'was shock enough to kill her. If she lives through that, she's proof against all else until her full time comes. We are a durable kind, Brother Cadfael, very durable.'

Cadfael turned aside from leaving by the passage to the street, and entered Walter Aurifaber's workshop by the side door. Here Walter would have let himself in, when he came burdened with several choice items in gold and silver, enamel and fine stones, to lock them up with his other wealth in the strong-box; from which, in all likelihood, Mistress Margery would have had much ado to get them out again for her wearing. Unless, of course, that soft and self-effacing shape concealed a spirit of unsuspected toughness. Women can be very deceptive.

As he entered the shop from the passage, the street door was on his left, there was a trestled show-table, cloth-covered, and the rear part of the room was all narrow shelving, the small furnace, cold, and the work-benches, at which Daniel was working on a setting for a clouded mossagate, brows locked in a gloomy knot. But his fingers were deft enough with the fine tools, for all his preoccupation with the family misfortunes. The journeyman was bent over a scale on the bench beside the furnace, weighing small tablets of silver. A sturdy, compact person, this Iestyn, by the look of him about twenty-seven or twenty-eight years old, with cropped, straight dark hair in a thick cap. He turned his head, hearing someone entering, and his face was broad but bony, dark-skinned, thick-browed, deep-eyed, wholly

Welsh. A better-humoured man than his master, though not so comely.

At sight of Cadfael, Daniel put his tools aside. 'You've seen them both? How is it with them?'

'The pair of them will do well enough for this time,' said Cadfael. 'Master Walter is under his own physician, and held to be out of any danger, if his memory is shaken. Dame Juliana is over this fit, but any further shock could be mortal, it's only to be expected. Few reach such an age.'

By the young man's face, he was pondering whether any ever should. But for all that, he knew she favoured him, and had a use for her indulgence. He might even be fond of her, after his fashion, and as far as affection was possible between sour age and impatient youth. He did not seem altogether a callous person, only spoiled. Sole heirs of merchant houses can be as deformed by their privilege as those of baronies.

In the far corner of the shop Walter's pillaged strong-box stood, a big, iron-banded wooden coffer, securely bolted to floor and wall. Intent on impressing the magnitude of the crime upon any representative of the abbey that insisted on sheltering the felon, Daniel unlocked the double locks and heaved up the lid to display what was left within, a few heavy dishes of plate, too cumbersome to be concealed about the person. The tale he told, and would tell and retell indignantly as often as he found a listener, matched Susanna's account. Iestyn, called to bear witness at every other aggrieved sentence, could only nod his black head solemnly, and confirm every word.

'And you are all sure,' said Cadfael, 'that the jongleur must be the guilty man? No thought of any other possible thief? Master Walter is known to be a wealthy man. Would a stranger know how wealthy? I daresay there are some here in the town may well envy a craftsman better-off then themselves.'

'That's a true word,' agreed Daniel darkly. 'And there's one no farther away than the width of the yard that I might

37

have wondered about, if he had not been there in my eye every minute of the time. But he was, and there's an end. I fancy he was the first to hit on it that it was the jongleur we wanted.'

'What, your tenant the locksmith? A harmless soul enough, I should have thought. Pays his rent and minds his shop, like the rest.'

'His man John Boneth minds the shop,' said Daniel, with a snort of laughter, 'and the daft lad helps him. Peche is more often out poking his long nose into other people's business, and carrying the gossip round the ale-houses than tending to his craft. A smiling, sneaking toady of a man to your face, and back-biting as soon as you turn away. There's no sneak-thievery I'd put past him, if you want to know. But he was there in the hall the whole time, so it was not he. No, make no mistake, we were on the right trail when we set the pack after that rogue Liliwin, and so it will be proved in the end.'

They were all in the same story, and the story might well be true. There was but one point to be put to them counter: where would a stranger to the town, and out in the dark, stow away so valuable a booty safely enough and secretly enough to hide it from all others, and yet be able to recover it himself? The aggrieved family might brush that aside. Cadfael found it a serious obstacle to belief.

He was withdrawing by the same door at which he had entered, and drawing it closed after him by the iron latch, when the draught of the movement and the lengthening shaft of sunlight piercing the passage fluttered and illumined a single primrose-coloured thread, waving at the level of his eyes from the doorpost. The doorpost now on his right, on his left when he entered, but then out of range of the sun's rays. Pale as flax, and long and shining. He took it between finger and thumb, and plucked it gently from the wood, and a little blotch of dark, brownish red which had gummed it to the post came away with it, a second, shorter hair coiled and stuck in the blot. Cadfael stared at it for an instant, and cast one glance back over his shoulder before he closed the door.

From here the coffer in the far corner was plainly in view, and so would a man be, bending over it.

A small thing, to make so huge a hole in the defence a man put up for his life. Someone had stood pressed against that doorpost, looking in, someone about Cadfael's own height — a small man with flaxen hair, and a bloodied graze on the left side of his head.

# Three

Saturday, from Noon to Night

CADFAEL WAS STILL STANDING WITH THE TINY, OMINOUS speck in his palm when he heard his name called from the hall door, and in the same moment a freshening puff of wind took the floating hairs and carried them away. He let them go. Why not? They had already spoken all too eloquently, they had nothing to add. He turned to see Susanna withdrawing into the hall, and the little maidservant scurrying towards him, with a knotted bundle of cloth held out before her.

'Mistress Susanna says, Dame Juliana wants these out of the house.' She opened the twist of cloth, and showed a glimpse of painted wood, scarred from much use. 'They belong to Liliwin. She said you would take them to him.' The great dark eyes that dwelt unwaveringly on Cadfael's face dilated even more. 'Is it true?' she asked, low and urgently. 'He's safe, there in the church? And you'll protect him? You won't let them fetch him away?'

'He's with us, and safe enough,' said Cadfael. 'No one dare touch him now.'

'And they haven't hurt him?' she questioned earnestly.

'No worse than will mend now, in peace. No need to fret for a while. He has forty days grace. I think,' he said, studying the thin face, the delicate, staring cheekbones under the wide-set eyes, 'you like this young man.'

'He made such lovely music,' said the child wistfully. 'And he spoke me gently, and was glad of being with me in the kitchen. It was the best hour I ever spent. And now I'm frightened for him. What will happen to him when the forty days are up?'

'Why, if it goes so far — for forty days is time enough to change many things — but even if it goes so far, and he must come forth, it will be into the hands of the law, not into the hands of his accusers. Law is grim enough, but tries to be fair. And by then those who accuse him will have forgotten their zeal, but even if they have not, they cannot touch him. If you want to help him, keep eyes and ears open, and if you learn of anything to the purpose, then speak out.' Clearly the very thought terrified her. Who ever listened to anything she might say? 'To me you may speak freely,' he said. 'Do you know anything of what went on here last night?'

She shook her head, casting wary glances over her shoulder. 'Mistress Susanna sent me away to my bed. I sleep in the kitchen, I never even heard . . . I was very tired.' The kitchen was set well apart from the house for fear of fire, as was customary with these close-set and timber-framed town houses, she might well sleep through all the alarm after her long hours of labour. 'But I do know this,' she said, and lifted her chin gallantly, and he saw that for all her youth and frailty it was a good chin, with a set to it that he approved. 'I know Liliwin never harmed anyone, not my master nor any other man. What they say of him is not true.'

'Nor ever stole?' asked Cadfael gently.

She was no way put down, she held him steadily in her great lamps of eyes. 'To eat, yes, perhaps, when he was hungry, an egg from under a hen somewhere, a partridge in the woods, even a loaf . . . that may be. He has been

41

hungry all his life.' She knew, for much of her life so had she. 'But steal more than that? For money, for gold? What good would that do him? And he is not like that . . . never!'

Cadfael was aware of the head emerging from the hall door before Rannilt was, and warned her softly: 'There, run! Say I kept you with questions, and you knew no answers.'

She was very quick, she had whirled and was speeding back when Susanna's voice pealed impatiently: 'Rannilt!'

Cadfael did not wait to see her vanish within on the heels of her mistress, but turned at once to resume his way along the passage to the street.

Baldwin Peche was sitting with a pot of ale on the steps of his shop. The fact that the street was narrow, and the frontages here faced north-west and were in deep shadow, suggested that he had a reason beyond idleness and ease for being where he was at this hour. No doubt all those townsmen who had been guests at the Aurifaber wedding were up and alert this morning, as soon as they could shake off the effects of their entertainment, roused and restored by the sensational gossip they had to spread, and the possibility of further revelations.

The locksmith was a man in his fifties; short, sturdy, but beginning to grow a round paunch, a noted fisherman along the Severn, but a weak swimmer, unusually for this river-circled town. He had, truly enough, a long nose that quivered to every breath of scandal, though he was cautious in the use he made of it, as though he enjoyed mischief for its own sake rather than for any personal profit. A cold, inquisitive merriment twinkled in his pale-blue eyes, set in a round, ruddy and smiling face. Cadfael knew him well enough to pass the time of day, and gave him good morrow as though making the approach himself, whereas he was well apprised Peche had been waiting to make it.

'Well, Brother Cadfael,' said the locksmith heartily,

'you'll have been tending these unlucky neighbours of mine. I trust you find them bearing up under their griefs? The lad tells me they'll make good recoveries, the both of them.'

Cadfael said what was required of him, which was rather enquiry than response, and kept his mouth shut and his ears open to listen to the tale all over again, with more and richer detail, since this was Peche's chosen craft. The journeyman locksmith, a fine-looking young man who lived with his widowed mother a street or two away in the town, looked out once from the shop doorway, cast a knowledgeable eye on his master, and withdrew, assured of having work to himself, as he preferred it. By this time John Boneth knew everything his skilled but idle tutor could teach him, and was quite capable of running the business single-handed. There was no son to inherit it, he was trusted and depended on, and he could wait.

'A lucky match, mark,' said Peche, prodding a knowing finger into Brother Cadfael's shoulder, 'especially if this treasury of Walter's is really lost, and can't be recovered. Edred Bele's girl has money enough coming to her to make up the half, at least. Walter's worked hard to get her for his lad, and the old dame's done her share, too. Trust them!' He rubbed finger and thumb together suggestively, and nudged and winked. 'And the girl no beauty and without graces — neither sings nor dances well, and dumb in company. No monster, though, she'll pass well enough, or that youngster would never have been brought to . . . not with what he has in hand!'

'He's a fine-looking lad,' said Cadfael mildly, 'and they say not unskilled. And a good inheritance waiting for him.'

'Ah, but short *now!*' whispered Baldwin, leaning closer still and stabbing with a stiff forefinger, his knowing face gleeful. 'It's the waiting is hard to bear. Young folk live now, not tomorrow, and this side marriage — you take my meaning? — not t'other. Oh, the old dame may dote on him, the sun shines out of his tail for her, but she keeps her hold on the purse and doles out sweets very sparingly. Not enough for the sort *he* fancies!'

It occurred to Cadfael, rather belatedly, that it was hardly becoming behaviour in one of his habit to listen avidly to local scandal, but if he did nothing to encourage confidences, he certainly did not stop listening. Encouragement, in any case, was unnecessary. Peche had every intention of making the most of his probings.

'I wouldn't say,' he breathed into Cadfael's ear, 'but he's had his fingers in her purse a time or two, for all her sharpness. His present fancy comes expensive, not to speak of the game there'll be if ever her husband gets to know of their cantrips. It's a fair guess the bride's dowry, as much of it as he can get his hands on, will go to deck out another wench's neck. Not that he had any objections to this match — not he, he likes the girl well enough, and he likes her money a good deal better. But he likes somebody else best of all. No names, no revenges! But you should have seen her as a guest last night! Bold as a royal whore, and the old man puffed up beside her, proud of owning the handsomest thing in the hall, and she and the bridegroom eyeing each other fit to laugh out loud at the old fool. As well I was the only one there had sharp enough eyes to see the sparks pass!'

'As well, indeed!' said Cadfael almost absently, for he was busy reflecting how understandable it was that Daniel should view his father's tenant with such ill-will. No need to doubt Peche's information, really devoted pryers make sure of their facts. Doubtless, though never a word need have been said, certain quiverings of that inquisitive nose and knowing glances from those coldly merry eyes had warned Daniel, evidently not quite a fool, that his gallivantings were no secret.

And the other, the old fool, welcome guest at the wedding — of consequence, therefore, among the merchants of Shrewsbury and with a young, bold, handsome wife . . . A second marriage, then, on the man's part? The town was not so great that Cadfael had to look very far. Ailwin Corde, widowed a few years ago and married again, against his grown son's wishes, to a fine, flaunting beauty a third his age, called Cecily . . .

'I'd keep your tongue within your teeth,' he advised amiably. 'Wool merchants are a power in this town, and not every husband will thank you for opening his eyes.'

'What, I? Speak out of turn?' The merry eyes sparkled with all the cordiality of ice, and the long nose twitched. 'Not I! I have a decent landlord and a snug corner, and no call to overturn what suits me well. I take my fun where I find it, Brother, but quietly and privately. No harm in what does none.'

'None in the world,' agreed Cadfael, and took his leave peaceably, and went on towards the winding descent of the Wyle, very thoughtful, but none too sure of what he should be thinking. For what had he learned? That Daniel Aurifaber was paddling palms, and probably more, with mistress Cecily Corde, whose wool-merchant husband collected fleeces from the bordering district of Wales, and traded them into England, and therefore was often absent for some days at a time, and that the lady, however fond, was accustomed to gifts, and did not come cheaply, whereas the young man was baulked by equally parsimonious father and grandmother, and was reputed already to be filching such small sums as he could get his fingers on. And no easy matter, either! And had his father not gone to lock up at least half of the bride's dowry out of reach? Out of reach now in good earnest — or had last night's events snugged it away well *within* reach? Such things can happen in families.

What else? That Daniel held no good opinion, reasonably enough, of the tenant who spent his leisure so inconveniently, and claimed he would have held him to be a prime suspect, if he had not been in full view throughout the time when the deed was done.

Well, time would show. They had forty days in hand.

High Mass was over when Cadfael had crossed the bridge and made his way back to the gatehouse and the great court.

Prior Robert's shadow, Brother Jerome, was hovering in the cloister to intercept him when he came.

'The lord abbot asks that you will wait upon him before dinner.' Jerome's pinched, narrow nose quivered with a suggestion of deprecation and distaste which Cadfael found more offensive than Baldwin Peche's full-blooded enjoyment of his own mischief. 'I trust, Brother, that you mean to let time and law take their course, and not involve our house beyond the legal obligations of sanctuary, in so sordid a matter. It is not for you to take upon yourself the burdens that belong to justice.'

Jerome, if he had not explicit orders, had received his charge from Prior Robert's knotted brow and quivering nostril. So low and ragged and miserable a manifestation of humanity as Liliwin, lodged here within the pale, irked Robert like a burr working through his habit and fretting his aristocratic skin. He would have no peace while the alien body remained, he wanted it removed, and the symmetry of his life restored. To be fair, not merely his own life, but the life of this house, which fretted and itched with the infection thus hurled in from the world without. The presence of terror and pain is disruptive indeed.

'All the abbot wants from me is an account of how my patients fare,' said Cadfael, with unwonted magnanimity towards the narrow preoccupations of creatures so uncongenial to him as Robert and his clerk. For their distress, however strange to him, was still comprehensible. The walls did, indeed, tremble, the sheltered souls did quake. 'And I have burdens enough with them, and am hardly looking for any others. Is that lad fed and doctored? That's all my business with him.'

'Brother Oswin has taken care of him,' said Jerome.

'That's well! Then I'll go pay my respects to the lord abbot, and get to my dinner, for I missed breakfast, and those up there in the town are too distraught to think of offering a morsel.'

He wondered, however, as he crossed the court to the abbot's lodging, how much of what he had gleaned he was about to impart. Salacious gossip can be of no interest to ab-batial ears, nor was there much to be said about a tiny plaque of dried blood tethering a couple of flaxen hairs; not, at least, until the vagabond, with every hand against him and his life at stake, had exercised the right to answer for himself.

Abbot Radulfus received without surprise the news that the entire wedding party was united in insisting on the jongleur's guilt. He was not, however, quite convinced that Daniel, or any other of those attending could be certain who had, or had not, been in full view throughout.

'With a hall full of so many people, so much being drunk, and over so many hours of celebration, who can say how any man came and went? Yet so many voices all in one tale cannot be disregarded. Well, we must do our part, and leave the law to deal with the rest. The sergeant tells me his master the sheriff is gone to arbitrate in a dispute between neighbour knights in the east of the shire, but his deputy is due in the town before night.'

That was good news in Cadfael's ear. Hugh Beringar would see to it that the search for truth and justice should not go sliding down the easiest way, and erase such minor details as failed to fit the pattern. Meantime, Cadfael had just such a detail to take up with Liliwin, besides restoring him the tools of his juggling trade. After dinner he went to look for him, and found him sitting in the cloister, with borrowed needle and thread, trying to cobble together the rents in his coat. Beneath the bandaged brow he had washed his face scrupulously, it showed pale and thin but clear-skinned, with good, even delicate features. And if he could not yet wash the dust and mire from his fair hair, at least he had combed it into decent order.

The sop first, perhaps, and then the switch! Cadfael sat down beside him, and dumped the cloth bundle in his lap. 'Here's a part of your property restored you, for an earnest. There, open it!'

But Liliwin already knew the faded wrapping. He sat

gazing down for a moment in wonder and disbelief, and then untied the knotted cloth and sank his hand among his modest treasures with affection and pleasure, faintly flushing and brightening, as though for the first time recovering faith that some small comforts and kindnesses existed for him in the world.

'But how did you get them? I never thought I should see them again. And you thought to ask for them . . . for me . . . That was kind!'

'I did not even have to ask. That old dame who struck you, terror though she may be, is honest. She won't keep what is not hers, if she won't forgo a groat of what is. She sends them back to you.' Not graciously, but no need to go into that. 'There, take it for a good sign. And how do you find yourself today? Have they fed you?'

'Very well! I'm to fetch my food from the kitchen at breakfast, dinner and supper.' He sounded almost incredulous, naming three meals a day. 'And they've given me a pallet in the porch here. I'm afraid to be away from the church at night.' He said it simply and humbly. 'They don't all like it that I'm here. I stick in their craw like a husk.'

'They're accustomed to calm,' said Cadfael sympathetically. 'It is not calm you bring. You must make allowances, as they must. At least from tonight you may sleep secure. The deputy sheriff should be in town by this evening. In his authority, I promise you, you can trust.'

Trust would still come very hardly to Liliwin, after all he had experienced in a short life, but the toys he had tucked away so tenderly under his pallet were a promise. He bent his head over his patient stitching, and said no word.

'And therefore,' said Cadfael briskly, 'you'd best consider on the half-tale you told me, and own to the part you left out. For you did not creep away so docilely as you let us all think, did you? What were you doing, hugging the door-post of Master Walter's workshop, long after you claim you had made off into the night? With the door open, and your head against the post, and the goldsmith's coffer in full view . . . and also open? And he bending over it!'

Liliwin's needle had started in his fingers and pricked his left hand. He dropped needle, thread and coat, and sat sucking his pierced thumb, and staring at Brother Cadfael with immense, frightened eyes. He began to protest shrilly: 'I never went there . . . I know nothing about it . . .' Voice and eyes sank together. He blinked down at his open hands, lashes long and thick as a well-bred cow's brushing his staring cheekbones.

'Child,' said Cadfael, sighing, 'you were there in the doorway, peering in. You left your mark there. A lad your size, with a bloodied head, leaned long enough against that door-post to leave a little clot of his blood, and two flax-white hairs gummed into it. No, no other has seen it, it's gone, blown away on the wind, but I saw it, and I know. Now tell me truth. What passed between you and him?'

He did not ask why Liliwin had lied in omitting this part of his story, there was no need. What, place himself there on the spot, there where the blow had been struck? Innocence would have avoided admission every bit as desperately as guilt.

Liliwin sat and shivered, fluttering like a leaf in that same wind which had carried off his stray hairs. Here in the cloister the air was still chilly, and he had only a patched shirt and hose on him, the half-mended coat lying on his knees. He swallowed hard and sighed.

'It's true, I did wait . . . It was not fair!' he blurted, shaking. 'I stayed there in the dark. They were not all as hard as she, I thought I might plead . . . I saw him go to the shop with a light and I followed. He was not so furious when the pitcher was broken, he did try to calm her, I dared approach him. I went in and pleaded for the fee I was promised, and he gave me a second penny. He gave it to me and I went. I swear it!'

He had sworn the other version, too. But fear does so, the fear bred of a lifetime's hounding and battering.

'And then you left? And you saw no more of him? More to the point still, did you see ought of any other who may have been lurking as you did, and entered to him afterwards?'

'No, there was no one. I went, I was glad to go, it was all over. If he lives, he'll tell you he gave me the second penny.'

'He lives, and will,' said Cadfael. 'It was not a fatal blow. But he's said nothing yet.'

'But he will, he will, he'll tell you how I begged him, and how he took pity on me. I was afraid,' he said quivering, 'I was afraid! If I'd said I went there, it would have been all over with me.'

'Well, but consider,' said Cadfael reasonably, 'when Walter is his own man again, and comes forth with that very tale, how would it look if he brought it out when you had said no word of it? And besides, when his wits settle and he recalls what befell, it may well be that he'll be able to name his attacker, and clear you of all blame.'

He was watching closely as he said it, for to an innocent man that notion would come as powerful comfort, but to a guilty one as the ultimate terror; and Liliwin's troubled countenance gradually cleared and brightened into timid hope. It was the first truly significant indication of how far he should be believed.

'I never thought of that. They said murdered. A murdered man can't accuse or deliver. If I'd known then he was well alive I would have told the whole truth. What must I do now? It will look bad to have to own I lied.'

'What you should do for the best,' Cadfael said after some thought, 'is let me take this word myself to the lord abbot, not as my discovery — for the evidence is gone with a puff of wind — but as your confession. And if Hugh Beringar comes tonight, as I hope and hear he may, then you may tell the tale over again to him in full, yourself. Whatever follows then, you may rest out your days of grace here with a clear conscience and truth will speak on your side.'

Hugh Beringar of Maesbury, deputy sheriff of the shire, reached the abbey for Vespers, after a long conference with the sergeant concerning the lost treasury. In search of it, every yard of ground between the goldsmith's house and the bushes from which Liliwin had been flushed at midnight had been scoured without result. Every voice in the town declared confidently that the jongleur was the guilty man, and had successfully hidden his plunder before he was sighted and pursued.

'But you, I think,' said Beringar, walking back towards the gatehouse with Cadfael beside him and twitching a thin dark eyebrow at his friend, 'do not agree. And not wholly because this enforced guest of yours is young and hungry and in need of protection. What is it convinces you? For I do believe you are convinced he's wronged.'

'You've heard his story,' said Cadfael. 'But you did not see his face when I put it into his head that the goldsmith may get back his memory of the night in full, and be able to put a name or a face to his assailant. He took that hope to him like a blessed promise. The guilty man would hardly do so.'

Hugh considered that gravely and nodded agreement. 'But the fellow is a player, and has learned hard to keep command of his face in all circumstances. No blame to him, he has no other armour. To appear innocent of all harm must now be his whole endeavour.'

'And you think I am easily fooled,' said Cadfael drily.

'Far from it. Yet it is well to remember and admit the possibility.' And that was also true, and Hugh's dark smile, slanted along his shoulder, did nothing to blunt the point. 'Though I grant it would be nothing new for you to be the only creature who holds against the grain, and makes his wager good.'

'Not the only one,' said Cadfael almost absently, with Rannilt's wan, elfin face before his mind's eye. 'There's one other more certain than I.' They had reached the arch of the gatehouse, the broad highway of the Foregate crossed beyond, and the evening was just greening and dimming towards twilight. 'You say you found the place where the lad bedded down for the night? Shall we take a look there together?'

They passed through the arch, an odd pair to move so congenially side by side, the monk squat and square and sturdy, rolling in his gait like a seaman, and well launched into his sixtieth year, the sheriff's deputy more than thirty year younger and half a head taller, but still a small man, of graceful, nimble movements and darkly saturnine features. Cadfael had seen this young man win his appointment fairly, and a wife to go with it, and had witnessed the christening of their first son only a few months ago. They understood each other better than most men ever do, but they could still take opposing sides in a matter of the king's justice.

They turned towards the bridge that led into the town, but turned aside again on the right, a little way short of the riverside, into the belt of trees that fringed the road. Beyond, towards the evening gleam of the Severn, the ground declined to the lush level of the main abbey gardens, along the meadows called the Gaye. They could see the green, clear light through the branches as they came to the place where Liliwin had settled down sadly to sleep before leaving this unfriendly town. And it was a nest indeed, rounded and coiled into the slope of thick new grass, and so small, like the haunt of a dormouse.

'He started up in alarm, in one leap clear of his form, like a flushed hare,' said Hugh soberly. 'There are young shoots broken here — do you see? — where he crashed through. This is unquestionably the place.' He looked round curiously, for Cadfael was casting about among the bushes, which grew thickly here for cover. 'What are you seeking?'

'He had his rebec in a linen bag on his shoulder,' said Cadfael. 'In the dark a branch caught the string and jerked it away, and he dared not stop to grope after it. So he told me,

52

like a man bereaved. I am sure that was truth. I wonder what became of it?'

He found the answer that same evening, but not until he had parted from Hugh and was on his way back to the gatehouse. It was a luminous evening and Cadfael was in no hurry to go in, and had plenty of time before Compline. He stood to watch the leisurely evening walk of the Foregate worthies, and the prolonged games of the urchins of the parish of Holy Cross reluctant to go home to their beds, just as he was. A dozen or so of them swept by in a flurry of yelling and laughter, shrill as starlings, some still half-naked from the river, but not yet so cold that they must make for the home hearth. They were kicking a shapeless rag ball among them, and some of them swiping at it with sticks, and one with something broader and shorter. Cadfael heard the impact of hollow wood, and the thrumming reverberation of one surviving string. A lamentable sound, like a cry for help with little expectation that the plea would be heard.

The imp with this weapon loitered, dragging his implement in the dust. Cadfael pursued, and drew alongside like a companion ship keeping station rather than a pirate boarding. The brat looked up and grinned, knowing him. He had but a short way to go home, and was tired of his plaything.

'Now what in the world have you found there?' said Cadfael amicably. 'And where did you happen on such an odd thing?'

The child waved a hand airily back towards the trees that screened the Gaye. 'It was lying in there, in a cloth bag, but I lost that down by the water. I don't know what it is. I never saw a thing like it. But it's no use that I can see.'

'Did you find,' asked Cadfael, eyeing the wreckage, 'a stick, with fine hairs stretched along it, that went with this queer thing?'

The child yawned, halted, and abandoned his hold on his toy, letting it drop into the dust. 'I hit Davey with that when he tripped me in the water, but it broke. I threw it away.' So he would, having proved its uselessness, just as he walked away from this discarded weapon, leaving it lying, and went off scrubbing at sleepy eyes with the knuckles of a grimy fist.

Brother Cadfael picked up the sorry remnant and examined ruefully its stove-in ribs and trailing, tangled strings. No help for it, this was all that remained of the lost rebec. He took it back with him, only too well aware of the grief he was about to cause its luckless owner. Say that Liliwin came alive in the end out of his present trouble, still he must emerge penniless, and deprived now even of his chief means of livelihood. But there was more in it even than that. He knew it even before he presented the broken instrument to Liliwin's appalled hands, and watched the anguish and despair mantle like bleak twilight over his face. The boy took the ruin in his hands and fondled it, rocked it in his arms, bowed his head to its splintered frame, and burst into tears. It was not the loss of a possession so much as the death of a sweetheart.

Cadfael sat down apart, in the nearest carrel of the scriptorium, and kept decently silent until the storm passed, and Liliwin sat drained and motionless, hugging his broken darling, his thin shoulders hunched against the world.

'There are men,' said Cadfael then mildly, 'who understand such arts as repairing instruments of music. I am not one of them, but Brother Anselm, our precentor, is. Why should we not ask him to look at your fiddle and see what can be done to make it sing again?'

'*This?*' Liliwin turned on him passionately, holding out the pathetic wreck in both hands. 'Look at it — no better than firewood. How could anyone restore it?'

'Do you know that? Do I? What's lost by asking the man who may? And if this is past saving, Brother Anselm can make one new.'

Bitter disbelief stared back at him. Why should he credit that anyone would go out of his way to do a kindness to so despised and unprofitable a creature as him-

54

self? Those within here held that they owed him shelter and food, but nothing more, and even that as a duty. And no one without had ever offered him any benefit that cost more than a crust.

'As if I could ever pay for a new one! Don't mock me!'

'You forget, we do not buy and sell, we have no use for money. But show Brother Anselm a good instrument damaged, and he'll want to heal it. Show him a good musician lost for want of an instrument, and he'll be anxious to provide him a new voice. Are you a good musician?'

Liliwin said: 'Yes!' with abrupt and spirited pride. In one respect, at least, he knew his worth.

'Then show him you are, and he'll give you your due.'

'You mean it?' wondered Liliwin, shaken between hope and doubt. 'You will truly ask him? If he would teach me, perhaps I could learn the art.' He faltered there, losing his momentary brightness with a suddenness that was all too eloquent. Whenever he took heart for the future, the bleak realisation came flooding over him afresh that he might have no future. Cadfael cast about hurriedly in his mind for some crumb of distraction to ward off the recurrent despair.

'Never suppose that you're friendless, that's black ingratitude when you have forty days of grace, a fair-minded man like Hugh Beringar enquiring into your case, and one creature at least who stands by you stoutly and won't hear a word against you.' Liliwin kindled a little at that, still doubtfully, but at least it had put the gallows and the noose out of his mind for the moment. 'You'll remember her — a girl named Rannilt.'

Liliwin's face at once paled and brightened. It was the first smile Cadfael had yet seen from him, and even now tentative, humble, frightened to reach for anything desired, for fear it should vanish like melting snow as he clutched it.

'You've see her? Talked to her? And she does not believe what they all say of me?'

'Not a word of it! She affirms — she *knows* — you never did violence nor theft in that house. If all the tongues in

55

Shrewsbury cried out against you, she would still stand her ground and speak for you.'

Liliwin sat cradling his broken rebec, as gently and shyly as if he clasped a sweetheart indeed. His faint, frightened smile shone in the dimming light within the cloister.

'She is the first girl who ever looked kindly at me. You won't have heard her sing — such a small, sweet voice, like a reed. We ate in the kitchen together. It was the best hour of my life, I never thought . . . And it's true? Rannilt believes in me?'

# Four

LILIWIN FOLDED AWAY HIS BRYCHANS AND MADE HIMSELF presentable before Prime on the sabbath, determined to cause as little disruption as possible in the orderly regime within these walls. In his wandering life he had had little opportunity to become familiar with the offices of the day, and Latin was a closed book to him, but at least he could attend and pay his reverences, if that would make him more acceptable.

After breakfast Cadfael dressed the gash in the young man's arm again, and unwound the bandage from the graze on his head. 'This is healing well,' he said approvingly. 'We'd best leave it uncovered, and let in the air to it now. Good clean flesh you have, boy, if something too little of it. And you've lost that limp that had you going sidewise. How is it with all those bruises?'

Liliwin owned with some surprise that most of his aches and pains were all but gone, and performed a few startling contortions to prove it. He had not lost his skills. His fingers itched for the coloured rings and balls he used for his juggling, safely tucked away in their knotted cloth

57

under his bed, but he feared they would be frowned on here. The ruin of his rebec also reposed in the corner of the porch next the cloister. He returned there after his breakfast to find Brother Anselm turning the wreck thoughtfully in his hands, and running a questing finger along the worst of the cracks.

The precentor was past fifty, a vague, slender, short-sighted person who peered beneath an untidy brown tonsure and bristling brows to match, and smiled amiably and encouragingly at the owner of this disastrous relic.

'This is yours? Brother Cadfael told me how it had suffered. This has been a fine instrument. You did not make it?'

'No. I had it from an old man who taught me. He gave it to me before he died. I don't know,' said Liliwin, 'how to make them.'

It was the first time Brother Anselm had heard him speak since the shrill terror of the first invasion. He looked up alertly, tilting his head to listen. 'You have the upper voice, very true and clear. I could use you, if you sing? But you must sing! You have not thought of taking the cowl, here among us?' He recalled with a sigh why that was hardly likely under present circumstances. 'Well, this poor thing has been villainously used, but it is not beyond help. We may try. And the bow is lost, you say.' Liliwin had said no such thing, he was mute with wonder. Evidently Brother Cadfael had given precise information to a retentive enthusiast. 'The bow, I must say, is almost harder to perfect than the fiddle, but I have had my successes. Have you skills on other instruments?'

'I can get a tune out of most things,' said Liliwin, charmed into eagerness.

'Come,' said Brother Anselm, taking him firmly by the arm, 'I will show you my workshop and you and I between us, after High Mass, will try what can best be done for this rebec of yours. I shall need a helper to tend my resins and gums. But this will be slow and careful work, mind, and matter for prayer, not to be hastened for any

58

cause. Music is study for a lifetime, son — a lifetime however long.'

He blew so like a warm gale that Liliwin went with him in a dream, forgetting how short a lifetime could also be.


Walter Aurifaber woke up that morning with a lingering headache, but also with a protesting stiffness in his limbs and restless animation in his mind that made him want to get up and stretch, and stamp, and move about briskly until the dullness went out of him. He growled at his patient, silent daughter, enquired after his journeyman, who had had the sense to make sure of his Sunday rest by vanishing from both shop and town for the day, and sat down to eat a substantial breakfast and stare his losses in the face.

Things were coming back to him, however foggily, including one incident he would just as soon his mother should not hear about. Money was money, of course, the old woman had the right of it there, but it's not every day a man marries off his heir, and marries him, moreover, to a most respectable further amount of money. A little flourish towards a miserable menial might surely be forgiven a man, in the circumstances. But would she think so? He regretted it bitterly himself, now, reflecting on the disastrous result of his rare impulse of generosity. No, she must not hear of it!

Walter nursed his thick head and vain regrets, and took some small comfort in seeing his son and his new daughter-in-law off to church at Saint Mary's, in their best clothes and properly linked, Margery's hand primly on Daniel's arm. The money Margery had brought with her, and would eventually bring, mattered now more than anything else until the lost contents of his strong-box could be recovered. His head ached again fiercely when he thought of it. Whoever had done that to the house of Aurifaber should and must hang, if there was any justice in this world.

When Hugh Beringar came, with a sergeant in attendance, to hear for himself what the aggrieved victim had to tell, Walter was ready and voluble. But he was none too pleased when Dame Juliana, awaiting Brother Cadfael's visit, and foreseeing more strictures as to her behaviour if she wanted to live long, took it into her head to forestall the lecture by being downstairs when her mentor came and stumped her way down, cane in hand, prodding every tread before her and scolding Susanna away from attempting to check her. She was firmly settled on her bench in the corner, propped with cushions, when Cadfael came, and challenged him with a bold, provocative stare. Cadfael chose not to gratify her with homilies, but delivered the ointment he had brought for her, and reassured himself of the evenness of her breathing and heart, before turning to a Walter grown unaccountably short of words.

'I'm glad to see you so far restored. The tales they told of you were twenty years too soon. But I'm sorry for your loss. I hope it may yet be recovered.'

'Faith, so do I,' said Walter sourly. 'You tell me that rogue you have in sanctuary has no part of it on him, and while you hold him fast within there he can hardly unearth and make off with it. For it must be somewhere, and I trust the sheriff's men here to find it.'

'You're very certain of your man, then?' Hugh had got him to the point where he had taken his valuables and gone to stow them away in the shop, and there he had suddenly grown less communicative. 'But he had already been expelled some time earlier, as I understand it, and no one has yet testified to seeing him lurking around your house after that.'

Walter cast a glance at his mother, whose ancient ears were pricked and her faded but sharp eyes alert. 'Ah, but he could well have stayed in hiding, all the same. What was there to prevent it in the dark of the night?'

'So he could,' agreed Hugh unhelpfully, 'but there's no man so far claims he did. Unless you've recalled something no one else knows? Did *you* see anything of him after he was thrown out?'

Walter shifted uneasily, looked ready to blurt out a whole

indictment, and thought better of it in Juliana's hearing. Brother Cadfael took pity on him.

'It might be well,' he said guilelessly, 'to take a look at the place where this assault was made. Master Walter will show us his workshop, I am sure.'

Walter rose to it thankfully, and ushered them away with alacrity, along the passage and in again at the door of his shop. The street door was fast, the day being Sunday, and he closed the other door carefully behind them, and drew breath in relief.

'Not that I've anything to conceal from you, my lord, but I'd as lief my mother should not have more to worrit her than she has already.' Plausible cover, at any rate, for the awe of her in which he still went. 'For this is where the thing happened, and you see from this door how the coffer lies in the opposite corner. And there was I, with the key in the lock and the lid laid back against the wall, wide open, and my candle here on the shelf close by. The light shining straight down into the coffer — you see? — and what was within in plain view. And suddenly I hear a sound behind me, and there's this minstrel, this Liliwin, creeping in at the door.'

'Threateningly?' asked Hugh, straight-faced. If he did not wink at Cadfael, his eyebrow was eloquent. 'Armed with a cudgel?'

'No,' admitted Walter, 'rather humbly, to all appearance. But then I'd heard him and turned. He was barely into the doorway, he could have dropped his weapon outside when he saw I was ware of him.'

'But you did not hear it fall? Nor see any sign of such?'

'No, that I own.'

'Then what had he to say to you?'

'He begged me to do him right, for he said he had been cheated of two thirds of his promised fee. He said it was hard on a poor man to be so blamed and docked of his money, and pleaded with me to make it good as promised.'

'And did you?' asked Hugh.

'I tell you honestly, my lord, I could not say he had been hardly used, considering the worth of the pitcher, but I did think him a poor, sad creature who had to live, whatever the rights or wrongs of it. And I gave him another penny — good silver, minted in this town. But not a word of this to Dame Juliana, if you'll be so good. She'll have to know, now it's all come back to me, that he dared creep in and ask, but no need for her to know I gave him anything. She would be affronted, seeing she had denied him.'

'Your thought for her does you credit,' said Hugh gravely. 'What then? He took your bounty and slunk out?'

'He did. But I wager *he* has not told you anything of this begging visit. A poor return I got for the favour!' Walter was sourly vengeful still.

'You mistake, for he has. He has told us this very same tale that you now tell. And confided to the abbey's keeping, while he remains there, the two silver pence which is all he has on him. Tell me, had you closed the lid of the coffer as soon as you found yourself observed?'

'I did!' said Walter fervently. 'And quickly! But he had seen. I never gave him another thought at the time but — see here, my lord, how it follows! As soon as he was gone, or I thought he was gone, I opened the coffer again, and was bending over it laying Margery's dowry away, when I was clouted hard from behind, and that's the last I knew till I opened an eye in my own bed, hours later. If it was two minutes after that fellow crept out of the door, when someone laid me flat, it was not a moment more. So who else could it be?'

'But you did not actually *see* who struck you?' Hugh pressed. 'Not so much as a glimpse? No shadow cast, to give him a shape or size? No sense of a bulk heaving up behind you?'

'Never a chance.' Walter might be vindictive, but he was honest. 'See, I was stooping over the coffer when it seemed the wall fell on me, and I pitched asprawl, head-down into the box, clean out of the world. I heard nothing and saw nothing, not even a shadow, no — the last thing I recall was the candle flickering, but what is there in that? No, depend on it, that rogue had seen what I had in my store before I clapped down the lid. Was he going tamely away with his penny, with all that money there to take? Not he! Nor hide nor hair of any other did I see in here that night. You may be certain of it, the jongleur is your man.'

'And it may still be so,' admitted Hugh, parting from Cadfael on the bridge some twenty minutes later. 'Enough to tempt any poor wretch with but two coins to rub together. Whether he had any such thought in his head before the candle shone on our friend's hoard or no. Equally, I grant the lad may not even have realised what lay beneath his hand, or seen anything but his own need and the thin chance of getting a kinder reception from the goldsmith than from that ferocious mother of his. He may have crept away thanking God for his penny and never a thought of wrong. Or he may have picked up a stone or a stave and turned back.'

At about that same time, in the street outside Saint Mary's church, which was the common ground for exchanging civilities and observing fashions on a fine Sunday morning after Mass, Daniel and Margery Aurifaber in their ceremonial progression, intercepted by alternate well-wishers and commiserators — wedding and robbery being equally relished subjects of comment and speculation in Shrewsbury — came face to face with Master Ailwin Corde, the wool-merchant, and his wife, Cecily, and halted by general consent to pass the time of day as befitted friends and neighbours.

This Mistress Cecily looked more like a daughter to the merchant, or even a granddaughter, than a wife. She was twenty-three years old to his sixty, and though small and slender of stature, was so opulent in colouring, curvature and gait, and everything that could engage the eye, that she managed to loom large as a goddess and dominate whatever scene she graced with her presence. And her elderly husband took pleasure in decking her out with sumptuous fabrics and fashions the gem he should rather have shrouded in secretive, plain linens. A gilt net gathered on her head its weight of auburn hair, and a great ornament of enamel and gemstones jutted before her, calling attention to a resplendent bosom.

Faced with this richness, Margery faded, and knew that she faded. Her smile became fixed and false as a mask, and her voice tended to sharpen like a singer forced off-key. She tightened her clasp on Daniel's arm, but it was like trying to hold a fish that slid through her fingers without even being aware of restraint.

Master Corde enquired solicitously after Walter's health, was relieved to hear that he was making a good recovery, was sad, nonetheless, to know that so far nothing had been found of all that had been so vilely stolen. He sent his condolences, while thanking God for life and health spared. His wife echoed all that he said, modest eyes lowered, and voice like distant wood-doves.

Daniel, his eyes wandering more often to Mistress Cecily's milk-and-roses face than to the old man's flabby and self-satisfied countenance, issued a hearty invitation to Master Corde to bring his wife and take a meal with the goldsmith as soon as might be, and cheer him by his company. The wool-merchant thanked him, and wished it no less, but must put off the pleasure for a week or more, though he sent his sympathetic greetings and promised his prayers.

'You don't know,' confided Mistress Cecily, advancing a small hand to touch Margery's arm, 'how fortunate you are in having a husband whose trade is rooted fast at home. This man of mine is for ever running off with his mules and his wagon and his men, either west into Wales or east into England, over business with these fleeces and cloths of his, and I'm left lonely days at a time. Now tomorrow early he's off again, if you please, as far as Oxford, and I shall lack him for three or four days.'

Twice she had raised her creamy eyelids during this complaint, once ruefully at her husband, and once, with a miraculously fleeting effect which should have eluded Margery, but did not, at Daniel, eyes blindingly bright in the one flash that shot from them, but instantly veiled and serene.

'Now, now, sweet,' said the wool-merchant indulgently, 'you know how I shall hurry back to you.'

'And how long it will take,' she retorted, pouting. 'Three or four nights solitary. And you'd better bring me something nice to sweeten me for it when you return.'

As she knew he would. He never came back from any journey but he brought her a gift to keep her sweet. He had bought her, but there was enough of cold sense in him, below his doting, to know that he had to buy her over and over again if he wanted to keep her. The day he acknowledged it, and examined the implications, she might well go in fear for her slender throat, for he was an arrogant and possessive man.

'You say very truly, madam!' said Margery, stiff-lipped. 'I do know, indeed, how fortunate I am.'

Only too well! But every man's fortune, and every woman's too, can be changed given a little thought, perseverance and cunning.

Liliwin had spent his day in so unexpected and pleasant a fashion that for an hour and more at a time he had forgotten the threat hanging over him. As soon as High Mass was over, the precentor had hustled him briskly away to the corner of the cloister where he had already begun to pick apart, with a surgeon's delicacy and ruthlessness, the fractured shards of the rebec. Slow, devoted work that demanded every particle of the pupil's attention, if he was to assist at a resurrection. And excellent therapy against the very idea of death.

'We shall put together what is here broken,' said Brother Anselm, intent and happy, 'for an avowal on our part. No matter if the product, when achieved, turns out to be flawed,

65

yet it shall speak again. If it speaks with a stammering voice, then we shall make another, as one generation follows its progenitor and takes up the former music. There is no absolute loss. Hand me here that sheet of vellum, son, and mark in what order I lay these fragments down.' Mere splinters, a few of them, but he set them carefully in the shape they should take when restored. 'Do you believe you will play again upon this instrument?'

'Yes,' said Liliwin, fascinated, 'I do believe.'

'That's well, for faith is necessary. Without faith nothing is accomplished.' He mentioned this rare tool as he would have mentioned any other among those laid out to his hand. He set aside the fretted bridge. 'Good workmanship, and old. This rebec had more than one master before it came to you. It will not take kindly to silence.'

Neither did he. His brisk, gentle voice flowed like a placid stream while he worked, and its music lulled like the purling of water. And when he had picked apart and set out in order all the fragments of the rebec, and placed the vellum that held them in a safe corner, covered with a linen cloth, to await full light next day, he confronted Liliwin at once with his own small portative organ, and demanded he should try his hand with that. He had no need to demonstrate its use, Liliwin had seen one played, but never yet had the chance to test it out for himself.

He essayed the fingering nimbly enough at his first attempt, but concentrated so totally on the tune he was playing that he forgot to work the little bellows with his left hand, and the air ran out with a sigh into silence. He caught himself up with a startled laugh, and tried again, too vigorously, his playing hand slow on the keys. At the third try he had it. He played with it, entranced, picked out air after air, getting the feel of it, balancing hand against hand, growing ambitious, attempting embellishments. Five fingers can do only so much.

Brother Anselm presented to him a curious, figured array of signs upon vellum, matched by written symbols which he knew to be words. He could not read them, since he could not read in any tongue. To him this meant nothing more than a pleasing pattern, such as a woman might draw for her embroidery.

'You never learned this mystery? Yet I think you would pick it up readily. This is music, set down so that the eye, no less than the ear, may master it. See here, this line of neums here! Give me the organ.'

He took it and played a long line of melody. 'That — what you have heard — that is written down here. Listen again!' And again he plucked it jubilantly forth. 'There, now sing me that!'

Liliwin flung up his head and paid him back the phrase.

'Now, follow me still . . . answer as I go.'

It was an intoxication, line after line of music to copy and toss back. Within minutes Liliwin had begun to embellish, to vary, to return a higher echo that chorded with the original.

'I could make of you a singer,' said Brother Anselm, sitting back in high content.

'I *am* a singer,' said Liliwin. He had never before understood fully how proud he was of being able to say so.

'I do believe it. Your music and mine go different ways, but both of them are made up of these same small signs here, and the sounds they stand for. If you stay a little, I shall teach you how to read them,' promised Anselm, pleased with his pupil. 'Now, take this, practise some song of your own with it, and then sing it to me.'

Liliwin reviewed his songs, and was somewhat abashed to discover how many of them must be suppressed here as lewd and offensive. But not all were so. He had a favourite, concerned with the first revelation of young love, and recalling it now, he recalled Rannilt, as poor as himself, as unconsidered, in her smoky kitchen and coarse gown, with her cloud of black hair and pale, oval face lit by radiant eyes. He fingered out the tune, feeling his way, his left hand now deft and certain on the bellows. He played and sang it, and grew so intent upon the singing that he scarcely noticed how busily Brother Anselm was penning signs upon his parchment.

'Will you believe,' said Anselm, delightedly proffering the leaf, 'that what you have just sung to me is written down here? Ah, not the words, but the air. This I will explain to you hereafter, you shall learn both how to inscribe and how to decypher. That's a very pleasant tune you have there. It could be used for the ground of a Mass. Well, now, that's enough for now, I must go and prepare for Vespers. Let be until tomorrow.'

Liliwin set the organetto tenderly back on its shelf, and went out, dazed, into the early evening. A limpid, pale-blue day was drifting away into a deeper blue twilight. He felt drained and gentle and fulfilled, like the day itself, silently and hopefully alive. He thought of his battered wooden juggling rings and balls, tucked away under his folded brychans in the church porch. They represented another of his skills, which, if not practised, would rust and be damaged. He was so far buoyed up by his day that he went to fetch them, and carried them away hopefully into the garden, which opened out level below level to the pease-fields that ran down to the Meole brook. There was no one there at this hour, work was over for the day. He untied the cloth, took out the six wooden balls and the rings after them, and began to spin them from hand to hand, testing his wrists and the quickness of his eye.

He was still stiff from bruises and fumbled at first, but after a while the old ease began to return to him, and his pleasure in accomplishment. This might be a very humble skill, but it was still an achievement, and his, and he cherished it. Encouraged, he put the balls and rings away, and began to try out the suppleness of his thin, wiry body, twisting himself into grotesque knots. That cost him some pain from muscles trampled and beaten, but he persisted, determined not to give up. Finally he turned cartwheels all along the headland across the top of the pease-fields, coiled himself into a ring and rolled down the slope to the banks of the brook, and made his way up again, the slope being gentle enough, in a series of somersaults.

Arrived again at the level where the vegetable gardens and the enclosed herbarium began, he uncurled himself, flushed and pleased, to find himself gazing up at a couple of yards distance into the scandalised countenance of a sour-faced brother almost as meagre as himself. He stared, abashed, into eyes rounded and ferocious with outrage.

'Is this how you reverence this holy enclave?' demanded Brother Jerome, genuinely incensed. 'Is such foolery and lightmindedness fit for our abbey? And have you, fellow, so little gratitude for the shelter afforded you here? You do not deserve sanctuary, if you value it so lightly. How dared you so affront God's enclosure?'

Liliwin shrank and stammered, out of breath and abased to the ground. 'I meant no offence. I am grateful, I do hold the abbey in reverence. I only wanted to see if I could still master my craft. It is my living, I must practise it! Pardon if I've done wrong!' He was easily intimidated, here where he was in debt, and in doubt how to comport himself in a strange world. All his brief gaiety, all the pleasure of the music, ebbed out of him. He got to his feet almost clumsily, who had been so lissome only moments ago, and stood trembling, shoulders bowed and eyes lowered.

Brother Jerome, who seldom had business in the gardens, being the prior's clerk and having no taste for manual labour, had heard from the great court the small sound, strange in these precincts, of wooden balls clicking together in mid-air, and had come to investigate in relative innocence. But once in view of the performance, and himself screened by bushes fringing Brother Cadfael's herb-garden, he had not called a halt at once and warned the offender of his offence, but remained in hiding, storing up a cumulative fund of indignation until the culprit uncoiled at his feet. It may be that a degree of guilt on his own part rendered more extreme the reproaches he loosed upon the tumbler.

'Your *living,*' he said mercilessly, 'ought to engage you rather in prayers and self-searchings than in these follies. A man who has such charges hanging over him as you have must concern himself first with his soul's welfare, for whether he has a living to make hereafter or none, he has a soul to save when his debt in this world is paid. Think on that, and go put your trumpery away, as long as you are sheltered here. It is not fitting! It is blasphemy! Have you not enough already unpaid on your account?'

Liliwin felt the terror of the outer world close in on him: it could not be long evaded. As some within here wore hovering haloes, so he wore a noose, invisible but ever-present.

'I meant no harm,' he whispered hopelessly and turned, half-blind with misery, to grope for his poor bundle of toys and blunder hastily away.

'Tumbling and juggling, there in our gardens,' Jerome reported, still burning with offence, 'like a vagabond player at a fair. How can it be excused? Sanctuary is lawful for those who come in proper deference, but this . . . I reproved him, of course. I told him he should be thinking rather of his eternal part, having so mortal a charge against him. "My living," he says! And he with a life owing!'

Prior Robert looked down his patrician nose, and maintained the fastidious and grieved calm of his noble countenance. 'Father Abbot is right to observe the sanctity of sanctuary, it may not be discarded. We are not to blame, and need not be concerned, for the guilt or innocence of those who lay claim to it. But we are, indeed, concerned for the good order and good name of our house, and I grant you this present guest is little honour to us. I should be happier if he took himself off and submitted himself to the law, that is true. But unless he does so, we must bear with him. To reprove where he offends is not only our due, but our duty. To use any effort to influence or eject him is far beyond either.

Unless he leaves of his own will,' said Prior Robert, 'both you and I, Brother Jerome, must succour, shelter and pray for him.'

How sincerely, how resolutely. But how reluctantly!

# Five

SUNDAY PASSED, CLEAR AND FINE, AND MONDAY CAME UP no less sunnily, a splendid washing day, with a warm air and a light breeze, and bushes and turf dry and springy. The Aurifaber household was always up and active early on washing days, which were saved up two or three weeks at a time, to make but one upheaval of the heating of so much water, and such labour of scrubbing and knuckling with ash and lye. Rannilt was up first, to kindle the fire under the brick and clay boiler and hump the water from the well. She was stronger than she looked and used to the weight. What burdened her far more, and to that she was not used, was the terror she felt for Liliwin.

It was with her every moment. If she slept, she dreamed of him, and awoke sweating with fear that he might be hunted out already and taken and she none the wiser. And while she was awake and working, his image was ever in her mind, and a great stone of anxiety hot and heavy in her breast. Fear for yourself crushes and compresses you from without, but fear for another is a monster, a ravenous rat gnawing within, eating out your heart.

What they said of him was false, could not under any circumstances be true. And it was his life at stake! She could not help hearing all that was said of him among them, how they all united to accuse him, and promised themselves he should hang for what he had done. What she was certain in her heart and soul he had *not* done! It was not in him to strike down any man, or rob any man's coffers.

The locksmith, up early for him, heard her drawing up the bucket from the well, and came out from his back door to stroll down into the garden in the sunlight and pass the time of day. Rannilt did not think he would have troubled if he had known it was only the maidservant. He made a point of being attentive to his landlord's family, and never missed the common neighbourly courtesies, but his notice seldom extended to Rannilt. Nor did he linger on this fine morning, but took a short turn about the yard and returned to his own door. There he looked back, eyeing for a moment the obvious preparations at the goldsmith's house, the great mound of washing in hand, and the normal bustle just beginning.

Susanna came down with her arms full of linen, and went to work with her usual brisk, silent competence. Daniel ate his breakfast and went to his workshop, leaving Margery solitary and irresolute in the hall. Too much had happened on her wedding night, she had had no time to grow used to house and household, or consider her own place in it. Wherever she turned to make herself useful, Susanna had been before her. Walter lay late, nursing his sore head, and Dame Juliana kept her own chamber, but Margery was too late to carry food and drink to either, it was already done. There was no need yet to think of cooking, and in any case all the household keys were on Susanna's girdle. Margery turned her attention to the one place where she felt herself and her own wishes to be dominant, and set to work to rearrange Daniel's bachelor chamber to her own taste, and clear out the chest and press which must now make room for her own clothes and stores of linen. In the process she discovered much evidence of Dame Juliana's noted parsimony. There were garments which must have belonged to Daniel as a growing boy, and could certainly never again be worn by him. Neatly mended again and again, they had all been made to last as long as possible, and even when finally outgrown, had still been folded away and kept. Well, she was now Daniel's wife, she would have this chamber as she wanted it, and be rid of these useless and miserly reminders of the past. Today the household might still be running on its customary wheels, as though she had no part to play, but it would not always be so. She was in no haste, she had a great deal of thinking to do before she took action.

On her knees in the yard, Rannilt scrubbed and pummelled, her hands sore from the lye. By mid-morning the last of the washing was wrung and folded and piled into a great wicker basket. Susanna hoisted it on her hip and bore it away down the slope of the garden, and through the deep arch in the town wall, to spread it out on the bushes and the smooth plane of grass that faced almost due south to the sun. Rannilt cleared away the tub and mopped the floor, and went in to tend the fire and set the salt beef simmering for dinner.

Here quiet and alone, she was suddenly so full of her pain on Liliwin's account that her eyes spilled abrupt tears into the pot, and once the flow began she could not dam it. She groped blindly about the kitchen, working by touch, and shedding helpless tears for the first man who had caught her fancy, and the first who had ever fancied her.

Absorbed into her misery, she did not hear Susanna come quietly into the doorway behind her, and halt there at gaze, watching the fumbling hands feeling their way, and the half-blind eyes still streaming.

'In God's name, girl, what is it with you now?'

Rannilt started and turned guiltily, stammering that it was nothing, that she was sorry, that she was getting on with her work, but Susanna cut her off sharply:

'It is not nothing! I'm sick of seeing you thus moping and useless. You've been limp as a sick kitten this two days past, and I know why. You have that miserable little thief on your mind — I know! I know he wound about you with his soft voice and his creeping ways, I've watched you. Must you be fool enough to fret over a guilty wretch the like of that?'

She was not angry; she was never angry. She sounded impatient, even exasperated, but still contemptuously kind, and her voice was level and controlled as ever. Rannilt swallowed the choking residue of tears, shook the mist from her eyes, and began to be very busy with her pots and pans, looking hurriedly about her for a distraction which would turn attention from herself at any cost. 'It came over me just for a minute: I'm past it now. Why, you've got your feet and the hem of your gown wet,' she exclaimed, seizing gratefully on the first thing that offered. 'You should change your shoes.'

Susanna shrugged the diversion scornfully aside. 'Never mind my wet feet. The river's up a little, I was not noticing until I went too near the edge, leaning to hang a shirt on the bushes. What of your wet eyes? That's more to the point. Oh, fool girl, you're wasting your fancy! This is a common rogue of the roads, with many a smaller deed of the kind behind him, and he'll get nothing but his due in the noose that's waiting for him. Get sense, and put him out of your mind.'

'He is not a rogue,' said Rannilt, despairingly brave. 'He did not do it, I know it, I know *him,* he could not. It isn't in him to do violence. And I do fret for him, I can't help it.'

'So I see,' said Susanna resignedly. 'So I've seen ever since they ran him to ground. I tire of him and of you. I want you in your wits again. God's truth, must I carry this household on my back without even your small help?' She gnawed a thoughtful lip, and demanded abruptly: 'Will it cure you if I let you go see for yourself that the tumbler is alive and whole, and out of our reach for a while, more's the pity? Yes, and likely to worm his way out of even this tangle in the end!'

She had spoken magical words. Rannilt was staring up at her dry-eyed, bright as a candle-flame. 'See? See him? You mean I could go there?'

'You have legs,' said Susanna tartly. 'It's no distance. They don't close their gates against anyone. You may even come back in your right senses, when you see how little store he sets by *you*, while you're breaking your fool heart for him. You may get to know him for what he is, and the better for you. Yes, go. Go, and be done with it! This once I'll manage without you. Let Daniel's wife start making herself useful. Good practice for her.'

'You mean it?' whispered Rannilt, stricken by such generosity. 'I may go? But who will see to the broth here, and the meat?'

'I will. I have often enough, God knows! I tell you, go, go quickly, before I change my mind, stay away all day long, if that will send you back cured. I can very well do without you this once. But wash your face, girl, and comb your hair, and do yourself and us credit. You can take some of those oat-cakes in a basket, if you wish, and whatever scraps were left from yesterday. If he felled my father,' said Susanna roughly, turning away to pick up the ladle and stir the pot simmering on the hob, 'there's worse waiting for him in the end, no need to grudge him a mouthful while he is man alive.' She looked back over a straight shoulder at Rannilt, who still hovered in a daze. 'Go and visit your minstrel, I mean it, you have leave. I doubt if he even remembers your face! Go and learn sense.'

Lost in wonder, and only half believing in such mercies, Rannilt washed her face and tidied her tangle of dark hair with trembling hands, seized a basket and filled it with whatever morsels were brusquely shoved her way, and went out through the hall like a child walking in its sleep. It was wholly by chance that Margery was coming down the stairs, with a pile of discarded garments on her arm. She marked the small, furtive figure flitting past below, and in surprised good will, since this waif was alien and lonely here as she was, asked: 'Where are you sent off to in such a hurry, child?'

Rannilt halted submissively, and looked up into Margery's rounded, fresh countenance. 'Mistress Susanna gave me leave. I'm going to the abbey, to take this provision to Liliwin.' The name, so profoundly significant to her, meant nothing to Margery. 'The minstrel. The one they say struck down Master Walter. But I'm sure he did not! She said I may go, see for myself how he's faring — because I was crying . . .''

'I remember him,' said Margery. 'A little man, very young. They're sure he's the guilty one, and you are sure he is not?' Her blue eyes were demure. She hunted through the pile of garments on her arm, and very faintly and fleetingly she smiled. 'He was not too well clothed, I recall. There is a cotte here that was my husband's some years ago, and a capuchon. The little man could wear them, I think. Take them with you. It would be a pity to waste them. And charity is approved of in Heaven, even to sinners.'

She sorted them out gravely, a good dark-blue coat outgrown while it was still barely patched, and a much-mended caped hood in russet brown. 'Take them! They're of no use here.' None, except for the satisfaction it gave her to despatch them to the insignificant soul condemned by every member of her new family. It was her gesture of independence.

Rannilt, every moment more dazed, took the offerings and tucked them into her basket, made a mute reverence, and fled before this unprecedented and hardly credible vein of good will should run out, and food, clothing, holiday and all fall to ruin round her.

Susanna cooked, served, scoured and went about her circumscribed realm with a somewhat grim smile on her lips. The provisioning of the house under her governance was discreetly more generous than ever it had been under Dame Juliana, and on this day there was enough and to spare, even after she had carried his usual portion to Iestyn in the workshop, and sat with him for company while he ate, to bring back the dish to the kitchen afterwards. What remained was not worth keeping to use up another day, but there was enough for one. She shredded the remains of the boiled salt beef into it, and took it across to the locksmith's shop, as she had sometimes done before when there was plenty.

John Boneth was at work at his bench, and looked up as she entered, bowl in hand. She looked about her, and saw everything in placid order, but no sign of Baldwin Peche, or the boy Griffin, probably out on some errand.

'We have a surfeit, and I know your master's no great cook. I brought him his dinner, if he hasn't eaten already.'

John had come civilly to his feet, with a deferential smile for her. They had known each other five years, but always at this same discreet distance. The landlord's daughter, the rich master-craftsman's girl, was no meat for a mere journeyman.

'That's kind, mistress, but the master's not here. I've not seen him since the middle of the morning, he's left me two or three keys to cut. I fancy he's off for the day. He said something about the fish rising.'

There was nothing strange in that. Baldwin Peche relied on his man to take charge of the business every bit as competently as he could have done himself, and was prone to taking holidays whenever it suited his pleasure. He might be merely making the round of the ale-houses to barter his own news for whatever fresh scandal was being whispered, or he might be at the butts by the riverside, betting on a good marksman, or out in his boat, which he kept in a yard near the watergate, only a few minutes down-river. The young salmon must be coming up the Severn by this time. A fisherman might well be tempted out to try his luck.

'And you don't know if he'll be back?' Susanna read his face, shrugged and smiled. 'I know! Well, if he's not here to eat it . . . I daresay you have still room to put this away, John?' He brought with him, usually, a hunk of bread and a strip of salt bacon or a piece of cheese, meat was festival fare in his mother's house. Susanna set down her bowl before him on the bench, and sat down on the customer's stool opposite, spreading her elbows comfortably along the boards. 'It's his loss. In an ale-house he'll pay more for poorer fare. I'll sit with you, John, and take back the bowl.'

Rannilt came down the Wyle to the open gate of the town, and passed through its shadowed arch to the glitter of sunlight on the bridge. She had fled in haste from the house, for fear of being called back, but she had lingered on the way through the town for fear of what lay before her. For the course was fearful, to one unschooled, half-wild, rejected by Wales and never welcomed in England but as a pair of labouring hands. She knew nothing of monks or monasteries, and none too much even of Christianity. But there inside the abbey was Liliwin, and thither she would go. The gates, Susanna had said, were never closed against any.

On the far side of the bridge she passed close by the copse where Liliwin had curled up to sleep, and been hunted out at midnight. On the other side of the Foregate lay the mill pool, and the houses in the abbey's grant, and beyond, the wall of the enclave began, and the roofs of infirmary and school and guest-hall within, and the tall bulk of the gatehouse. The great west door of the church, outside the gates, confronted her in majesty. But once timidly entering the great court, she found reassurance. Even at this hour, perhaps the quietest of the day, there was a considerable bustle of coming and going within there, guests arriving and departing, servants ambling about on casual errands, petitioners begging, packmen taking a mid-day rest, a whole small world of people, some of them as humble as herself. She could walk in there among them, and never be noticed. But still she had to find Liliwin, and she cast about her for the most sympathetic source of information.

She was not blessed in her choice. A small man, in the habit of the house, scurrying across the court; she chose him because he was as small and slight as Liliwin, and his shoulders had a discouraged droop which reminded her of Liliwin, and because someone who looked so modest and disregarded must surely feel for others as insignificant as himself. Brother Jerome would have been deeply offended if he had known. As it was, he was not displeased at the low reverence this suppliant girl made to him, and the shy whisper in which she addressed him.

'Please, sir, I am sent by my lady with alms for the young man who is here in sanctuary. If you would kindly teach me where I may find him.'

She had not spoken his name because it was a private thing, to be kept jealously apart. Jerome, however he might regret that any lady should be so misguided as to send alms to the offender, was somewhat disarmed by the approach. A maid on an errand was not to be blamed for her mistress's errors.

'You will find him there, in the cloister, with Brother Anselm.' He indicated the direction grudgingly, disapproving of Brother Anselm's complacent usage with an accused man, but not censuring Rannilt, until he noted the brightening of her face and the lightness of her foot as she sprang to follow where he pointed. Not merely an errand-girl, far too blithe! 'Take heed, child, what message you have to him must be done decorously. He is on probation of a most grave charge. You may have half an hour with him, you may and you should exhort him to consider on his soul. Do your errand and go!'

She looked back at him with great eyes, and was very still for one instant in her flight. She faltered some words of submission, while her eyes flamed unreadably, with a most disquieting brilliance. She made a further deep reverence, to the very ground, but sprang from it like an angel soaring, and flew to the cloister whither he had pointed her.

It seemed vast to her, four-sided in stony corridors about an open garden, where spring flowers burst out in gold and white and purple on a grassy ground. She flitted the length of one walk between terror and delight, turned along the second in awe of the alcove cells furnished with slanted tables and benches, empty but for one absorbed scholar copying wonders, who never lifted his head as she passed by. At the end of this walk, echoing from such another cell, she heard music. She had never before heard an organ played, it was a magical sound to her, until she heard a sweet, lofty voice soar happily with it, and knew it for Liliwin's.

He was bending over the instrument, and did not hear her come. Neither did Brother Anselm, equally absorbed in fitting together the fragments of the rebec's back. She stood timidly in the opening of the carrel, and only when the song ended did she venture speech. At this vital moment she did not know what her welcome would be. What proof had she that he had thought of her, since that hour they had spent together, as she had thought ceaselessly of him? It might well be that she was fooling herself, as Susanna had said.

'If you please . . .' began Rannilt humbly and hesitantly.

Then they both looked up. The old man viewed her with mildly curious eyes, unastonished and benign. The young one stared, gaped and blazed, in incredulous joy, set aside his strange instrument of music blindly on the bench beside him, and came to his feet slowly, warily, all his movements soft almost to stealth, as though any sudden start might cause her to quiver and dissolve into light, vanishing like morning mist.

'Rannilt . . . It *is* you?'

If this was indeed foolery, then she was not the only fool. She looked rather at Brother Anselm, whose devoted fingers were held poised, not to divert by the least degree the touch he had suspended on his delicate operations.

'If you please, I should like to speak with Liliwin. I have brought him some gifts.'

'By all means,' said Brother Anselm amiably. 'You hear, boy? You have a visitor. There, go along and be glad of her. I shall not need you now for some hours. I'll hear your lesson later.'

They moved towards each other in a dream, wordless, took hands and stole away.


'I swear to you, Rannilt, I never struck him, I never stole from him, I never did him wrong.' He had said it at least a dozen times, here in the shadowy porch where his brychans were folded up, and his thin pallet spread, and the poor tools of his craft hidden away in a corner of the stone bench as though some shame attached to them. And there had never been any need to say it even once, as she a dozen times had answered him.

'I know, I know! I never believed for a moment. How could you doubt it? I know you are good. They will find it out, they will have to own it.'

They trembled together and kept fast hold of hands in a desperate clasp, and the touch set their unpractised bodies quivering in an excitement neither of them understood.

'Oh, Rannilt, if you knew! That was the worst of all, that you might shrink from me and believe me so vile . . . *They* believe it, all of them. Only you . . .'

'No,' she said stoutly, 'I'm not so sure. The brother who comes to physic Dame Juliana, the one who brought back your things . . . And that kind brother who is teaching you . . . Oh, no, you are not abandoned. You must not think it!'

'No!' he owned thankfully. 'Now I do believe, I do trust, if *you* are with me . . .' He was lost in wonder that anyone in that hostile household should send her to him. 'She was good, your lady! I'm so beholden to her . . .'

Not for the gifts of food, orts to her, delicacies to him. No, but for this nearness that clouded his senses in a fevered warmth and delight and disquiet he had never before experienced, and which could only be love, the love he had sung by rote for years, while his body and mind were quite without understanding.

Brother Jerome, true to what he felt to be his duty, had marked the passing of time, and loomed behind them, approaching inexorably along the walk from the great court. His sandals silent on the flagstones, he observed as he came the shoulders pressed close, the two heads, the flaxen and the black, inclined together with temples almost touching. Certainly it was time to part them, this was no place for such embraces.

'It will all be well in the end,' said Rannilt, whispering. 'You'll see! Mistress Susanna — she says as they say, and

82

yet she let me come. I think she doesn't really believe . . .
She said I might stay away all day long . . .'

'Oh, Rannilt . . . Oh, Rannilt, I do so love you . . .'

'Maiden,' said Brother Jerome, harshly censorious behind them, 'you have had time enough to discharge your
mistress's errand. There can be no further stay. You must
take your basket and depart.'

A shadow no bigger than Liliwin's, there behind them
black against the slanting sun of mid-afternoon, and yet he
cast such a darkness over them as they could hardly bear.
They had only just linked hands, barely realised the possi-
bilities that lie within such slender bodies, and they must be
torn apart. The monk had authority, he spoke for the abbey,
and there was no denying him. Liliwin had been granted
shelter, how could he then resist the restrictions laid upon
him?

They rose, tremulous. Her hand in his clung convul-
sively, and her touch ran through him like a stiffening fire,
drawn by a great, upward wind that was his own desperation
and anger.

'She is going,' said Liliwin. 'Only give us, for pity's
sake, some moments in the church together for prayer.'

Brother Jerome found that becoming, even disarming,
and stood back from them as Liliwin drew her with him, the
basket in his free hand, in through the porch to the dark inte-
rior of the church. Silence and dimness closed on them.
Brother Jerome had respected their privacy and remained
without, though he would not go far until he saw one of
them emerge alone.

And it might be the last time he would ever see her! He
could not bear it that she should go so soon, perhaps to be
lost for ever, when she had leave to be absent all day long.
He closed his hand possessively on her arm, drawing her
deep into the shadowy, stony recesses of the transept chapel
beyond the parish altar. She should not go like this! They
were not followed, there was no one else here within at this
moment, and Liliwin was well acquainted now with every
corner and cranny of this church, having prowled it rest-

lessly and fearfully on his first night here alone, when his ears were still pricked for sounds of pursuit, and he was afraid to sleep on his pallet in the porch.

'Don't go, don't go!' His arms were clasped tightly about her as they pressed together into the darkest corner, and his lips were whispering agitatedly against her cheek. 'Stay with me! You can, you can, I'll show you a place . . . No one will know, no one will find us.'

The chapel was narrow, the altar wide, all but filling the space between its containing columns, and stood out somewhat from the niche that tapered behind it. There was a little cavern there, into which only creatures as small and thin as they could creep. Liliwin had marked it down as a place to which he might retreat if the hunters broke in, and he knew his own body could negotiate the passage, so for her it would be no barrier. And within there was darkness, privacy, invisibility.

'Here, slip in here! No one will see. When he's satisfied, when he goes away, I'll come to you. We can be together until Vespers.'

Rannilt went where he urged her; she would have done anything he asked, her hunger was as desperate as his. The empty basket was drawn through the narrow space after her. Her wild whisper breathed back from the darkness: 'You will come? Soon?'

'I'll come! Wait for me . . .'

Invisible and still, she made no murmur nor rustle. Liliwin turned, trembling, and went back past the parish altar, and out at the south porch into the east walk of the cloisters. Brother Jerome had had the grace to withdraw into the garth, to keep his jealous watch a little less blatantly, but his sharp eyes were still on the doorway, and the emergence of the solitary figure, head drooping and shoulders despondent, appeared to satisfy him. Liliwin did not have to feign dejection, he was already in tears of excitement, compounded of joy and grief together. He did not turn along the scriptorium to go back to Brother Anselm, but went straight past the bench in the porch, where the gifts of food and clothing lay on his folded brychans, and out into the court and the garden beyond. But not far, only into cover among the first bushes, where he could look back and see Brother Jerome give over his vigil, and depart briskly in the direction of the grange court. The girl was gone, from the west door of the church; the disturbing presence was removed, monastic order restored, and Brother Jerome's authority had been properly respected.

Liliwin flew back to his pallet in the porch, rolled up food and clothing in his blankets, and looked round carefully to make sure there was now no one paying any attention to him, either within or without the church. When he was certain, he slipped in with his bundle under his arm, darted into the chapel, and slid as nimbly as an eel between altar and pillar into the dark haven behind. Rannilt's hands reached out for him, her cheek was pressed against his, they shook together, almost invisible even to each other, and by that very mystery suddenly loosed from all the restraints of the outer world, able to speak without speech, delivered from shyness and shame, avowed lovers. This was something quite different even from sitting together in the porch, before Jerome's serpent hissed into their Eden. There they had never got beyond clasping hands, and even those clasped hands hidden between them, as if a matter for modesty and shame. Here there was neither, only a vindicated candour that expanded in darkness, giving and receiving passionate, inexpert caresses.

There was room there to make a nest, with the blankets and the basket and Daniel's outgrown clothes, and if the stone floor was thick with a generation or more of soft, fine dust, that only helped to cushion the couch they laid down for themselves. They sat huddled together with their backs against the stone wall, sharing their warmth, and the morsels Susanna had discarded, and holding fast to each other for reassurance, until they drifted into a dream-like illusion of safety where reassurance was unnecessary.

They talked, but in few and whispered words.

Are you cold?'

'No.'

'Yes, you're trembling.' He shifted and drew her into his arm, close against his breast, and with his free hand plucked up a corner of the blanket over her shoulder, binding her to him. She stretched up her arm within the rough wool, slipped her hand about his neck, and embraced him with lips and cheek and nestling forehead, drawing him down with her until they lay breast to breast, heaving as one to great, deep-drawn sighs.

There was some manner of lightning-stroke, as it seemed, that convulsed them both, and fused them into one without any coherent action on their part. They were equally innocent, equally knowing. Knowing by rote is one thing. What they experienced bore no resemblance to what they had thought they knew. Afterwards, shifting a little only to entwine more closely and warmly, they fell asleep in each other's arms, to quicken an hour or more later to the same compulsion, and love again without ever fully awaking. Then they slept again, so deeply, in such an exhaustion of wonder and fulfilment, that even the chanting of Vespers in the choir did not disturb them.

'Shall I fetch in the linen for you?' Margery offered in the afternoon, making a conciliatory foray into Susanna's domain, and finding that composed housekeeper busy with preparations for the evening's supper.

'Thank you,' said Susanna, hardly looking up from her work, 'but I'll do that myself,' Not one step is she going to advance towards me, thought Margery, damped. *Her* linen, *her* stores, *her* kitchen! And at that Susanna did look up, even smiled; her usual, wry smile, but not unfriendly. 'If you wish me well, do take charge of my grandmother. You are new to her, she'll take more kindly to you, and be more biddable. I have had this some years, she and I wear out each other. We are too like. You come fresh. It would be a kindness.'

Margery was silenced and disarmed. 'I will,' she said heartily, and went away to do her best with the old woman, who, true enough, undoubtedly curbed her malevolence with the newcomer.

Only later in the evening, viewing Daniel across the trestle table, mute, inattentive and smugly glowing with some private satisfaction, did she return to brooding on her lack of status here, and reflecting at whose girdle the keys were hung, and whose voice bound or loosed the maidservant who was still absent.

'I marvel,' said Brother Anselm, coming out from the refectory after supper, 'where my pupil can have got to. He's been so eager, since I showed him the written notes. An angel's ear, true as a bird, and a voice the same. And he has not even been to the kitchen for his supper.'

'Nor come to have his arm dressed,' agreed Brother Cadfael, who had spent the whole afternoon busily planting, brewing and compounding in his herbarium. 'Though Oswin did look at it earlier, and found it healing very well.'

'There was a maidservant here bringing him a basket of dainties from her mistress's table,' said Jerome, one ear pricked in their direction. 'No doubt he felt no appetite for our simple fare. I had occasion to admonish them. He may have taken some grief, and be moping solitary.'

It had not occurred to him, until then, that he had not seen the unwanted guest since the boy had come out of the church alone; now it seemed, moreover, that Brother Anselm, who had had more reason to expect to spend time with his pupil, had not seen hide or hair of him, either. The abbey enclave was extensive, but not so great that a man virtually a prisoner should disappear in it. If, that is, he was still within it?

Jerome said no word more to his fellows, but spent the final half-hour before Compline making a rapid search of every part of the enclave, and ended at the south porch. The pallet on the stone bench was bare and unpressed, the brychans unaccountably missing. He did not notice the small cloth bundle tucked under a corner of the straw. As far as he could see, there was no sign left of Liliwin's presence.

He reported as much to Prior Robert, returning breathless

just before Compline was due to begin. Robert did not exactly smile, his ascetic face remained benign and bland as ever, but he did somehow radiate an air of relief and cautious pleasure.

'Well, well!' said Robert. 'If the misguided youth has been so foolish as to quit his place of safety on account of a woman, it is his own choice. A sad business, but no blame lights upon any within here. No man can be wise for another.' And he led the procession into the choir with his usual impressive gait and saintly visage, and breathed the more easily now that the alien burr had been dislodged from his skin. He did not warn Jerome to say no word yet to anyone else within here; there was no need, they understood each other very well.

# Six

*Monday night to Tuesday afternoon*

LILIWIN AWOKE WITH A JOLTING SHOCK TO DARKNESS, THE unmistakable sound of Brother Anselm's voice leading the chanting in the choir, a wild sense of fear, and the total remembrance of the wonderful and terrible thing he and Rannilt had done together, that revelation of bliss that was at the same time so appalling and unforgivable a blasphemy. Here, behind the altar, in the presence of relics so holy, the sin of the flesh, natural and human as it might be out in some meadow or coppice, became mortal and damning. But the immediate terror was worse than the distant smell of hellfire. He remembered where he was, and everything that had passed, and his senses, sharpened by terror and dismay, recognized the office. Not Vespers! Compline! They had slept for hours. Even the evening was spent, the night closing in.

He groped with frantic gentleness along the brychan, to lay a hand over Rannilt's lips, and kissed her cheek to awaken her. She started instantly and fully out of the depths of sleep. He felt her lips move, smiling, against his palm. She remembered, but not as he did; she felt no guilt and she was not afraid. Not yet! That was still to come.

With his lips close to her ear, in the tangle of her black hair, he breathed: 'We've slept too long . . . it's night, they're singing Compline.'

She sat up abruptly, braced and listening with him. She whispered: 'Oh mercy! What have we done? I must go . . . I shall be so late . . .'

'No, not alone . . . you can't. All that way in the dark!'

'I'm not afraid.'

'But I won't let you! There are thieves and villains in the night. You shan't go alone, I'm coming with you.'

She put him off from her with a hand flattened against his breast, her fluttering whisper agitated but still soft on his cheek: 'You can't! You can't, you mustn't leave here, they're watching outside, they'd take you.'

'Wait . . . wait here a moment, let me look.' The faint light from the choir, shut off by stone walls from their cranny, but feebly reflected into the chapel, had begun to show in a pallid outline the shape of the altar behind which they crouched. Liliwin slipped round it, and padded across to peer round a sheltering column into the nave. There were a number of elderly women of the Foregate who attended even non-parochial services regularly, having their souls in mind, their homes only a few paces distant, and nothing more interesting to do with their evenings in these declining years. Five of them were present on this fine, mild night, kneeling in the dimness just within Liliwin's view, and one of them must have brought a young grandson with her, while another, fragile enough to need or demand a prop, had a young man in his twenties attendant on her. Enough of them to provide a measure of cover, if God, or fate, or whatever held the dice, added the requisite measure of luck.

Liliwin fled back into the dark chapel, and reached a hand to draw Rannilt out from their secret nest.

'Quick, leave the brychans,' he whispered feverishly, 'but give me the clothes — the cotte and capuchon. No one has ever seen me but in these rags . . .'

Daniel's old coat was ample for him, and worn over his own clothes gave him added bulk, as well as respectability.

The nave was lit by only two flares close to the west door, and the rust-brown capuchon, with its deep shoulder-cape, widened his build and hid his face to some extent even before he could hoist it over his head on quitting the church.

Rannilt clung to his arm, trembling and pleading. 'No, don't . . . stay here, I'm afraid for you . . .'

'Don't be afraid! We shall go out with all those people, no one will notice us.' And whether in terror or no, they would be together still a while longer, arms linked, hands clasped.

'But how will you get in again?' she breathed, lips against his cheek.

'I will. I'll follow someone else through the gate.' The office was ending, in a moment the brothers would be moving in procession down the opposite aisle to the night stairs. 'Come, now, close to the people there . . .'

The ancient, holy women of the Foregate waited on their knees, faces turned towards the file of monks as they passed, shadowy, towards their beds. Then they rose and began their leisurely shuffle towards the west door, and after them, emerging unquestioned from shadow, went Liliwin and Rannilt, close and quiet, as though they belonged.

And it was unbelievably easy. The sheriff's officers had a guard of two men constantly outside the gatehouse, where they could cover both the gate itself and the west door of the church, and they had torches burning, but rather for their own pleasure and convenience than as a means of noting Liliwin's movements, since they had to while away the hours somehow on their watch, and you cannot play either dice or cards in the dark. By this time they did not believe that the refugee would make any attempt to leave his shelter, but they knew their duty and kept their watch faithfully enough. They stood to watch in silence as the worshippers left the church, but they had no orders to scrutinise those who went in, and so had not either counted them or observed them closely, and noted no discrepancy in the numbers leaving. Nor was there any sign here of the jongleur's faded and threadbare motley, but neat, plain burgess clothing. Having no knowledge that a young girl had made her way in, intent on seeing the accused man, they thought nothing of watching her make her way out in his company. Two insignificant young people passed and dwindled into the night on the heels of the old women. What was there in that?

They were out, they were past, the lights of the torches dimmed behind them, the cool darkness closed round them, and the hearts that had fluttered up wildly into their throats, like terrified birds shut into a narrow room, settled back gradually into their breasts, still beating heavily. By luck two of the old women, and the young man who supported the elder, inhabited two of the small houses by the mill, as pensioners of the abbey, and so had to turn towards the town, and Liliwin and Rannilt did not have to go that way alone from the gate, or they might have been more conspicuous. When the women had turned aside to their own doors, and they two alone were stealing silently between mill-pool on one hand and the copses above the Gaye on the other, and the stone rise of the bridge showed very faintly before them, Rannilt halted abruptly, drawing him round face to face with her in the edge of the trees.

'Don't come into the town! Don't! Turn here, to the left, this side the river, there's a track goes south, they won't be watching there. Don't come through the gate! And don't go back! You're out now, and none of them know. They won't, not until tomorrow. Go, go, while you can! You're free, you can leave this place . . .' Her whisper was urgent, resolute with hope for him, desolate with dismay on her own account. Liliwin heard the one as clearly as the other, and for a moment he, too, was torn.

He drew her deeper into the trees, and shut his arms about her fiercely. 'No! I'm coming with you, it isn't safe for you alone. You don't know what things can happen by night in a dark alley. I'll see you to your own yard. I must, I will!'

'But don't you see . . .' She beat a small fist against his shoulder in desperation. 'You could go now, escape, put this town behind you. A whole night to get well away. There'll be no second chance like this.'

'And put you behind me, too? And make myself seem

what they say I am?' He put a shaking hand under her chin, and turned up to him none too gently the face he saw only as a pale oval in the darkness. 'Do you *want* me to go? Do you want never to see me again? If that's what you want, say it, and I'll go. But say truth! Don't lie to me!'

She heaved a huge sigh, and embraced him in passionate silence. In a moment she breathed: 'No! No . . . I want you safe . . . But I want you!''

She wept briefly, while he held her and made soft, inarticulate sounds of comfort and dismay; and then they went on, for that was settled, and would not lightly be raised again. Over the bridge, with lambent light flickering up from the Severn's dimpling surface on either side, and the torches burning down redly in the side-pillars of the town gate before them. The watchmen at the gate were easy, bestirring themselves only when brawlers or obstreperous drunks rolled in upon them. Two humble but respectable young people hurrying home got only a glance from them, and an amiable goodnight.

'You see,' said Liliwin, on their way up the dark slope and curve of the Wyle, 'it was not so hard.'

Very softly she said: 'No.'

'I shall go in again just as simply. Late travellers come, I shall tread in on their heels. If there are none, I can sleep rough over the night, and in these clothes I can slip in when the morning traffic begins.'

'You could still go from here,' she said, 'when you leave me.'

'But I will not leave you. When I go from here, you will go with me.'

He was flying his small pennon of defiance against the wind, and knew it, but he meant it with all his heart. It might all end ignominiously, he might still fall like the heron to the fowler, but he had had until now a name, however humble, never traduced with accusation of theft and violence, and it was worth a venture to keep that; and now he had a still dearer stake to win or lose. He would not go. He would abide to win or lose all.

At the High Cross they turned to the right, and were in narrower and darker places, and once, at least, something furtive and swift turned aside from their path, perhaps wary of two, where one might cry out loud enough to rouse others, even if the second could be laid out with the first blow. Shrewsbury was well served in its watchmen, but every solitary out at night is at the mercy of those without scruples, and the watch cannot be everywhere. Rannilt did not notice. Her fear for Liliwin was not of any immediate danger to him here.

'Will they be angry with you?' he wondered anxiously, as they drew nearer to Walter Aurifaber's shop-front, and the narrow passage through into the yard.

'She said I might stay all day, if it would cure me.' She smiled invisibly in the night, far from cured, but armed against any questioning. 'She was kind, I'm not afraid of her, she'll stand by me.'

In the deep darkness of a doorway opposite he drew her to him, and she turned and clung. It came upon them both alike that this might be the last time, but they clung, and kissed and would not believe it.

'Now go, go quickly! I shall watch until you're within.' They stood where he could gaze deep into the passage, and mark the faint glow from an unshuttered window within. He put her away from him, turned her about, and gave her a push to start her on her way. 'Run!'

She was gone, across the street and into the passage, scurrying obediently, blotting out for a moment the inner glow. Then she was into the yard, and the small light picked out the shape of her for one instant as she flew past the hall door and was gone indeed.

Liliwin stood motionless in the dark doorway, staring after her for a long time. The night was very still and quiet about him. He did not want to move away. Even when the dull spark within the yard was quenched, he still stood there, straining blindly after the way she had gone.

But he was wrong, the spark had not been quenched, only blotted out from sight for the minute or so it took for a man's form to thread the passage silently and emerge into the street. A tall, well-built man, young by his step, in a hurry by the way he hurtled out of the passage, and about some private and nefarious business by the agility and stealth with which he slid in and out of the deepest shadows as he made off along the lane, with his capuchon drawn well forward and his head lowered.

There were but two young men who habited within that burgage at night, and a man who had played and sung and tumbled a long evening away in their company had no difficulty in distinguishing between them. In any case, the fine new coat marked him out, for all his furtive procedure. Only three days married, where was Daniel Aurifaber off to in such a hurry, late at night?

Liliwin left his station at last, and went back along the narrow street towards the High Cross. He saw no more of that flitting figure. Somewhere in this maze of by-streets Daniel had vanished, about what secret business there was no knowing. Liliwin made his way down the Wyle to the gate, and was hardly shaken at being halted by a guard wider awake than his fellows.

'Well, well, lad, you're back soon. Wanting out again at this hour? You're back and forth like a dog at a fair.'

'I was seeing my girl safe home,' said Liliwin, truth coming both welcome and easy. 'I'm away back to the abbey now. I'm working there.' And so he was, and would work the harder the next day for having deserted Brother Anselm on this one.

'Oh, you're in their service, are you?' The guard was benevolent. 'Take no unwary vows, lad, or you'll lose that girl of yours. Off you go then, and goodnight to you.'

The cavern of the gateway, reflecting torchlight from its stony vault, fell behind him, the arch of the bridge, with liquid silver on either side, opened before him, and above there was a light veil of cloud pierced here and there by a stray star. Liliwin crossed, and slipped again into the bushes that fringed the roadway. The silence was daunting. When he drew nearer to the abbey gatehouse he was afraid to stir out of cover, and cross the empty street to brave the scrutiny beyond. Both the west door of the church and the open wicker of the gate seemed equally inaccessible.

He stood deep in cover, watching the Foregate, and it came back to him suddenly and temptingly that he was, indeed, out of sanctuary undetected, and the whole of the night before him to put as many miles as possible between himself and Shrewsbury, and hide himself as deeply as possible among men to whom he was unknown. He was small and weak and fearful, and very greedy for life, and the ache to escape this overhanging peril was acute. But all the time he knew he would not go. Therefore he must get back to the one place where for thirty-seven more days he was safe, here within reach of the house where Rannilt slaved and waited and prayed for him.

He had luck in the end, and not even long to wait. One of the lay servants of the abbey had had his new son christened that day, and opened his house to the assembly of his relatives and friends to celebrate the occasion. The abbey stewards, shepherds and herdsmen who had been his guests came back along the Foregate in a flock, well-fed and merry, to return to their quarters in the grange court. Liliwin saw them come, spanning the street with their loose-knit chain, and when they drew near enough, and closed at leisure on the gatehouse, those bound within taking spacious leave of those living without, so that he was sure of the destination of perhaps a third of their number, he slipped out of the bushes and mingled with the fringes of the group. One more in the dimness made no matter. He went in unquestioned by any, and in the unhurried dispersal within he slipped away silently into the cloister, and so to his deserted bed in the south porch.

He was within the fold, and it was over. He sidled thankfully into the empty church — a good hour yet before Matins — and went to retrieve his blankets from behind the altar in the chancel chapel. He was very tired, but so agonisingly awake that sleep seemed very far off. Yet when he had spread his bedding again on his pallet, tucked away under the straw his new capuchon and cotte, and stretched himself out, still trembling, along the broad stone bench, sleep came on him so abruptly that all he knew of it was the descent, fathoms deep, into a well of darkness and peace.

Brother Cadfael rose well before Prime to go to his workshop, where he had left a batch of troches drying overnight. The bushes in the garden, the herbs in the enclosed herbarium, all glimmered softly with the lingering dew of a brief shower, and reflected back the dawn sunlight from thousands of tiny facets of silver. Another fine, fresh day beginning. Excellent for planting, moist, mild, the soil finely crumbled after the intense frosts of the hard winter. There could be no better auguries for germination and growth.

He heard the bell rousing the dortoir for Prime, and went directly to the church as soon as he had put his troches safely away. And there in the porch was Liliwin, his bedding already folded tidily away, his ill-cobbled motley exchanged for his new blue cotte, and his pale hair damp and flattened from being plunged in the bowl where he had washed. Cadfael took pleasure in observing him from a distance, himself unobserved. So wherever he had been hiding himself yesterday, he was still here in safety, and, moreover, developing a wholly creditable self-respect, with which guilt, or so it seemed to Cadfael, must be incompatible.

Brother Anselm, detecting the presence of his truant in church only when a high, hesitant voice joined in the singing, was similarly reassured and comforted. Prior Robert heard the same voice, looked round in incredulous displeasure, and frowned upon a dismayed Brother Jerome, who had so misled him. They still had the thorn in the flesh, thanksgiving had been premature.

The lay brothers were planting out more seedlings in a large patch along the Gaye that day, and sowing a later field of pease for succession, to follow when those by the Meole brook were harvested. Cadfael went out after dinner to view the work. After the night's soft shower the day was brilliant, sunlit and serene, but the earlier rains were still coming down the river from the mountains of Wales in their own good time, and the water was lapping into the grass where the meadow sloped smoothly down, and gnawing gently under the lip of the bank where it could not reach the turf. The length of a man's hand higher since two days ago, but always with this sunlit innocence upon it, as if it would be ashamed to endanger the swimming urchins, and could not possibly be thought capable of drowning any man. And this as perilous a river as any in the land, as treacherous and as lovely.

It was a pleasure to walk along the trodden path that was only a paler line in the turf, following the fast, quiet flood downstream. Cadfael went with his eyes on the half-turgid, half-clear eddies that span and murmured under the lip of green, a strong current here hugging this shore. Across the stream, so silent and so fast, the walls of Shrewsbury loomed, at the crest of a steep green slope of gardens, orchards and vineyard, and further downstream fused into the solid bulk of the king's castle, guarding the narrow neck of land that broke Shrewsbury's girdle of water.

On this near shore Cadfael had reached the limit of the abbey orchards, where lush copses began, fringing the abbey's last wheat-field, and the old, disused mill jutted over the river. He passed, threading the trees and bushes, and went on a short way, to where the level of land dipped to water-level in a little cove, shallowly covered by clear water now, the driving current spinning in and out again just clear of disturbing the gravel bottom. Things tended to come in here and be cast ashore if the Severn was in spate, and enclosing shoulders of woodland screened whatever came.

And something wholly unforeseen had come, and was lying here in uneasy repose, sprawled face-down, head butted into the gravelly calm of the bank. A solid body in good homespun cloth, shortish and sturdy, a round bullish head with floating, grizzled brown hair, thinning at the crown. Splayed arms, languidly moving in the gentle stir of the shallows, clear of the deadly purposeful central flow, fingered and fumbled vaguely at the fine gravel. Squat legs, but drawn out by the hungry current tugging at their toes, stretched towards open water. Cast up dead, all four limbs stirred and strained to prove him living.

Brother Cadfael kilted his habit to the knee, plunged down the gentle slope into the water, took the body by the bunched capuchon swaying at his neck and the leather belt at his waist, and hoisted him gradually clear of the surface, to disturb as little as possible the position in which he had been swept ashore, and whatever traces the river had spared in his clothing, hair and shoes. No haste to feel for any life here, it had been gone for some time. Yet he might have something to tell even in his final silence.

The dead weight sagged from Cadfael's hands. He drew it, streaming, up the first plane of grass, and there let it sink in the same shape it had had in the river. Who knew where it had entered the water and how?

As for naming him, there was no need to turn up that sodden face to the light of day, not yet. Cadfael recognised the russet broadcloth, the sturdy build, the round, turnip head with its thinning crown and bushy brown hedge of hair all round the shiny island of bone. Only two mornings ago he had passed the time of day with this same silenced tongue, very fluent and roguish then, enjoying its mischief without any great malice.

Baldwin Peche had done with toothsome scandal, and lost his last tussle with the river that had provided him with so many fishing sorties, and hooked him to his death in the end.

Cadfael hoisted him by the middle, marked the derisory flow from his mouth, barely moistening the grass, and let him down carefully in the same form. He was a little puzzled to find so meagre a flow, since even the dead may give back the water they have swallowed, for at least a brief while after their death. This one had left a shallow shape scooped in the gravel of the cove, which was hardly disturbed by currents. His outlines in the grass now duplicated the outline he had abandoned there.

Now how had Baldwin Peche come to be beached here like a landed fish? Drunk and careless along the riverside at night? Spilled out of a boat while fishing? Or fallen foul of a footpad in one of the dark alleys and tipped into the water for the contents of his purse? Such things did occasionally happen even in a well-regulated town on dark enough nights, and there did seem to be a thicker and darker moisture in the grizzled hair behind Peche's right ear, as though the skin beneath was broken. Scalp wounds tend to bleed copiously, and even after some hours in the water or cast up here traces might linger. He was native-born, he knew the river well enough to respect it, all the more as he acknowledged he was a weak swimmer.

Cadfael threaded the belt of bushes to have a clear view over the Severn, upstream and down, and was rewarded by the sight of a coracle making its way against the current, turning and twisting to make use of every eddy, bobbing and dancing like a shed leaf, but always making progress. There was only one man who could handle the paddle and read the river with such ease and skill, and even at some distance the squat, dark figure was easily recognisable. Madog of the Dead-Boat was as Welsh as Cadfael himself, and the best-known waterman in twenty miles of the Severn's course, and had got his name as a result of the cargo he most often had to carry, by reason of his knowledge of all the places where missing persons, thought to have been taken by the river whether in flood or by felony, were likely to fetch up. This time he had no mute passenger aboard; his natural quarry was here waiting for him.

Cadfael knew him well and for no ascertainable reason, except the customary association of Madog with drowned men, took for granted that even in this case the connection must hold good. He raised a hail and waved an arm as the coracle drew nearer, picking its feathery way across the mid-stream current where it was diffused and moderate. Madog looked up, knew the man who beckoned him in, and with a sweep of his paddle brought his boat inshore, clear of the deceitfully silent and rapid thrust that sped down-river, leaving this cove so placid and clear. Cadfael waded into the shallows to meet him, laying a hand to the rim of hide as Madog hopped out nimbly to join him, his brown feet bare.

'I thought I knew that shaven sconce of yours,' he said heartily, and hoisted his cockle-shell of withies and hide on to his shoulder to heft it ashore. 'What is it with you? When you call me, I take it there's a sound reason.'

'Sound enough,' said Cadfael. 'I think I may have found what you were looking for.' He jerked his head towards the plane of grass above, and led the way up without more words. They stood together over the prone body in thoughtful silence for some moments. Madog had taken note in one glance of the position of the head, and looked back to the gravelled shore under its liquid skin of water. He saw the shadowy shape left in the fine shale, and the mute, contained violence of the current that swept past only a man's length away from that strange calm.

'Yes. I see. He went into the water above. Perhaps not far above. There's a strong tow under that bank, upstream from here a piece, under the castle. Then it could have brought him across and thrown him up here just as he lies. A good, solid weight, head-first into the bank. And left him stranded.'

'So I thought,' said Cadfael. 'You were looking for him?' People along the waterside who had kin go missing usually sought out Madog before they notified the provost or the sheriff's sergeant.

'That journeyman of his sent after me this morning. It seems his master went off yesterday before noon, but nobody wondered, he did the like whenever he chose, they were used to it. But this morning he's never been back. There's a boy sleeps in his shop, he was fretting over it, so when Boneth came to work and no locksmith he sent the lad to me. This one here liked his bed, even if he sometimes came to it about dawn. Not the man to go hungry or dry, either, and the ale-house he favoured hadn't seen him.'

'He has a boat,' said Cadfael. 'A known fisherman.'

'So I hear. His boat was not where he keeps it.'

'But you've found it,' said Cadfael with conviction.

'A half-mile down-river, caught in the branches where the willows overhang. And his rod snagged by the hook and trailing. The boat had overturned. He ran a coracle, like me. I've left it beached where I found it. A tricky boat,' said Madog dispassionately, 'if he hooked a lusty young salmon. The spring ones are coming. But he knew his craft and his sport.'

'So do many and take the one chance that undoes them.'

'We'd best get him back,' said Madog, minding his business like any good master-craftsman. 'To the abbey? It's the nearest. And Hugh Beringar will have to know. No need to mark this place, you and I both know it well, and his marks will last long enough.'

Cadfael considered and decided. 'You'll get him home best afloat, and it's your right. I'll follow ashore and meet you below the bridge, we shall make much the same time of it. Keep him as he lies, Madog, face-down, and note what signs he leaves aboard.'

Madog had at least as extensive a knowledge of the ways of drowned men as Cadfael. He gave his friend a long, thoughtful look, but kept his thoughts to himself, and stooped to lift the shoulders of the dead man, leaving Cadfael the knees. They got him decently disposed into the light craft. There was a fee for every Christian body Madog brought out of the river, he had indeed a right to it. The duty had edged its way in on him long ago, almost unaware, but other men's dying was the better part of his living now. And an honest, useful, decent art, for which many a family had been thankful.

Madog's paddle dipped and swung him across the contrary flow, to use the counter-eddies in moving up-river. Cadfael took a last look at the cove and the level of grass above it, memorised as much of the scene as he could, and set off briskly up the path to meet the boat at the bridge.

The river was fast and self-willed, and by hurrying, Cadfael won the race, and had time to recruit three or four novices and lay brothers by the time Madog brought his coracle into the ordered fringes of the Gaye. They had an improvised litter ready, they lifted Baldwin Peche onto it, and bore him away up the path to the Foregate and across to the gatehouse of the abbey. A nimble and very young novice had been sent in haste to carry word to the deputy-sheriff to come to the abbey at Brother Cadfael's entreaty.

But for all that, no one knew how, somehow the word had gone round. By the time Madog arrived, so had a dozen idle observers, draped over the downstream parapet of the bridge. By the time the bearers had got their burden to the level of the Foregate and turned towards the abbey, the dozen had become a score, and drifted in ominous quietness towards the end of the bridge, and there were a dozen more gradually gathering behind them, emerging from the town gate. When they reached the abbey gatehouse, which could not well be closed against any who came in decorous silence and apparent peace, they had between forty and fifty souls hovering at their heels and following them within. The weight of their foreboding, accusation and self-righteousness lay heavy on the nape of Cadfael's neck as the litter was set down in the great court. When he turned to view the enemy, for no question but they were the enemy, the first face he saw, the first levelled brow and vengeful eye, was that of Daniel Aurifaber.

# Seven

*Tuesday: from afternoon to night*

THEY CAME CROWDING CLOSE, PEERING ROUND MADOG and Cadfael to confirm what they already knew. They passed the word back to those behind, in ominous murmurs that swelled into excited speculation in a matter of moments. Cadfael caught at the sleeve of the first novice who came curiously to see what was happening.

'Get Prior Robert and sharp about it. We're likely to need some other authority before Hugh Beringar gets here.' And to the litter-bearers, before they could be completely surrounded: 'Into the cloister with him, while you can, and stand ready to fend off any who try to follow.'

The sorry cortège obediently made off into cover in some haste, and though one or two of the younger fellows from the town were drawn after by gaping curiosity to the threshold of the cloister, they did not venture further, but turned back to rejoin their friends. An inquisitive ring drew in about Cadfael and Madog.

'That was Baldwin Peche the locksmith you had there,' said Daniel, not asking, stating. 'Our tenant. He never came home last night. John Boneth has been hunting high and low for him.'

'So have I,' said Madog, 'at that same John's urging. And between the two of us here we've found both the man and his boat.'

'Dead.' That was not a question either.

'Dead, sure enough.'

By that time Prior Robert had been found, and came in haste with his dutiful shadow at his heels. Of the interruptions to his ordered, well-tuned life within here, it seemed, there was to be no end. He had caught an unpleasant murmur of 'Murder!' as he approached, and demanded in dismay and displeasure what had happened to bring this inflamed mob into the great court. A dozen voices volunteered to tell him, disregarding how little they themselves knew about it.

'Father Prior, we saw our fellow-townsman carried in here, dead . . .'

'No one had seen him since yesterday . . .'

'My neighbour and tenant, the locksmith,' cried Daniel. 'Father robbed and assaulted, and now Master Peche fetched in dead!'

The prior held up a silencing hand, frowning them down. 'Let one speak. Brother Cadfael, do you know what this is all about?'

Cadfael saw fit to tell the bare facts, without mention of any speculations that might be going on in his own mind. He took care to be audible to them all, though he doubted if they would be setting any limits to their own speculations, however careful he might be. 'Madog here has found the man's boat overturned, down-river past the castle,' he concluded. 'And we have sent to notify the deputy-sheriff, the matter will be in his hands now. He should be here very soon.'

That was for the more excitable ears. There were some wild youngsters among them, the kind who are always at leisure to follow up every sensation, who might well lose their heads if they sighted their scapegoat. For the implication was already there, present in the very air. Walter robbed and battered, now his tenant dead, and all evil must light upon the same head.

'If the unfortunate man drowned in the river, having fallen from his boat,' said Robert firmly, 'there can be no possibility of murder. That is a foolish and wicked saying.'

They began to bay from several directions. 'Father Prior, Master Peche was not a foolhardy man . . .' 'He knew the Severn from his childhood . . .'

'So do many,' said Robert crisply, 'who fall victim to it in the end, men no more foolhardy than he. You must not attribute evil to what is natural misfortune.'

'And why should natural misfortune crowd so on one house?' demanded an excited voice from the rear. 'Baldwin was a guest the night Walter was struck down and his coffer emptied.'

'And next-door neighbour, and liked to nose out whatever was hidden. And who's to say he didn't stumble on some proof that would be very bad news to the villain that did the deed, and lurks here swearing to his innocence?'

It was out, they took it up on all sides. 'That's how it was! Baldwin found out something the wretch wouldn't have been able to deny!'

'And he's killed the poor man to stop his mouth . . .'

'A knock on the head and souse into the river . . .'

'No trick to turn his boat loose for the river to take down after him . . .'

Cadfael was relieved to see Hugh Beringar riding briskly in at the gatehouse then with a couple of officers behind him. This was getting all too predictable. When men have elected a villain, and one from comfortably outside their own ranks, without roots or kin, they need feel nothing for him, he is hardly a man, has no blood to be shed or heart to be broken, and whatever else needs a scapegoat will be laid on him heartily and in the conviction of righteousness. Nor will reason have much say in the matter. But he raised his voice powerfully to shout them down: 'The man you accuse is absolutely clear of this, even if it were murder. He is in sanctuary here, dare not leave the precinct, and has not left it. The king's officers wait for him outside, as you all know. Be ashamed to make such senseless charges!'

He said afterwards, rather resignedly than bitterly, that it was a precise measure of Liliwin's luck that he should appear innocently from the cloister at that moment, bewildered and shocked by the incursion of a dead body into the pale, and coming anxiously to enquire about it, but utterly ignorant of any connection it might be thought to have with him. He came hastening out of the west walk, solitary, apart, marked at once by two or three of the crowd. A howl went up, hideously triumphant. Liliwin took it like a great blast of cold wind in his face, shrank and faltered, and his countenance, healing into smooth comeliness these last two days, collapsed suddenly into the disintegration of terror.

The wildest of the young bloods moved fast, hallooing, but Hugh Beringar moved faster. The raw-boned grey horse, his favourite familiar, clattered nimbly between quarry and hounds, and Hugh was out of the saddle with a hand on Liliwin's shoulder, in a grip that could have been ambiguously arrest or protection, and his neat, dark, saturine visage turned blandly towards the threatening assault. The foremost hunters froze discreetly, and thawed again only to draw back by delicate inches from challenging his command.

The nimble young novice had acquitted himself well, and shown an excellent grasp of his charge, for Hugh had the half of it clear in his mind already and understood its perilous application here. He kept his hold — let them read it however they would — on Liliwin throughout the questioning that followed, and listened as narrowly to Daniel Aurifaber's heated witness as to Cadfael's account.

'Very well! Father Prior, it would be as well if you yourself would convey this in due course to the lord abbot. The drowned man I must examine, as also the place where he was cast ashore and that where his boat came to rest. I must call upon the help of those who found out these matters. For the rest of you, if you have anything to say, say it now.'

Say it they did, intimidated but still smouldering, and determined to pour out their heat. For this was no chance death in the river, of that they were certain. This was the killing of a witness, close, curious, likely of all men to uncover some irrefutable evidence. He had found proof of the jongleur's strenuously-denied guilt, and he had been slipped into the Severn to drown before he could open his mouth. They began by muttering it, they ended by howling it. Hugh let them rave. He knew they were no such monsters as they made themselves out to be, but knew, too, that given a following wind and a rash impulse, they could be, to their own damage and that of every other man.

They ran themselves out of words at length, and dwindled like sails bereft of wind.

'My men have been camped outside the gates here,' said Hugh then, calmly, 'all this while and have seen no sign of this man you accuse. To my knowledge he has not set foot outside these walls. How, then, can he have had any hand in any man's death?'

They had no answer ready to that, though they sidled and exchanged glances and shook their heads as though they knew beyond doubt that there must be an answer if they could only light on it. But out of the prior's shadow the insinuating voice of Brother Jerome spoke up mildly:

'Pardon, Father Prior, but is it certain that the young man has been every moment within here? Only recall, last night Brother Anselm was enquiring after him and had not seen him since just after noon, and remarked, moreover, that he did not come to the kitchen for his supper as is customary. And being concerned for any guest of our house, I felt it my duty to look for him and did so everywhere. That was just when twilight was falling. I found no trace of him anywhere within the walls.'

They took it up gleefully on the instant and Liliwin, as

108

Cadfael observed with a sigh, shook and swallowed hard, and could not get out a word, and drops of sweat gathered on his upper lip and ran down, to be licked off feverishly.

'You see, the good brother says it! He was not here! He was out about his foul business!'

'Say rather,' Prior Robert reproached gently, 'that he could not be found.' But he was not altogether displeased.

'And go without his supper? A half-starved rat scorn his food unless he had urgent business elsewhere?' cried Daniel fiercely.

'Very urgent! He took his life in his hands to make sure Baldwin should not live to speak against him.'

'Speak up!' said Hugh drily, shaking Liliwin by the shoulder. 'You have a tongue, too. Did you leave the abbey enclave at any time?'

Liliwin gulped down gall, hung in anguished silence a moment, and got out in a great groan: 'No!'

'You were within here yesterday, when you were sought and could not be found?'

'I didn't want to be found. I hid myself.' His voice was firmer when he had at least a morsel of truth to utter. But Hugh pressed him still.

'You have not once set foot outside this pale since you took refuge here?'

'No, never!' he gasped, and dragged in breath as though he had run a great way.

'You hear?' said Hugh crisply, putting Liliwin aside and behind him. 'You have your answer. A man penned securely here cannot have committed murder outside, even if this proves to be murder, as at this moment there is no proof whatsoever. Now go, get back to your own crafts, and leave to the law what is the law's business. If you doubt my thoroughness, try crossing me.' And to his officers he said simply: 'Clear the court of those who have no business here. I will speak with the provost later.'

In the mortuary chapel Baldwin Peche lay stripped naked, stretched now on his back, while Brother Cadfael, Hugh

Beringar, Madog of the Dead-Boat and Abbot Radulfus gathered about him attentively. In the corners of his eyes, now closed, traces of ingrained mud lingered, drying, like the pigments vain women use to darken and brighten their eyes. From his thick tangle of grizzled brown hair Cadfael had coaxed out two or three strands of water crowfoot, cobweb-fine stems with frail white flowers withering into veined brown filaments as they died, and a broken twig of alder leaves. There was nothing strange in either of those. Alders clustered in many places along the riverside, and this was the season when delicate rafts of crowfoot swayed and trembled wherever there were shallows or slower water.

'Though the water where I found him,' said Cadfael, 'runs fast, and will not anchor these flowers. The opposite bank I fancy, harbours them better. That is reasonable — if he launched his boat to go fishing it would be from that bank. And now see what more he has to show us.'

He cupped a palm under the dead man's cheek, turned his face to the light, and hoisted the bearded chin. The light falling into the stretched cavities of the nostrils showed them only as shallow hollows silted solid with river mud. Cadfael inserted the stem of the alder twig into one of them, and scooped out a smooth, thick slime of fine gravel and a wisp of crowfoot embedded within it.

'So I thought, when I hefted him to empty out the water from him and got only a miserable drop or two. The drainings of mud and weed, not of a drowned man.' He inserted his fingers between the parted lips, and showed the teeth also parted, as if in a grimace of pain or a cry. Carefully he drew them wider. Tendrils of crowfoot clung in the large, crooked teeth. Those peering close could see that the mouth within was clogged completely with the debris of the river.

'Give me a small bowl,' said Cadfael, intent, and Hugh was before Madog in obeying. There was a silver saucer under the unlighted lamp on the altar, the nearest receptacle, and Abbot Radulfus made no move to demur. Cadfael eased the stiffening jaw wider, and with a probing finger drew out into the bowl a thick wad of mud and gravel, tinted with minute fragments of vegetation. 'Having drawn in this, he could not draw in water. No wonder I got none out of him.' He felt gently about the dead mouth, probing out the last threads of crowfoot, fine as hairs, and set the bowl aside.

'What you are saying,' said Hugh, closely following, 'is that he did not drown.'

'No, he did not drown.'

'But he did die in the river. Why else these river weeds deep in his throat?'

'True. So he died. Bear with me, I am treading as blindly as you. I need to know, like you, and like you, I must examine what we have.' Cadfael looked up at Madog, who surely knew all these signs at least as well as any other man living. 'Are you with me so far?'

'I am before you,' said Madog simply. 'But tread on. For a blind man you have not gone far astray.'

'Then, Father, may we now turn him again on his face, as I found him?'

Radulfus himself set his two long, muscular hands either side of the head, to steady the dead man over, and settled him gently on one cheekbone.

For all his self-indulgent habits of life, Baldwin Peche showed a strong, hale body, broad-shouldered, with thick, muscular thighs and arms. The discolorations of death were beginning to appear on him now, and they were curious enough. The broken graze behind his right ear, that was plain and eloquent, but the rest were matter for speculation.

'That was never got from any floating branch,' said Madog with certainty, 'nor from being swept against a stone, either, not in that stretch of water. Up here among the islands I wouldn't say but it might be possible, though not likely. No, that was a blow from behind, before he went into the water.'

'You are saying,' said Radulfus gravely, 'that the charge of murder is justified.'

'Against someone,' said Cadfael, 'yes.'

'And this man was indeed next-door neighbour to the

household that was robbed, and may truly have found out something, whether he understood its meaning or not, that could shed light on that robbery?'

'It is possible. He took an interest in other men's business,' agreed Cadfael cautiously.

'And that would certainly be a strong motive for his removal, if the guilty man got to know of it,' said the abbot, reflecting. 'Then since this cannot be the work of one who was here within our walls throughout, it is strong argument in favour of the minstrel's innocence of the first offence. And somewhere at large is the true culprit.'

If Hugh had already perceived and accepted the same logical consequence, he made no comment on it. He stood looking down at the prone body in frowning concentration. 'So it would seem he was hit on the head and tossed into the river. And yet he did not drown. What he drew in, in his fight for breath — in his senses or out — was mud, gravel, weed.'

'You have seen,' said Cadfael. 'He was smothered. Held down somewhere in the shallows, with his face pressed into the mud. And set afloat in the river afterwards, with the intent he should be reckoned as one more among the many drowned in Severn. A mistake! The current cast him up before the river had time to wash away all these evidences of another manner of death.'

He doubted, in fact, if they would ever have been completely washed away, however long the body had been adrift. The stems of crowfoot were very tenacious. The fine silt clung tightly where it had been inhaled in the struggle for breath. But what was more mysterious was the diffused area of bruising that spread over Peche's back at the shoulder-blades, and the two or three deep indentations in the swollen flesh there. In the deepest the skin was broken, only a tiny lesion, as though something sharp and jagged had pierced him. Cadfael could make nothing of these marks. He memorised them and wondered.

There remained the contents of the silver bowl. Cadfael took it out to the stone basin in the middle of the garth and carefully sluiced away the fine silt, drawing aside and retaining the fragments of weed. Fine threads of crowfoot, a tiny, draggled flower, a morsel of an alder leaf. And something else, a sudden speck of colour. He picked it out and dipped it into the water to wash away the dirt that clouded it, and there it lay glistening in the palm of his hand, a mere scrap, two tiny florets, the tip of a head of flowers of a reddish purple colour, speckled at the lip with a darker purple and a torn remnant of one narrow leaf, just large enough to show a blackish spot on its green.

They had followed him out and gathered curiously to gaze. 'Fox-stones, we call this,' said Cadfael, 'for the two swellings at its root like pebbles. The commonest of its kind, and the earliest, but I don't recall seeing it much here. This, like the broken twig of alder, he took down with him when he was pushed into the water. It might be possible to find that place somewhere on the town bank — where crowfoot and alder and fox-stones all grow together.'

The place where Baldwin Peche had been cast ashore had little to tell beyond what it had already told. The spot where Madog had turned down the dead man's coracle on the meadow grass was well down-river, and so feather-light a boat, loose without a man's weight aboard, might well have gone on bobbing gaily downstream a mile or more beyond, before the first strong curve and encroaching sandbank would inevitably have arrested it. They would have to comb the town bank, Madog reckoned, from below the watergate, to establish where he had been assaulted and killed. A place where crowfoot grew inshore under alders, and fox-stones were in flower close to the very edge of the water.

The first two could be found together all along the reach. The third might occur in only one place.

Madog would search the riverside, Hugh would question the Aurifaber household and the immediate neighbours, as well as the tavern-keepers of the town, for everything they knew about the recent movements of Baldwin Peche: where he had last been seen, who had spoken with him, what he had had to say. For someone, surely, must have seen him after he left his shop about mid-morning of the previous day, which was the last John Boneth knew of him.

Meantime, Cadfael had business of his own, and much to think about. He came back from the riverside too late for Vespers, but in time to visit his workshop and make sure all was in order there before supper. Brother Oswin, left in charge alone, was developing a deft touch and a proprietorial pride. He had not broken or burned anything for several weeks.

After supper Cadfael went in search of Liliwin, and found him sitting in deep shadow in the darkest corner of the porch, drawn up defensively against the stone with his arms locked about his knees. At this hour the light was too far gone for work to proceed on the mending of his rebec, or his new studies under Brother Anselm, and it seemed that the day's alarms had driven him back into distrust and despair, so that he hunched himself as small as possible into his corner and kept a wary face against the world. Certainly he gave Cadfael a bright, nervous, sidelong flash of his eyes as the monk hitched his habit comfortably and sat down beside him.

'Well, young man, have you fetched your supper tonight?' said Cadfael placidly.

Liliwin acknowledged that with a silent nod, watching him warily.

'It seems you did not yesterday, and Brother Jerome tells us that a maidservant came to visit you in the afternoon and brought you a basket of food from her lady's table. He had, he said, occasion to admonish you both.' The silence beside him was charged and uneasy. 'Now, granted Brother Jerome is uncommonly good at finding grounds for admonishment, yet I fancy there is but one maidservant whose presence here would have caused him qualms for the propriety of your conduct — let alone the well-being of your soul.' It was said with a smile in his voice, but he did not miss the slight shudder that convulsed the thin body beside him or the stiffening of the hands that were clasped so tightly round Liliwin's knees. Now why in the world should the lad quake at the mention of his soul's health, just when Cadfael was becoming more and more convinced that he had no guilt whatever upon his conscience, bar an understandable lie or two.

'Was it Rannilt?'

'Yes,' said Liliwin, just audibly.

'She came with good leave? Or of her own accord?'

Liliwin told him, in as few words as possible.

'So that was how it befell. And Jerome bade her do her errand and go, and stood over you to make sure she obeyed. And it was from that hour, as I understand — after he had witnessed her going — that no one saw *you* again until Prime this morning. Yet you say you were here within the pale and what you say, that I accept. Did you speak?'

'No,' said Liliwin, none too happily. Not speech, exactly, but a small, shamed sound hurriedly suppressed.

'You let her go somewhat tamely, did you not?' remarked Cadfael critically. 'Seeing the magnitude of the step she had taken for you.'

The evening was closing down tranquilly all round them, there was no one else to hear, and Liliwin had spent much of the day wrestling alone with the belated conviction of his mortal sin. Terror of men was surely enough to bear, without being suddenly visited by the terror of damnation, let alone the awful sense of having brought about the damnation of another person as dear to him as himself. He uncurled abruptly from his dark corner, slid his legs over the edge of the stone bench, and clutched Cadfael impulsively by the arm.

'Brother Cadfael, I want to tell you . . . I must tell someone! I did — *we* did, but the fault was mine! — we did a terrible thing. I never meant it, but she was going away from me, and I might never see her again, and so it happened. A mortal sin and I've caused her to share in it!' The words spurted out like blood from a new wound, but the first flow eased him. From incoherent he grew quiet, and his shaking subsided and was gone. 'Let me tell you, and then do whatever you think is just. I couldn't bear it that she must go so soon, and it might be for ever. We went through the church, and I hid her within there, behind the altar in the transept chapel. There's a space behind there, I found it when I came new here and was afraid they might come for me in the night. I knew I could creep in there, and she is smaller than I. And when that brother had gone away, I went back to her there. I took my blankets in with me, and the new clothes she brought me — it's hard and chill on the stone. All I wanted,' said Liliwin simply, 'was to be with her as long as we dared. We did not even talk very much. But then we forgot where we were, and what was due . . .'

Brother Cadfael said no word either to help or check him, but waited in silence.

'I couldn't think of anything but that she would go away, and I might never be with her again,' blurted Liliwin miserably, 'and I knew she was in the selfsame pain. We never intended evil, but we committed a terrible sacrilege. Here in the church, behind one of the holy altars — we couldn't bear it . . . We lay together as lovers do!'

He had said it, it was out, the very worst of it. He sat humbly waiting for condemnation, resigned to whatever might come, even relieved at having shifted the burden to other shoulders. There was no exclamation of horror, but this brother was not so given to prodigal admonishment as that sour one who had frowned on Rannilt.

'You love this girl?' asked Cadfael after some thought, and very placidly.

'Yes, I *do* love her! With all my heart I want her for my wife. But what is there for her if I am brought out of here to trial and the matter goes blackly for me? As they mean it should! Don't let it be known that she has been with me. Her hopes of marriage are wretched enough, a poor servant-girl without folk of her own. I don't want to damage them further. She may still get a decent man, if I . . .' He let that die away unfinished. It was no comforting thought.

'I think,' said Cadfael, 'she would rather have the man she has already chosen. Where mutual love is, I find it hard to consider any place too holy to house it. Our Lady, accord-

ing to the miracles they tell of her, has been known to protect even the guilty who sinned out of love. You might try a
few prayers to her, that will do no harm. Don't trouble too
much for what was done under such strong compulsion and
pure of any evil intent. And how long, then,' enquired Cadfael, eyeing his penitent tolerantly, 'did you remain hidden
there? Brother Anselm was worried about you.'

'We fell asleep, both of us.' Liliwin shook again at the
memory. 'When we roused, it was late and dark, they were
singing Compline. And she had to go back all that way into
the town in the night!'

'And you let her go alone?' demanded Cadfael with deceitful indignation.

'I did not! What do you take me for?' Liliwin had flared
and fallen into the snare before he stopped to think, and it
was too late to take it back. He sat back with a deflated sigh,
stooping his face into deeper shadow.

'What do I take you for?' Cadfael's smile was hidden by
the dusk. 'A bit of a rogue, perhaps, but no worse than the
most of us. A bit of a liar when the need's great enough, but
who isn't? So you did slip out of here to take the child home.
Well, I think the better of you for it, it must have cost you
some terrors.' And provided a salutary stiffening of self-
respect, he thought but did not say.

In a small and perversely resentful voice Liliwin asked:
'How did you know?'

'By the effort it cost you to get the denial out. For you will
never make a really *good* liar, lad, and the more you hate
doing it, the worse you'll manage, and it seems to me
you've taken strongly against lying these last few days.
How did you contrive to get out and in again?'

Liliwin took heart and told him, how the new clothes had
got him past the guards on the heels of the worshippers, and
how he had taken Rannilt to her very doorway, and made his
way back under cover of the returning lay servants. What
had passed between himself and Rannilt on the way he kept
to himself, and it did not enter his mind to say any word of

what else he had noticed, until Cadfael took him up alertly on that very subject.

'So you were there, outside the shop, about an hour after Compline?' Night is the favoured time for ridding oneself of enemies, and this was the one night that had passed since Baldwin Peche was last seen alive.

'Yes, I watched her safe into the courtyard. Only I fret,' said Liliwin, 'over what sort of welcome she may have found. Though her lady did say she might stay the day out. I hope no one was angry with her.'

'Well, since you were there, did you see ought of anything or anyone stirring about the place?'

'I did see one man who was out and about,' said Liliwin, remembering. 'It was after Rannilt had gone in. I was standing opposite, in a dark doorway, and Daniel Aurifaber came out through the passage, and went away to the left along the lane. He can't have gone far without turning aside, for when I went back to the Cross and down the Wyle he was gone already, I never saw sign of him after.'

'Daniel? You're sure it was he?' That young man had been very prompt and present this afternoon, as soon as the usual idlers saw a body being lifted ashore under the bridge. Very prompt and very forward to lead the accusers who made haste to fling this, like the other offences, on the stranger's head, reason or no reason, sanctuary or no sanctuary.

'Oh, yes, there's no mistaking him.' He was surprised that such a point should be made of it. 'Is it important?'

'It may be. But no matter now. One thing you haven't said,' pointed out Cadfael gravely, 'and yet I'm sure you are not so dull but you must have thought on it. Once you were out of here and no alarm, and the night before you, you might have made off many miles from here, and got clean away from your accusers. Were you not tempted?'

'So *she* prompted me, too,' said Liliwin, remembering, and smiled. 'She urged me to go while I could.'

'Why did you not?'

Because she did not truly want me to, thought Liliwin,

with a joyful lift of the heart for all his burdens. And because if ever she does come to me, it shall not be to an accused felon, but to a man acknowledged honest before the world. Aloud he voiced only the heart of that revelationary truth: 'Because now I won't go without her. When I leave — *if* I leave — I shall take Rannilt with me.'

# Eight

HUGH SOUGHT OUT CADFAEL AFTER CHAPTER THE NEXT morning for a brief conference in his workshop in the herbarium.

'They're all in a tale,' said Hugh, leaning back with a cup of Cadfael's latest-broached wine under the rustling bunches of last year's harvest of herbs. 'All insistent that this death must be linked to what happened at the young fellow's wedding feast. But since they're all of them obsessed with money, *their* money — except, perhaps, the daughter, who curls her lip very expressively but says little, and certainly nothing against her kin — they can think of nothing but their grievance and every other man must be as intent on it as they are. Yet there's profit and profit, and this locksmith's business does very nicely for itself, and now there's no kith nor kin to take it over, and it seems to be common knowledge the man had commended his journeyman to take the shop over after him. This young Boneth has been doing most of the work now above two years, he deserves he should get the credit. As right and virtuous a young man as ever I saw, to all appearances, but who's to be sure he didn't get tired of waiting? And we'd best bear in mind another truth — it was Baldwin Peche made the lock and keys for that strong-box of Aurifaber's.'

'There's a boy runs the errands and sleeps there in the shop,' said Cadfael. 'Has he ought to say?'

'The dark boy, the simpleton? I wouldn't say his memory goes back farther than a day or so, but he's positive his master did not come back to his shop after he looked in at mid-morning, the day before he was fished out of the Severn. They were used to his absences by day, but the boy was anxious when there was no return at twilight. He didn't sleep. I would take his word for it there was no disturbance, no prowling about that burgage during the night. Nor are we the nearer knowing just when the man died, though the night would seem to be when he was set adrift, and the boat, too. There was no overturned coracle sighted down the Severn during the day — either day.'

'You'll be going back there, I suppose,' said Cadfael. There had been very little time the previous day for hunting out all the neighbours to testify. 'I've an errand there myself to the old dame tomorrow, but no occasion to go that way today. Give an eye for me to the little Welsh girl, will you, see in what spirits she is, and whether they're being rough or smooth with her.'

Hugh cocked a smiling eye at him. 'Your countrywoman, is she? To judge by the way I heard her singing away about her pot-scouring, last night, she's in good enough heart.'

'Singing, was she?' That would come as very welcome news to that draggled sparrow in his sanctuary cage here. Evidently no hardship more than normal had fallen upon Rannilt for her day of freedom. 'Good, that answers me very properly. And, Hugh, if you'll take a nudge from me without asking any questions as to where I picked up the scent — probe around as to whether anyone on that street saw Daniel Aurifaber slipping out in the dark an hour past Compline, when he should have been snug in bed with his bride.'

Hugh turned his black head sharply, and gave his friend a long and quizzical look. '*That* night?'

'That night.'

'Three days married!' Hugh grimaced and laughed. 'I'd heard the young man has the name for it. But I take your meaning. There may be other reasons for leaving a new wife to lie cold.'

'When I spoke with him,' said Cadfael, 'he made no secret of it that he heartily disliked the locksmith. Though had his dislike had a solid core, and gone as far as congealing into hate, I think he might have been less voluble about it.'

'I'll bear that in mind, too. Tell me, Cadfael,' said Hugh, eyeing him shrewdly, 'how strong is the scent you got wind of? Say I find no such witness — no *second* such witness, ought I to say? — shall I be justified in wagering on the accuracy of your nose?'

'In your shoes?' said Cadfael cheerfully, '*I* would.'

'You seem to have found your witness in very short order,' remarked Hugh drily, 'and without leaving the precinct. So you got it out of him — whatever it was that had him choking on a simple lie. I thought you would.' He rose, grinning, and set down his cup. 'I'll take your confession later, I'm away now to see what I can get out of the new wife.' He clouted Cadfael amiably on the shoulder in passing, and looked back from the doorway. 'No need to fret for that weedy lad of yours, I'm coming round to your opinion. I doubt if he ever did worse in his life than sneak a few apples from an orchard.'

The journeyman, Iestyn, was working alone in the shop, repairing the broken clasp of a bracelet, when Hugh came to the Aurifaber burgage. It was the first time Hugh had spoken with this man alone, and in company Iestyn kept himself silent and apart. Either he was taciturn by nature, thought Hugh, or the family had taken care to make his status clear to him, and it was not theirs, and there should be no stepping over the line that divided them.

In answer to Hugh's question he shook his head, smiling and hoisting impassive shoulders.

'How would I see what goes on in the street after dark or

who's on the prowl when decent folks are in bed? I sleep in the back part of the undercroft, beneath the rear of the hall, my lord. Those outside stairs go down to my bed, as far from the lane as you can get. I neither see nor hear anything from there.'

Hugh had already noted the stairs that dived below the house at the rear, a shallow flight, since the ground dropped steadily away from the street level, and the undercroft, completely below-ground at the street end, was half above-ground at the back. From there, certainly, a man would be cut off from the world outside.

'At what hour did you go there, two nights ago?'

Iestyn knotted his thick black brows and considered. 'I'm always early, having to rise early. I reckon about eight that night, as soon as my supper had settled.'

'You had no late errands to do? Nothing that took you out again after that?'

'No, my lord.'

'Tell me, Iestyn,' said Hugh on impulse, 'are you content in your work here? With Master Walter and his family? You have fair treatment, and a good relationship?'

'One that suits me well enough,' said Iestyn cautiously. 'My wants are simple, I make no complaint. I never doubt time will bring me my due. First to earn it.'


Susanna met Hugh in the hall doorway, and bade him in with the same practical composure she would have used with any other. Questioned, she shrugged away all knowledge with a rueful smile.

'My chamber is here, my lord, between hall and store, the length of the house away from the street. Baldwin's boy did not come to us with his trouble, though he well could have done. At least he would have had company. But he didn't come, so we knew nothing of his master being still astray until the morning, when John came. I was sorry poor Griffin worried out the night alone.'

'And you had not seen Master Peche during the day?'

'Not since morning, when we were all about the yard and

123

the well. I went across to his shop at dinner with a bowl of broth, having plenty to spare, and it was then John told me he'd gone out. Gone since mid-morning and said something about the fish rising. To the best I know, that's the last known word of him.'

'So Boneth has told me. And no report of him from any shop or ale-house or friend's house since. In a town where every man knows every man, that's strange. He steps over his door-sill and is gone.' He looked up the broad, unguarded stairs that led up from beyond her door to the gallery and the rooms above. 'How are these chambers arranged? Who has the one on the street, above the shop?'

'My father. But he sleeps heavily. Yet ask him, who knows but he may have heard or seen something. Next to him my brother and his wife. Daniel is away to Frankwell, but Margery you'll find in the garden with my father. And then my grandmother has the nearest chamber. She keeps her room today, she's old and has had some trying seizures, perilous at her age. But she'll be pleased if you care to visit her,' said Susanna, with a brief, flashing smile, 'for all the rest of us grow very tedious to her, she's worn us out long ago, we no longer amuse her. I doubt if she can tell you anything that will help you, my lord, but the change would do marvels for her.'

She had wide eyes at once distant and brilliant, fringed with lashes russet as her coil of lustrous hair. A pity there should be grey strands in the russet, and fine wrinkles, whether of laughter or long-sighted pain, at the corners of the grey eyes, and drawn lines, like cobweb, about her full, firm mouth. She was, Hugh judged, at least six or seven years older than he, and seemed more. A fine thing spoiled for want of a little spending. Hugh had come by what was his as an only child, but he did not think a sister of his would have been left thus used and unprovided, to furnish a brother richly forth.

'I'll gladly present myself to Dame Juliana,' he said, 'when I have spoken with Master Walter and Mistress Margery.'

'That would be kind,' she said. 'And I could bring you wine, and that would give me the chance to bring her, with it, a dose she might otherwise refuse to take, even though Brother Cadfael comes tomorrow and she minds him more than any of us. Go down this way, then, my lord. I'll look for you returning.'

Either the goldsmith had nothing to tell, or else could not bring himself to spend even words. The one thing that haunted him day and night was his lost treasury, of which he had rendered an inventory piece by piece, almost coin by coin, in loving and grieving detail. The coins in particular were notable. He had silver pieces from before Duke William ever became King William, fine mintage not to be matched now. His father and grandfather, and perhaps one progenitor more, must have been of the same mind as himself, and lived for their fine-struck wealth. Walter's head might be healed now without, but his loss might well have done untold harm to the mind within.

Hugh stood patiently under the apple and pear trees of the orchard, pressing his few questions concerning the vanishing of Baldwin Peche. Almost it seemed to him that the name no longer struck any spark, that Walter had to blink and shake himself and think hard before he could recall the name or the face of his dead tenant. He could not see the one or remember the other for brooding on his voided coffer.

One thing was certain, if he knew of anything that could help to recover his goods, he would pour it out in a hurry. Another man's death, by comparison, meant little to him. Nor did it seem that he had yet hit upon one possibility that was hovering in Hugh's mind. If there was indeed a connection between the robbery and this death, need it be the one to which the town had jumped so nimbly? Robbers can also be robbed, and may even be killed in the robbing. Baldwin Peche had been a guest at the wedding, he had made the locks and keys for the strong-box, and who knew the house and shop better than he?

Margery had been feeding the fowls that scratched in a

narrow run under the town wall, at the bottom of the garden. Until a year previously Walter had even kept his two horses here within the town, but recently he had acquired a pasture and an old stable across the river, westward from Frankwell, where Iestyn was regularly sent to see that they were fed and watered and groomed, and exercise them if they were short of work. The girl was coming up the slope of the garden with the morning's eggs in a basket, the bulk of the wall in shadow behind her, and the narrow door in it closed. A short, rounded, insignificant young person to the view, with an untidy mass of fair hair. She made Hugh a wary reverence, and raised to him a pair of round, unwavering eyes.

'My husband is out on an errand, sir, I'm sorry. In half an hour or so he may be back.'

'No matter,' said Hugh truly, 'I can speak with him later. And you may well be able to speak for both, and save the time. You know on what business I'm engaged. Master Peche's death seems likely to prove no accident, and though he was missing most of the day, yet the night is the most favourable time for villainies such as murder. We need to know what every man was doing two nights ago, and whether he saw or heard anything that may help us lay hands on the culprit. I understand your chamber is the second one, back from the street, yet you may have looked out and seen someone lurking in the alley between the houses, or heard some sound that may have meant little to you then. Did you so?'

She said at once: 'No. It was a quiet night, like any other.'

'And your husband made no mention of noticing anything out of the way? No one out and about on the roads when law-abiding people are fast at home? Had he occasion to be in the shop late? Or any errand outside?'

Her rose and white countenance flushed very slowly a deeper rose, but her eyes did not waver, and she found a ready excuse for her colour. 'No, we retired in good time. Your lordship will understand — we are only a few days married.'

'I understand very well!' said Hugh heartily. 'Then I need hardly ask you if your husband so much as left your side.'

'Never for a moment,' she agreed, and voice and flush were eloquent, whether they told truth or no.

'The idea would never have entered my mind,' Hugh assured her urbanely, 'if we had not the testimony of a witness who says he saw your husband creeping out of the house and making off in haste about an hour after Compline that night. But of course, more's the unwisdom, not all witnesses tell the truth.'

He made her a civil bow, and turned and left her then, neither lingering nor hurrying, and strolled back up the garden path to the house. Margery stood staring after him with her underlip caught between her teeth, and the basket of eggs dangling forgotten from her hand.

She was waiting and watching for Daniel when he came back from Frankwell. She drew him aside into a corner of the yard, where they could not be overheard, and the set of her chin and brows stopped his mouth when he began to blurt out loud, incautious wonder at being thus waylaid. Instead, he questioned in an uneasy undertone, impressed by her evident gravity: 'What is it? What's the matter with you?'

'The sheriff's deputy has been here asking questions. Of all of us!'

'Well, so he must, what is there in that? And what, of all people, could you tell him?' The implied scorn did not escape her; that would change, and soon.

'I *could* have told what he asked me,' she spat, bitter and low, 'where you were all night on Monday. But could I? Do I even know? I know what I believed then, but why should I go on believing it? A man who was out of his bed and loose in the town that night may not have been bustling to another woman's bed after all — he *could* have been battering Baldwin Peche over the head and throwing him into the river! That's what *they* are thinking. And now what am I to believe? Bad enough if you left me to go to that woman while

127

her husband's away — oh, yes, I was there, do you remember when she told you, all nods and winks, the shameless whore! — that he was bound away for several days! But how do I know now that that's what you were about?'

Daniel was gaping at her, white-faced and aghast, and gripping her hand as if his senses at that moment had no other anchor. 'Dear God, they can't think that! *You* can't believe that of me? You know me better . . .'

'I don't know you at all! You pay me no attention, you're nothing but a stranger to me, you steal out at night and leave me in tears, and what do you care?'

'Oh, God!' babbled Daniel in a frantic whisper. 'What am I to do? And you told him? You told him I went out — the whole night?'

'No, I did not. I'm a loyal wife, if you're no proper husband to me. I told him you were with me, that you never left my side.'

Daniel drew breath deep, gawping at her in idiot relief, and began to smile, and jerk out praise and thanks incoherently while he wrung her hand, but Margery measured out her moment like a fencer, and struck the grin ruthlessly from his face.

'But he knows it is not true.'

'What?' He collapsed again into terror. 'But how can he? If you told him I was with you . . .'

'I did. I've perjured myself for you and all to no purpose. *I* gave nothing away, though God knows I owe you nothing. I put my soul in peril to save you from trouble! And then he tells me smoothly that there's a witness who saw you sneak out that night and has the hour right, too, so never think this was a trick. There *is* such a witness. You're known to have been out roving in the dark the night that man was murdered.'

'I never had ought to do with it,' he wailed softly. 'I told you truth . . .'

'You told me you had things to do that were no concern of mine. And everybody knows you had no love for the locksmith.'

'Oh, God!' moaned Daniel, gnawing his knuckles. 'Why did I ever go near the girl? I was mad! But I swear to you, Margery, that was all, it was to Cecily I went . . . and never again, never! Oh, girl, help me . . . what am I to do?'

'There's only one thing you can do,' she said forcefully. 'If that's truly where you were, you must go to this woman, and get her to speak up for you, as she ought. Surely she'll tell the truth, for your sake, and then the sheriff's men will let you alone. And I'll confess that I lied. I'll say it was for shame of being so slighted, though it was truly for love of you — however little you deserve it.'

'I will!' breathed Daniel, weak with fear and hope and gratitude all mingled, and stroking and caressing her hand as he had never done before. 'I'll go to her and ask her. And never see her again, I promise you, I swear to you, Margery.'

'Go after dinner,' said Margery, securely in the ascendancy, 'for you must come and eat and put a good face on it. You can, you must. No one else knows of this, no one but I, and I'll stand by you whatever it cost me.'


Mistress Cecily Corde did not brighten or bridle at the sight of her lover creeping in at the back door of her house early in the afternoon. She scowled as blackly as so golden a young woman could, hauled him hastily into a closed chamber where they could not possible be overlooked by her maid-servant, and demanded of him, before he had even got his breath back, what he thought he was doing there in broad daylight, and with the sheriff's men about the town as well as the usual loiterers and gossips. In a great, gasping out-pour Daniel told her what he was about, and why, and what he needed, entreated, must have from her, avowal that he had spent Monday night with her from nine of the evening until half an hour before dawn. His peace of mind, his safety, perhaps his life, hung on her witness. She could not deny him, after all they had meant to each other, all he had given her, all they had shared.

Once she had grasped what he was asking of her, Cecily

disengaged violently from the embrace she had permitted as soon as the door was closed, and heaved him off in a passion of indignation.

'Are you mad? Throw my good name to the four winds to save your skin? I'll do no such thing, the very idea of asking it of me! You should be ashamed! Tomorrow or the next day my man will be home, and very well you know it. You would not have come near me now, if you had any thought for me. And like this, in daylight, with the streets full! You'd better go, quickly, get away from here.'

Daniel clung, aghast, unable to believe in such a reception. 'Cecily, it may be my life! I *must* tell them . . .'

'If you dare,' she hissed, backing violently out of his desperate attempt at an embrace, 'I shall deny it. I shall swear that you lie, that you've pestered me, and I've never encouraged you. I mean it! Dare mention my name and I'll brand you liar, and bring witness enough to bear me out. Now go, go, I never want to see you again!'

Daniel fled back to Margery. She had the shrewd sense to be watching for him, having known very well what his reception must be, and spirited him competently away to their own chamber where, if they kept their voices down, they could not be heard. Dame Juliana, next door, slept in the afternoon and slept soundly. Their private business was safe from her.

In agitated whispers he poured out everything though he was telling her nothing she did not already know. She judged it time to soften against his shoulder, while keeping the mastery firmly in her own hands. He had been shocked out of his male complacency, and almost out of his skin, she felt pity and affection for him, but that was a luxury she could not yet afford.

'Listen, we'll go together. You have a confession to make, but so have I. We'll not wait for the Lord Beringar to come to us, we'll go to him. I'll own that I lied to him, that you left me alone all that night, knowing you were gone to a paramour. You'll tell him the same. I shall not know her name. And you will refuse to give it. You must say she is a married woman, and it would be her ruin. He'll respect you for it. And we'll say that we start anew, from this hour.'

She had him in her hand. He would go with her, he would swear to whatever she said. They would start anew from that hour; and she would be holding the reins.

In bed that night she clasped a devout, grateful husband, who could not fawn on her enough. Whether Hugh Beringar had believed their testimony or not, he had received it with gravity, and sent them away solemnly admonished but feeling themselves delivered. A Daniel eased of all fear that the eye of the law was turned ominously upon him would sit still where a hand could be laid on him at any moment.

'It's over,' Margery assured him, fast in his arms, and surprisingly contented there, considering all things. 'I'm sure you need not trouble any more. No one believes you ever harmed the man. I'll stand with you, and we have nothing to fear.'

'Oh, Margery, what should I have done without you?' He was drifting blissfully towards sleep, after extreme fear and the release of correspondingly great pleasure. Never before had he felt such devotional fervour, even to his mistresses. This might have been said to be his true wedding night. 'You're a good girl, loyal and true . . .'

'I'm your wife, who loves you,' she said, and more than half believed it, to her own mild surprise. 'And loyal you'll find me, whenever you call upon me. *I* shall not fail you. But you must also stand by me, for as your wife I have rights.' It was well to have him so complacent, but not to let him fall asleep, not yet. She took steps to rouse him; she had learned a great deal in one unsatisfactory week. While he was still glowing, she pursued very softly and sweetly: 'I am your wife now — wife to the heir, there's a status belongs to me. How can I live in a house and have no place, no duties that are mine by right?'

'Surely you have your place,' he protested tenderly. 'The place of honour, mistress of the house. What else? We all bear with my grandmother, she's old and set in her ways, but she doesn't meddle with the housekeeping.'

'No, I don't complain of her, of course we must reverence the elders. But your wife should be granted her due in responsibilities as well as privilege. If your mother still lived it would be different. But Dame Juliana has given up her direction of the household, being so old, to our generation. I am sure your sister has done her duty nobly by you all these years . . .'

Daniel hugged her close, his thick curls against her brow. 'Yes, so she has, and you can keep your hands white and take your ease, and be the lady of the house, why should you not?'

'That is not what I want,' said Margery firmly, gazing up into the dark with wide-open eyes. 'You're a man, you don't understand. Susanna works hard, no one could complain of her, she keeps a good table without waste, and all the linen and goods and provisions in fine order, I know. I give her all credit. But that is the *wife's* work, Daniel. Your mother, if she had lived. Your wife, now you have a wife.'

'Love, why should you not work together? Half the load is lighter to bear, and I don't want my wife worn out with cares,' he murmured smugly into the tangle of her hair. And thought himself very cunning, no doubt, wanting peace as men always want it, far before justice or propriety; but she would not let him get away with that sop.

'She won't give up any part of the load, she has had her place so long, she stands off any approach. Only on Monday I offered to fetch in the washing for her, and she cut me off sharply, *that* she would do herself. Trust me, my love, there cannot be two mistresses in one house, it never prospers. *She* has the keys at her girdle, *she* sees the store-bins kept supplied, and the linen mended and replaced, *she* gives the orders to the maid, *she* chooses the meats and sees them cooked as *she* wishes. *She* comes forth as hostess when visitors appear. All *my* rights, Daniel, and I want them. It is not fitting that the wife should be so put aside. What will our neighbours say of us?'

'Whatever you want,' he said with sleepy fervour, 'you shall have. I do see that my sister ought now to give up her office to you, and should have done so willingly, of her own accord. But she has held the reins here so long, she has not yet considered that I'm now a married man. Susanna is a sensible woman, she'll see reason.'

'It is not easy for a woman to give up her place,' Margery pointed out sternly. 'I shall need your support, for it's your status as well as mine in question. Promise me you will stand with me to get my rights.'

He promised readily, as he would have promised her anything that night. Of the two of them, she had certainly been the greater gainer from the day's crises and recoveries. She fell asleep knowing it, and already marshalling her skills to build on it.

# Nine

*Thursday: from morning to late evening*

DAME JULIANA TAPPED HER WAY DOWN THE BROAD wooden treads of the stairs to the hall in good time on the following morning, determined to greet Brother Cadfael when he came after breakfast with all the presence and assurance of a healthy old lady in full command of her household, even if she had to prepare her seat and surroundings in advance and keep her walking-stick handy. He knew that she was no such matter, and she knew that he knew it. She had a foot in the grave, and sometimes felt it sinking under her and drawing her in. But this was a final game they played together, in respect and admiration if not in love or even liking.

Walter was off to his workshop with his son this morning. Juliana sat enthroned in her corner by the stairs, cushioned against the wall, eyeing them all, tolerant of all, content with none. Her long life, longer than any woman should be called upon to sustain, trailed behind her like a heavy bridal train dragging at the shoulders of a child bride, holding her back, weighing her down, making every step a burden.

As soon as Rannilt had washed the few platters and set the bread-dough to rise, she brought some sewing to a stool in the hall doorway, to have the full light. A decent, drab brown gown, with a jagged tear above its hem. The girl was making a neat job of mending it. Her eyes were young. Juliana's were very old, but one part of her that had not mouldered. She could see the very stitches the maid put in, small and precise as they were.

'Susanna's gown?' she said sharply. 'How did she come to get a rent like that? And the hems washed out too! In my day we made things last until they wore thin as cobweb before we thought of discarding them. No such husbandry these days. Rend and mend and throw away to the beggars! Spendthrifts all!'

Plainly nothing was going to be right for the old woman today, she was determined to make her carping authority felt by everyone. It was better, on such days, to say nothing, or if answers were demanded, make them as short and submissive as possible.

Rannilt was glad when Brother Cadfael came in through the passage with dressings in his scrip for the ulcer that was again threatening to erupt on the old woman's ankle. The thin, eroded skin parted at the least touch or graze. He found his patient reared erect and still in her corner, waiting for him, silent and thoughtful for once, but at his coming she roused herself to maintain, in the presence of this friendly enemy, her reputation for tartness, obstinacy and grim wit, and for taking always, with all her kin, the contrary way. Whoever said black, Juliana would say white.

'You should keep this foot up,' said Cadfael, cleaning the small but ugly lesion with a pad of linen, and applying a new dressing. 'As you know very well, and have been told all too often. I wonder if I should not rather be telling you to stamp about upon it day-long — then you might do the opposite and let it heal.'

'I kept my room yesterday,' she said shortly, 'and am heartily sick of it now. How do I know what they get up to

135

behind my back while I'm shut away up there? Here at least I can see what goes on and speak up if I see cause — as I will, to the end of my days.'

'Small doubt!' agreed Cadfael, rolling his bandage over the wound and finishing it neatly. 'I've never known you baulk your fancy yet, and never expect to. Now, how is it with your breathing? No more chest pains? No giddiness?'

She would not have considered she had had her full dues unless she had indulged a few sharp complaints of a pain here, or a cramp there, and she did not grudge it that most of them he brushed away no less bluntly. It was all a means of beguiling the endless hours of the day that seemed so long in passing, but once past, rushed away out of mind like water slipping through the fingers.

Rannilt finished her mending, and carried off the gown into Susanna's chamber, to put it away in the press; and presently Susanna came in from the kitchen and stopped to pass the time of day civilly with Cadfael, and enquire of him how he thought the old woman did, and whether she should continue to take the draught he had prescribed for her after her seizure.

They were thus occupied when Daniel and Margery came in together from the shop. Side by side they entered, and there was something ceremonious in their approach, particularly in their silence, where they had certainly been talking together in low, intent tones on the threshold. They barely greeted Cadfael, not with any incivility, but rather as if their minds were fixed on something else, and their concentration on it must not be allowed to flag for a moment. Cadfael caught the tension and so, he thought, did Juliana. Only Susanna seemed to notice nothing strange, and did not stiffen in response.

The presence of someone not belonging to the clan was possibly an inconvenience, but Margery did not intend to be deflected or to put off what she was braced to say.

'We have been discussing matters, Daniel and I,' she

announced, and for a person who looked so soft and pliable her voice was remarkably firm and resolute. 'You'll understand, Susanna, that with Daniel's marriage there are sure to be changes in the order here. You have borne the burden of the house nobly all these years . . .' That was unwise, perhaps; it was all those years that had dried and faded what must once have been close to beauty, their signature was all too plain in Susanna's face. 'But now you can resign it and take your leisure and no reproach to you, it's well earned. I begin to know my way about the house, I shall soon get used to the order of the day here, and I am ready to take my proper place as Daniel's wife. I think, and he thinks too, that I should take charge of the keys now.'

The shock was absolute. Perhaps Margery had known that it would be. Every trace of colour drained out of Susanna's face, leaving her dull and opaque as clay, and then as swiftly the burning red flooded back, rising into her very brow. The wide grey eyes stared hard and flat as steel. For long moments she did not speak; Cadfael thought she could not. He might have stolen silently away and left them to their fight, if he had not been concerned for its possible effect on Dame Juliana. She was sitting quite still and mute, but two small, sharp points of high colour had appeared on her cheek bones, and her eyes were unusually bright. Or again, he might in any case have stayed, unobtrusive in the shadows, having more than his fair share of human curiosity.

Susanna had recovered her breath and the blood to man her tongue. Fire kindled behind her eyes, like a vivid sunset through a pane of horn.

'You are very kind, sister, but I do not choose to quit my charge so lightly. I have done nothing to be displaced, and I do not give way. Am I a slave, to be put to work as long as I'm needed, and then thrown out at the door? With nothing? *Nothing!* This house is my home, *I* have kept it, I *will* keep it: my stores, my kitchen, my linen-presses, all are *mine*. You are welcome here as my brother's bride,' she said, cooling formidably, 'but you come new into an old rule, in which *I* bear the keys.'

The quarrels of women are at all times liable to be bitter, ferocious and waged without quarter, especially when they bear upon the matriarchal prerogative. Yet Cadfael found it surprising that Susanna should have been so shaken out of her normal daunting calm. Perhaps this challenge had come earlier than she had expected, but surely she could have foreseen it and need not, for that one long moment, have stood so mute and stricken. She was ablaze now, claws bared and eyes sharp as daggers.

'I understand your reluctance,' said Margery, growing sweet as her opponent grew bitter. 'Never think there is any implied complaint, oh, no, I know you have set me an exemplary excellence to match. But see, a wife without a function is a vain thing, but a daughter who has borne her share of the burden already may relinquish it with all honour, and leave it to younger hands. I have been used to working, I cannot go idle. Daniel and I have talked this over, and he agrees with me. It is my right!' If she did not nudge him in the ribs, the effect was the same.

'So we have talked it over and I stand by Margery,' he said stoutly. 'She is my wife, it's right she should have the managing of this house which will be hers and mine. I'm my father's heir, shop and business come to me, and this household comes to Margery just as surely, and the sooner she can take it upon her, the better for us all. Good God, sister, you must have known it. Why should you object?'

'Why should I object? To be dismissed all in a moment like a thieving servant? I, who have carried you all, fed you, mended for you, saved for you, held up the house over you, if you had but the wit to know it or the grace to admit it. And my thanks is to be shoved aside into a corner to moulder, is it, or to fetch and carry and scrub and scour at the orders of a newcomer? No, that I won't do! Let your wife clerk and count for you, as she claims she did for her father, and leave my stores, my kitchen, my keys to me. Do you think I'll surrender tamely the only reason for living left to me? This family has denied me any other.'

Walter, if he had anticipated any of this, had been wise to keep well away from it, safe in his shop. But the likelihood was that he had never been warned or consulted, and was expendable until this dispute was settled.

'But you knew,' cried Daniel, impatiently brushing aside her lifelong grievance, seldom if ever mentioned so plainly before, 'you knew I should be marrying, and surely you had the sense to know my wife would expect her proper place in the house. You've had your day, you've no complaint. Of course the wife has precedence and requires the keys. And shall have them, too!'

Susanna turned her shoulder on him and appealed with flashing eyes to her grandmother, who had sat silent this while, but followed every word and every look. Her face was grim and controlled as ever, but her breathing was rapid and shallow, and Cadfael had closed his fingers on her wrist to feel the beat of her blood there, but it remained firm and measured. Her thin grey lips were set in a somewhat bitter smile.

'Madam grandmother, do you speak up! Your word still counts here as mine, it seems, cannot. Have I been so useless to you that you, also, want to discard me? Have I not done well by you all, all this while?'

'No one has found fault with you,' said Juliana shortly. 'That is not the issue. I doubt if this chit of Daniel's can match you, or do the half as well, but I suppose she has the good will and the perseverance to learn, if it has to be by her errors. What she has, and so I tell you, girl, is the right of the argument. The household rule is owing to her, and she will have to have it. I can say no other, like it or lump it. You may as well make it short and final, for it must happen.' And she rapped her stick sharply on the floor to make a period to the judgement.

Susanna stood gnawing at her lips and looking from face to face of all these three who were united against her. She

139

was calm now, the anger that filled her had cooled into bitter scorn.

'Very well,' she said abruptly. 'Under protest I'll do what's required of me. But not today. I have been the mistress here for years, I will not be turned out in the middle of my day's work, without time to make up my accounts. She shall not be able to pick flies here and there, and say, this was left unfinished, or, she never told me there was a new pan needed, or, here's a sheet was left wanting mending. No! Margery shall have a full inventory tomorrow, when I'll hand over my charge. She shall have it listed what stocks she inherits, to the last salt fish in the last barrel. She shall start with a fair, clean leaf before her. I have my pride, even if no other regards it.' She turned fully to Margery, whose round fair face seemed distracted between satisfied complacency and discomfort, as if she did not quite know, at this moment, whether to be glad or sorry of her victory. 'Tomorrow morning you shall have the keys. Since the store-room is entered through my chamber, you may also wish to have me move from there, and take that room yourself. Then you may. From tomorrow I won't stand in your way.'

She turned and walked away out of the hall door and round towards the kitchen, and the bunch of keys at her waist rang as if she had deliberately set them jangling in a last derisive spurt of defiance. She left a charged silence behind her, which Juliana was the first one bold enough to break.

'Well, children, make yourselves content,' she said, eyeing her grandson and his bride sardonically. 'You have what you wanted, make the most of it. There's hard work and much trouble goes into running a household.'

Margery hastened to ingratiate herself with thanks and promises. The old woman listened tolerantly, but with that chill smile so unnervingly like Susanna's still on her lips. 'There, be off now, and let Daniel get back to his work. Brother Cadfael, I can see, is none too pleased with seeing me roused. I'm likely to be getting some fresh potion poured into me to settle me down, through the three of you and your squabbles.'

They went gladly enough, they had much to say to each other privately. Cadfael saw the spreading grey pallor round Juliana's mouth as soon as she relaxed her obstinate self-control and lay back against her cushions. He fetched water from the cooling jar, and shook out a dose of the powdered oak mistletoe for her to take. She looked up at him over the cup with a sour grin.

'Well, say it! Tell me my granddaughter has been shabbily used!'

'There is no need for me to say it,' said Cadfael, standing back to study her the better and finding her hands steady, her breath even, and her countenance as hardy as ever, 'since you know it yourself.'

'And too late to mend it. But I've allowed her the one day she wanted. I could have denied her even that. When I gave her the keys, years ago, you don't think they were the only ones? What, leave myself unfurnished? No, I can still poke into corners, if I choose. And I do, sometimes.'

Cadfael was packing his dressings and unguents back into his scrip, but with an eye still intent on her. 'And do you mean to give up both bunches to Daniel's wife now? If you had meant mischief, you could have handed them to her before your granddaughter's face.'

'My mischief is almost over,' said Juliana, suddenly sombre. 'All keys will be wrested from me soon, if I don't give them up willingly. But these I'll keep yet a day or two. I still have a use for them.'

This was her house, her family. Whatever boiled within it, ripe for eruption, was hers to deal with. No outsider need come near.

In the middle of the morning, when Susanna and Rannilt were both busy in the kitchen, and would certainly be occupied for some time, and the men were at work in the shop, Juliana sent the only remaining witness, Margery, to fetch her a measure of a strong wine she favoured for mulling from a vintner's a satisfactory distance away across the town. When she had the hall to herself, she rose, bearing down heavily on her stick, and felt beneath her full skirt for the keys she kept hidden in a bag-pocket there.

Susanna's chamber door was open. A narrow rear door gave quick access here to the strip of yard which separated the kitchen from the house. Faintly Juliana could hear the voices of the two women, their words indistinguishable, their tones revealing. Susanna was cool, short and dry as always. The girl sounded anxious, grieved, solicitous. Juliana knew well enough about that truant day when the chit had come home hastily and in the dark. No one had told her, but she knew. The sharpness of her senses neither denied nor spared her anything. Shabbily used, and too late to mend! The girl had been listening, appalled, to the quarrel in the hall, and felt for the mistress who had shown her kindness. Young things are easily moved to generous indignation and sympathy. The old have no such easy grace.

The store-room with its heavy vats of salted food, jars of oil, crocks of flour and oatmeal and dry goods, tubs of fat, bunches of dried herbs, shared the width of the hall with Susanna's chamber, and opened out of it. This door was locked. Juliana fitted the key Baldwin Peche had cut for her before ever she gave up the original, and opened the door and went in, into the myriad fat, spicy, aromatic, salt smells of the pantry.

She was within for perhaps ten minutes, hardly more. She was ensconced in her cushioned corner under the staircase and the door locked again securely by the time Margery came back with her wine, and the spices needed to mull it to her liking for her indulgence at bedtime.

'I have been telling this youngster,' said Brother Anselm, fitting together curved shards of wood with the adroit delicacy appropriate to the handling of beloved flesh wounded, 'that should he consider taking vows as a novice here, his tenure would be assured. A life of dedication to the music of worship — what better could he seek, gifted as he is? And the world would withdraw its hand from him, and leave him in peace.'

Liliwin kept his fair head bent discreetly over the small mortar in which he was industriously grinding resins for the precentor's gum, and said never a word, but the colour rose in his neck and mounted his cheek and brow to the hair-line. What was offered might be a life secured and at peace, but it was not the life he wanted. Whatever went on inside that vulnerable and anxious head of his, there was not the ghost of a vocation for the monastic life there. Even if he escaped his present peril, even if he won his Rannilt and took her away with him, after more of the world's battering he might end as a small vagrant rogue, and she as what? His partner in some enforced thievery, picking pockets at fair and market in order to keep them both alive? Or worse, as his breadwinner by dubious means when all else failed? We have more to answer for here, thought Brother Cadfael, watching the work in silence, than the rights and wrongs of one local charge of robbery and assault. What we send out from here, in the end, must be armed against fate in something better than motley.

'A fast learner, too,' said Anselm critically, 'and very biddable.'

'Where he's busy with what he loves, no doubt,' agreed Cadfael, and grinned at seeing Liliwin's brief, flashing glance, which met his eyes and instantly avoided them, returning dutifully to the work in hand. 'Try teaching him his letters instead of the neums, and he may be less ardent.'

'No, you mistake, he has an appetite for either. I could teach him the elements of Latin if I had him for one year.'

Liliwin kept his head down and his mouth shut, grateful enough, and from the heart, for such praise, greedy to benefit by such generous teaching, enlarged and comforted by such simple kindness, and desirous of gratifying his tutor in return, if only he could. Now that his innocence began to be accepted as a probability, however uncertain as yet, these good people began also to make plans for his future. But his place was not here, but with his little dark girl, wherever their joint wanderings might take them about the world. Either that or out of the world, if the forty days of grace ebbed out without true vindication.

When the light faded too far to allow the fine work to continue, Brother Anselm bade him take the organetto and play and sing by ear to show off his skills to Brother Cadfacl. And when Liliwin somewhat forgot himself and launched into a love song, innocent enough but disturbing within these walls, Anselm showed no sign of perturbation, but praised the melody and the verses, but the melody above all, and noted it down briskly to be translated to the glory of God.

The Vesper bell silenced their private pleasure. Liliwin put away the organetto with hasty gentleness, and followed to pluck Cadfael by the sleeve.

'Did you see her? Rannilt? She came to no harm by me?'

'I saw her. She was mending a gown, altogether composed and in no trouble. You did her no harm. Yesterday, I hear, she was singing at her work.'

Liliwin released him with a thankful sigh and a whisper of gratitude for such news. And Cadfael went in to Vespers reflecting that he had told but the more welcome half of truth, and wondering if Rannilt felt much like singing this evening. For she had overheard the battle that sent Susanna away defeated, displaced, robbed of the only realm a parsimonious grandmother and sire had left her. And Susanna was the mistress who, if she had never shown her much warmth, had nevertheless kept her from cold, hunger and blows and, above all, had sent her to her strange marriage, so heretically blessed, and witnessed only by the saints whose relics sanctified her marriage bed. Tomorrow Susanna would give up the keys of her realm to a young rival. The little Welsh girl had a partisan heart, quicker to grief even than to joy. No, she would not feel like singing until tomorrow was over.

Rannilt crouched unsleeping on her pallet in the kitchen until all the house lights had been put out, except one, on which her attention was fixed. A miserly household goes early to bed to save lights and fuel, banking down the hearth-fire in the hall under small rubble, and snuffing all the candles and lamps. It was barely Compline, only just dark, but the young pair, quite full of each other now and cooing like doves, were happy enough to withdraw to their bed, and the others habitually fell asleep with the sun and awoke with it. Only in the store-room, showing a narrow chink of light downhill towards the kitchen, was there a candle still burning.

Rannilt had taken off neither shoes nor gown, but sat hugging herself for warmth and watching that meagre slit of light. When it was the only waking sign remaining, she got up and stole out across the few yards of hard-stamped earth between, and pressed herself against the narrow door that led into Susanna's chamber.

Her lady was there within awake, tireless, proud, going between her chamber and the store, hard at work as she had sworn, resolute to render account of every jar of honey, every grain of flour, every drop of oil or flake of fat. Rannilt burned and bled for her, but also she went in awe of her, she dared not go in and cry aloud her grief and indignation.

The steps that moved about within were soft, brisk and purposeful. All Susanna's movements were so, she did everything quickly, nothing in apparent haste, but now it did seem to Rannilt's anxious ear that there was something of bridled desperation about the way she took those few sharp paces here and there, about her last housewifely survey in this burgage. The slight went deep with her, as well it might.

The faint gleam of light vanished from the slit window of

the store-room, and reappeared at the chink of the shutter of the bed-chamber. Rannilt heard the door between closed, and the key turned in the lock. Even on this last night Susanna would not sleep without first securing the safety of her charge. But surely now she had finished, and would go to her bed and take what rest she could.

The light went out. Rannilt froze into stillness in the listening silence, and after a long moment heard the inner door into the hall opened.

On the instant there was a sharp, brief sound, a subdued cry that was barely audible, but so charged with dismay and anger that Rannilt put a hand to the latch of the door against which she stood pressed, half in the desire to hold fast to something solid and familiar, half wishful to go in and see what could have provoked so desolate and frustrated a sound. The door gave to her touch. Distant within the hall she heard a voice, the words indistinguishable, but the grim tones unmistakably those of Dame Juliana. And Susanna's voice replying, bitter and low. Two muted murmurs, full of resentment and conflict, but private as pillow confidences between man and wife.

Trembling, Rannilt pushed open the door, and crept across towards the open door into the hall, feeling her way in the dark. There was a feeble gleam of light high within the hall, it seemed to her to be shining from the head of the stairs. The old woman would not let anything happen in this house without prying and scolding. As though she had not done enough already, discarding her granddaughter and siding with the newcomer!

Susanna had half-closed the door of her room behind her, and Rannilt could see only the shadowy outline of her left side, from shoulder to hems, where she stood some three or four paces into the hall. But the voices had words now.

'Hush, speak low!' hissed the old woman, fiercely peremptory. 'No need to wake the sleepers. You and I are enough to be watching out the night.'

She must be standing at the head of the stairs, with her small night-lamp in one hand and shielded by the other,

Rannilt judged. She did not want to rouse any other member of the household.

'One more, madam, than is needed!'

'Should I leave you lone to your task, and you still hard at work so late? Such diligence! So strict in your accounting, and so careful in your providing!'

'Neither you nor she, grandmother, shall be able to claim that I left one measure of flour or one drop of honey unaccounted for,' said Susanna bitingly.

'Nor one grain of oatmeal?' There was a small, almost stealthy quiver of laughter from the head of the stairs. 'Excellent housewifery, my girl, to find your crock still above half-full, and Easter already past! I give you your due, you have managed your affairs well!'

'I learned from you, grandmother.' Susanna had vanished from the chink of the door, taking a step towards the foot of the staircase. It seemed to Rannilt that she was now standing quite still, looking up at the old woman above her, and spitting her soft, bitter protest directly into the ancient face peering down at her in the dimness. What light the small lamp gave cast her shadow along the boards of the floor, a wide black barrier across the doorway. By the shape of the shadow, Susanna had wrapped her cloak about her, as well she might, working late in the chill of the night. 'It is at your orders, grandmother,' she said, low and clearly, 'that I am surrendering my affairs. What did you mean to do with me now? Had you still a place prepared for me? A nunnery, perhaps?'

The shadow across the doorway was suddenly convulsed, as though she had flung out her arms and spread the cloak wide.

After those bitterly discreet exchanges the screech that tore the silence was so terrifying that Rannilt forgot herself, and started forward, hurling the inner door wide and bursting into the hall. She saw Dame Juliana, at the head of the stairs, shaken and convulsed as the black shadow had been, the lamp tilting and dripping oil in her left hand, her right clutching and clawing at her breast. The mouth that had just uttered that dreadful shriek was wrenched sidelong, the cheek above drawn out of shape. All this Rannilt saw in one brief glimpse, before the old woman lurched forward and fell headlong down the stairs, to crash to the floor below, and the lamp, flying from her hand, spat a jet of burning oil along the boards at Susanna's feet, and went out.

# Ten

*Thursday night to Friday dawn*

RANNILT SPRANG TO SMOTHER THE LITTLE SERPENT OF FIRE that had caught something burnable and sent up a spurt of flame. Blindly, fumbling, her hands found the hard corner of a cloth-wrapped bundle, there on the floor near the wall, and beat out the fire that had caught at the fraying end of the cord that bound it. A few sparks floated and found splinters of wood, and she followed on her knees and quenched them with the hem of her skirt, and then it was quite dark. Not for long, for everyone in the house must be awake now; but for this moment, utterly dark. Rannilt groped about her blindly on the floor, trying to find where the old woman lay.

'Stay still,' said Susanna, in the gloom behind her. 'I'll make light.'

She was gone, quick and competent again as ever, back into her own room, where she could lay her hands instantly on flint and tinder, always ready by her bed. She came with a candle, and lit the oil-lamp in its bracket on the wall. Rannilt got up from her knees and darted to where Juliana lay on her face at the foot of the stairs. But Susanna was before her,

149

kneeling beside her grandmother and running rapid hands over her in search of broken bones from her fall, before venturing to lift her over on to her back. Old bones are brittle, but it had not been a sheer fall, rather a rolling tumble from stair to stair.

Then they were all coming, clutching candles, gaping, crying questions, Daniel and Margery with one gown thrown hastily round the two of them, Walter bleared and querulous with sleep, Iestyn scurrying up the outdoor stairs from the undercroft and in by the rear door of Susanna's chamber, which Rannilt had left standing open. Light on light sprang up, the usual frugal rule forgotten.

They came crowding, demanding, incoherent with sleep, and alarm and bewilderment. The smoky flames and flickering shadows filled the hall with changing shapes that danced about the two figures quiet on the floorboards. What had happened? What was all the noise? What was the old woman doing out of her bed? Why the smell of burning? Who had done this?

Susanna slid an arm under her grandmother's body, cradled the grey head with her other palm, and turned her face upward. She cast up at the clamouring circle of her kin one cold, glittering glance in which Rannilt saw, as none of them did, the scorn in which she held all members of her family but this spent and broken one on her arm.

'Hold your noise, and make yourselves useful. Can you not see? She came out with her light to see how I was fairing, and she took another seizure like the last, and fell, and the last it may very well be. Rannilt can tell you. Rannilt saw her fall.'

'I did,' said Rannilt, quivering. 'She dropped the lamp and caught at her breast, and then she fell. The oil spilled and took fire, I put it out . . .' She looked towards the wall for the bundle, whatever it had been, that had offered an end of tow to the spark, but there was nothing there now. 'She's not dead . . . look, she's breathing . . . Listen!'

Certainly she was, for as soon as they hushed their clamour the air shook to her shallow-drawn, rattling breath. All one side of her face was dragged askew, the mouth grossly twisted, the eyes half-open and glaring whitely; and all her body on that side lay stiff as a board, the fingers of her hand contorted and rigid.

Susanna looked round them all, and made her dispositions, and no one now challenged her right. 'Father, and Daniel, carry her to her bed. She has no broken bones, she feels nothing. We cannot give her any of her draught, she could not swallow it. Margery, feed the little brazier in her room. I will get wine to mull for when she revives — if she does revive.'

She looked over Rannilt's shoulder to Iestyn, standing dumb and at a loss in the shadows. Her face was set as marble and as cold, but her eyes shone clear. 'Run to the abbey,' she said. 'Ask for Brother Cadfael to come to her. Sometimes he works late, if he has medicines making. But even if he has gone to his cell, the porter will call him. He said he would come if he was needed. He is needed now.'

Iestyn looked back at her without a word, and then turned as silently as he had come and ran as she had bade him.

It was not so late as all that. At the abbey the dortoir was still half awake, an uneasy stirring in certain cells, where the brothers found sleep difficult or remembrance all too strong. Brother Cadfael, having stayed late in his workshop to pound herbs for a decoction to be made next day, was just at his private prayers before sleep when the porter came edging along the passage between the cells to find him. He rose at once, and went silently down the night stairs and through the church, to confer with the messenger at the gatehouse.

'The old dame, is it?' He had no need to fetch anything from the herbarium, the best of what he could give her was already supplied and Susanna knew how to use it, if its use was still of any avail. 'We'd best hurry, then, if it's so grave.'

He set a sharp pace along the Foregate and over the

bridge, and asked such questions as were necessary as they went.

'How did she come to be up and active at this hour? And how did this fit come on?'

Iestyn kept station at his side and answered shortly. He had never many words to spare. 'Mistress Susanna was up late seeing to her stores, for she's forced to give up her keys. And Dame Juliana rose up, belike, to see what she was still about. The fit took her at the top of the stairs and she fell.'

'But the seizure came first? And caused the fall?'

'So the women say.'

'The women?'

'The maid was there and saw it.'

'What's her state now, then? The old dame? Has she bones broken? Can she move freely?'

'The mistress says nothing broken, but one side of her stiff as a tree, and her face drawn all on a skew.'

They were let in at the town gate without question. Cadfael occasionally had much later errands and was well known. They climbed the steep curve of the Wyle in silence, the gradient making demands on their breath.

'I warned her the last time,' said Cadfael, when the slope eased, 'that if she did not keep her rages in check the next fit might be the last. She was well in command of herself and all about her this morning, for all the mischief that was brewing in the house, but I had my doubts . . . What can have upset her tonight?'

But if Iestyn had any answer to that, he kept it to himself. A taciturn man, who did his work and kept his own counsel.

Walter was hopping about uneasily at the entrance to the passage, watching for them with a horn lantern in his hand. Daniel was huddled into his gown in the hall, with the spendthrift candles still burning unheeded around him, until Walter entered with the newcomers, and having seen them within, suddenly became aware of gross waste, and begun to go round and pinch out two out of three, leaving the smell of their hot wicks on the air.

'We carried her up to bed,' said Daniel, restless and wretched in this upheaval that disrupted his new content. 'The women are there with her. Go up, they're anxious for you.' And he followed, drawn to a trouble that must be resolved before he could take any comfort, and hovered in the doorway of the sick-chamber, but did not step within. Iestyn remained at the foot of the stairs. In all the years of service here, most likely, he had never climbed them.

A brazier burned in an iron basket set upon a wide stone, and a small lamp on a shelf jutting out from the wall. Here in the upper rooms there were no ceilings, the rooms went up into the vault of the roof, dark wood on all sides and above. On one side of the narrow bed Margery, mute and pale, drew hastily back into the shadows to let Brother Cadfael come close. On the other, Susanna stood erect and still, and her head turned only momentarily to ascertain who it was who came.

Cadfael sank to his knees beside the bed. Juliana was alive, and if one sense had been snatched from her, the others she still had, at least for a brief while. In the contorted face the ancient eyes were alive, alert and resigned. They met Cadfael's and knew him. The grimace could almost have been her old, sour smile. 'Send Daniel for her priest,' said Cadfael after one look at her, and without conceal. 'His errand here is more now than mine.' She would appreciate that. She knew she was dying.

He looked up at Susanna. No question now who held the mastery here; no matter how they tore each other, she of all these was Juliana's blood, kin and match. 'Has she spoken?'

'No. Not a word.' Yes, she even looked as this woman must have looked fifty years ago as a comely, resolute, able matron, married to a man of lesser fibre than her own. Her voice was low, steady and cool. She had done what could be done for the dying woman, and stood waiting for whatever broken words might fall from that broken mouth. She even leaned to wipe away the spittle that ran from its deformed lips at the downward corner.

'Have the priest come, for I am none. She is already promised our prayers, that she knows.' And that was for her, to ensure that she was alive within this dead body, and need not regret all her gifts to the abbey, doled out so watchfully. Her faded eyes had still a flash within them; she understood. Wherever she was gone, she knew what was said and done about her. But she had said no word, nor even attempted speech.

Margery had stolen thankfully out of the room, to send her husband for the priest. She did not come back. Walter was below, pinching out candles and fretting over the few that must remain. Only Cadfael on one side of the bed and Susanna on the other kept watch still by Dame Juliana's death.

The old woman's live eyes in her dead carcase clung to Cadfael's face, yet not, he thought, trying to convey to him anything but her defiant reliance on her own resources. When had she not been mistress of her own household? And these were still her family, no business of any other judge. Those outside must stay outside. This monk whom she had grown to respect and value, for all their differences, she admitted halfway, close enough to know and acknowledge her rights of possession. Her twisted mouth suddenly worked, emitted an audible sound, looked for a moment like a mouth that might speak memorable things. Cadfael stooped his ear close to her lips.

A laborious murmur, indistinguishable, and then: 'It was I bred them . . .' she said thickly, and again struggled with incommunicable thoughts, and rested with a rattling sigh. A tremor passed through her rigid body. A thread of utterance emerged almost clearly: 'But for all that . . . I should have liked to hold . . . my great-grandchild . . .'

Cadfael had barely raised his head when she closed her

eyes. No question but it was by her will they closed, no crippling weakness. But for the priest, she had done.

Even with the priest she did not speak again. She bore with his urgings, and made the effort to respond with her eyelids when he made his required probings into her sense of sin and need and hope for absolution. She died as soon as he had pronounced it, or only moments later.

Susanna stood by her to the end and never uttered a word. When all was done, she stooped and kissed the leather cheek and chilling brow somewhat better than dutifully, and still with that face of marble calm. Then she went down to see Brother Cadfael courteously out of the house, and thank him for all his attentions to the dead.

'She gave you, I know, more work than ever she repaid you for,' said Susanna, with the slight, bitter curl to her lips and the wry serenity in her voice.

'And is it you who tell me so?' he said, and watched the hollows at the corners of her lips deepen. 'I came to have a certain reverence for her, short of affection. Not that she ever required that of me. And you?'

Susanna stepped from the bottom stair, close to where Rannilt huddled against the wall, afraid to trespass, unwilling to abandon her devoted watch. Since Susanna had emerged from her room with the light, her cloak shed within now there was work to do, Rannilt had hovered attentive, waiting to be used.

'I doubt,' said Brother Cadfael, considering, 'whether there was any here who loved her half so well as you.'

'Or hated her half so well,' said Susanna, lifting her head with one measured flash of grey eyes.

'The two are often bed-fellows,' he said, unperturbed. 'You need not question either.'

'I will not. Now I must go back to her. She is my charge, I'll pay her what's due.' She looked round and said quite gently: 'Rannilt, take Master Walter's lantern, and light

Brother Cadfael out. Then go to your bed, there is no more for you to do here.'

'I'd rather stay and watch with you,' said Rannilt timidly.

'You'll need hot water and cloths, and a hand to lift her, and to run errands for you.' As if there were not enough of them, up there now about the bed, son, grandson, and grandson's woman, and how much grief among the lot of them? For Dame Juliana had outstayed her time by a number of years and was one mouth less to feed once her burial was accomplished; not to speak of the whiplash tongue and the too-sharp eye removed from vexing.

'So you may, then,' said Susanna, gazing long upon the small, childlike figure regarding her with great eyes from the shadows, where Walter had quenched all but one candle, but inadvertently left his lantern burning. 'You shall sleep tomorrow in the day, you'll be ready then for your bed and your mind quiet. Come up, when you've shown Brother Cadfael out to the lane. You and I will care for her together.'

'You were there?' asked Cadfael mildly, walking on the girl's heels along the pitch-dark passage. 'You saw what happened?'

'Yes, sir. I couldn't sleep. You were there this morning when they all turned against her, and even the old woman said she must yield her place . . . You know . . .'

'I know, yes. And you were aggrieved for her.'

'She — was never unkind to me . . .' How was it possible to say that Susanna had been kind, where the chill forbade any such word? 'It was not fair that they should turn and elbow her out, like that.'

'And you were watching and listening, and grieving. And you went in. When was that?'

She told him, as plainly as if she lived it again. She told him, as far as she could recall it, and that was almost word for word, what she had heard pass between grandmother and grandchild, and how she had heard the shriek that heralded the old woman's seizure, and burst in to see her panting and swaying and clutching her bosom, the lamp tilting out of her hand, before she rolled headlong down the stairs.

'And there was no other soul stirring then? No one within hand's-touch of her, there above?'

'Oh no, no one. She dropped the lamp just as she fell.' The little snake of fire, spitting sparks and sudden leaping flame as it found the end of tow, seemed to Rannilt to have nothing to do with what had happened. 'And then it was dark, and the mistress said keep still, and went for a light.'

Certain, then, yes quite certain she fell. No one was there to help her fall, the only witnesses were below. And if they had not gone to her aid at once, and sent as promptly for him, he would never have arrived here in time to see Dame Juliana die. Let alone hear the only words she had spoken before dying. For what they were worth! 'I bred them all . . . For all that, I should have liked to hold my great-grandchild . . .'

Well, her grandson, the only being she was reported to dote upon, was now a husband, her proud old mind might well strain forward to embrace a future generation.

'No, don't come out into the lane, child, time for you to be withindoors, and I know my way.'

She went, shy, wild and silent. And Cadfael made his way back thoughtfully to his own cell in the dortoir and took what comfort he might, and what enlightenment, but it was not much. In this death, at least, there was no question of foul play. Juliana had fallen when no other person was near by, and in an unquestionable seizure such as she had suffered twice before. The dissensions within the house, moreover, had broken out in a disturbing form that same day, cause enough for an old woman's body and heart and irascible nature to fail her. The wonder was this had not happened earlier. Yet for all he could do, Cadfael's mind could not separate this death from the first, nor that from the felony of which Liliwin stood accused. There was, there must be, a thread that linked them all together. Not by freakish chance was an ordinary burgess household thus suddenly stricken with blow after blow. A human hand had set off the chain; from that act all these later events stemmed, and where the impetus would finally run out and the sequence of fatalities end was a speculation that kept Cadfael awake half the night.

In Dame Juliana's death chamber the single lamp burned, a steady eye of fire, at the head of the bed. The night hung deep and silent over the town, past the mid-point between dusk and dawn. On a stool on one side Susanna sat, her own hands folded in her lap, quiet at last. Rannilt crouched at the foot of the bed, very weary but unwilling to go to her humble place, and certain that sleep would not come to her if she did. The lofty timbers of the roof soared above them into deep darkness. The three women, two living and one dead, were drawn together into a close, mute intimacy, for these few hours islanded from the world.

Juliana lay straight and austere, her grey hair combed into smooth order, her face uncovered, the sheet folded at her chin. Already the contortion was beginning to ease out of her features, and leave her at peace.

Neither of the two who watched beside her had spoken a word since their work was finished. Susanna had made no bones about dismissing Margery's reluctant offer of help, and had no difficulty in getting rid of all three of her kin. They were not sorry to return to their beds and leave all to her. Mistress and maid had the vigil to themselves.

'You're cold,' said Rannilt, breaking the silence very softly as she saw Susanna shiver. 'Shall I fetch up your cloak? You felt the want of it even about the store, when you were on the move, and now we sit here, and the night chiller than then. I'll creep down for it.'

'No,' said Susanna absently. 'It was a goose walking over my grave. I'm warm enough.' She turned her head and gave the girl a long, sombre stare. 'Were you so vexed for me that you must wake and watch into the night with me? I thought you came very quickly. Did you see and hear all?'

Rannilt trembled at the thought of having intruded uninvited, but Susanna's voice was equable and her face calm. 'No. I wasn't listening, but some part I couldn't help hearing. She praised your providing. Perhaps she was sorry then . . . It was strange she should take to thinking on such things, and suddenly take pride that you should still have the oatmeal crock above half-full . . . That I heard. Surely she was sorry in the end that you should be so misprised. She thought better of you than of any other.'

'She was returning to the days when she ruled all,' said Susanna, 'and had all on her shoulders, as I have had. The old go back, before the end.' Her eyes, large and intent upon Rannilt's face, gleamed in the dim, reflected light from the lamp. 'You've burned your hand,' she said. 'I'm sorry.'

'It's nothing,' said Rannilt, removing her hands hurriedly from sight into her lap. 'I was clumsy. The tow flared. It doesn't hurt.'

'The tow . . . ?'

'Tied round the bundle that was lying there. It had a frayed end and took the flame before I was aware.'

'A pity!' said Susanna, and sat silently for some moments, watching her grandmother's dead face. The corners of her lips curved briefly in what hardly had time to become a smile. 'There was a bundle there, was there? And I was wearing my cloak . . . yes! You noticed much, considering the fright we must have given you, between us.'

In the prolonged silence Rannilt watched her lady's face and went in great awe, having trodden where she had no right to go, and feeling herself detected in a trespass she had never intended.

'And now you are wondering what was in that bundle, and where it vanished to before ever we began lighting candles. Along with my cloak!' Susanna fixed her austere, half-smiling regard upon Rannilt's daunted face. 'It is only natural you should wonder.'

'Are you angry with me?' ventured Rannilt in a whisper.

'No. Why should I be angry? I believe, I do believe, you have sometimes felt for me as a woman for a woman. Is that true, Rannilt?'

'This morning . . .' faltered Rannilt, half-afraid, 'I could not choose but grieve . . .'

'I know. You have seen how I am despised here.' She went very gently and quietly, a woman speaking with a child, but a child whose understanding she valued. 'How I have always been despised. My mother died, my grandmother grew old, I was of value until my brother should take a wife. Yes, but barely a day longer. All those years gone for nothing, and I am left here husbandless and barren and out of office.'

There was another silence, for though Rannilt felt her breast bursting with indignant sympathy, her tongue was frozen into silence. In the lofty darkness of the roof-beams the faint, soft light quivered in a passing draught.

'Rannilt,' said Susanna gravely and softly, 'can you keep a secret?'

'Your secret I surely can,' whispered Rannilt.

'Swear never to breathe a word to any other, and I'll tell you what no one else knows.'

Rannilt breathed her vow devotedly, flattered and warmed at having such trust placed in her.

'And will you help me in what I mean to undertake? For I should welcome your help . . . I need your help!'

'I'll do anything in my power for you.' No one had ever expected or required of her such loyalty, no one had ever considered her as better than menial and impotent, no wonder her heart responded.

'I believe and trust you.' Susanna leaned forward into the light. 'My bundle and my cloak I made away out of sight before I brought the candle, and hid them in my bedchamber.

Tonight, Rannilt, but for this mortal stay, I meant to leave this place, to quit this house that has never done me right, and this town in which I have no honourable place. Tonight God prevented. But tomorrow night . . . tomorrow night I am going! If you will help me I can take with me more of my poor possessions than I can carry the first short piece of the way alone. Come nearer, child, and I'll tell you.' Her voice was very low and soft, a confiding breath in Rannilt's ear. 'Across the bridge, at my father's stable beyond Frankwell, someone who sets a truer value on me will be waiting . . .'

# Eleven

*Friday: from morning to late evening*

SUSANNA CAME TO THE TABLE AS THE SUBDUED HOUSE-
hold assembled next morning, with the keys at her girdle,
and with deliberation unfastened the fine chain that held
them, and laid them before Margery.

'These are now yours, sister, as you wished. From today
the management of this house belongs to you, and I will not
meddle.'

She was pale and heavy-eyed from a sleepless night,
though none of them were in much better case. They would
all be glad to make an early night of it as soon as the day's
light failed, to make up for lost rest.

'I'll come round kitchen and store with you this morning,
and show you what you have in hand, and the linen, and
everything I'm handing over to you. And I wish you well,'
she said.

Margery was almost out of countenance at such magnanimity, and took pains to be conciliatory as she was con-
ducted remorselessly round her new domain.

'And now,' said Susanna, shaking off that duty briskly

from her shoulders, 'I must go and bring Martin Bellecote to see about her coffin, and father will be off to visit the priest at Saint Mary's. But then — you'll hold me excused — I should like to get a little sleep, and so must the girl there, for neither of us has closed an eye.'

'I'll manage well enough alone,' said Margery, 'and take care not to disturb you in that chamber for today. If I may take out what's needed for the dinner now, then you can get your rest.' She was torn between humility and exultation. Having death in the house was no pleasure, but the gloom would lie heavy for only a few days, and then she was rid of all barriers to her own plans, free of the old, censorious eyes watching and disparaging her best efforts, free of this ageing virgin, who would surely absent herself from all participation in the running of the house hereafter, and mistress of a tamed husband who would dance henceforth to her piping.

Brother Cadfael spent the early part of that afternoon in the herb-garden, and having seen everything left in order there, went out to view the work along the Gaye. The weather continued sunny and warm, and the urchins of the town and the Foregate, born and bred by the water and swimmers almost before they could walk, were in and out of the shallows, and the bolder and stronger among them even venturing across where the Severn ran smoothly. The spring spate from the mountains was over now, the river showed a bland face, but these water-children knew its tricks, and seldom trusted it too far.

Cadfael walked through the flowering orchard, very uneasy in his mind after the night's alarms, and continued downstream until he stood somewhere opposite the gardens of the burgages along the approach to the castle. Halfway up the slope the tall stone barrier of the town wall crossed, its crest crumbled into disrepair in places, not yet restored after the rigours of the siege two years ago. Within his vision it was pierced by two narrow, arched doorways, easily barred in dangerous times. One of the two must be in the Aurifaber grounds, but he could not be sure which. Below the wall the greensward shone fresh and vivid, and the trees were in pale young leaf and snowy flower. The alders leaned over the shallows lissome and rosy with catkins. Willow withies shone gold and silver with the fur-soft flowers. So sweet and hopeful a time to be threatening a poor young man with hanging or bludgeoning a single household with loss and death.

The boys of the Foregate and the boys of the town were rivals by tradition, carring into casual warfare the strong local feeling of their sires. Their water-games sometimes became rough, though seldom dangerous, and if one rash spirit overstepped the mark, there was usually an older and wiser ally close by, to clout him off and haul his victim to safety. There was some horse-play going on in the shallows opposite as Cadfael watched. An imp of the Foregate had ventured the crossing, plunged into a frolic of town children before they were aware, and ducked one of them spluttering below the surface. The whole incensed rout closed on him and pursued him some way downstream, until he splashed ashore up a slope of grass to escape them, falling flat in the shallows in his haste, and clawing and scrambling clear in a flurry of spray. From a smooth greensward where he certainly had no right to be, he capered and crowed at them as they drew off and abandoned the chase.

It seemed that he had fished something up with him out of the shallow water and gravel under the bushes. He sat down and scrubbed at it in his palm, intent and curious. He was still busy with it when another boy hardly older than himself came naked out of the orchard above, dropping his shirt into the grass, and trotting down towards the water. He saw the intruder, and checked at gaze, staring.

The distance was not so great but Cadfael knew him, and knew, in consequence, at whose extended burgage he was looking. Thirteen years old, well-grown and personable; Baldwin Peche's simpleton boy, Griffin, let loose from his labours for an hour to run down through the wicket in the wall, and swim in the river like other boys.

Griffin had seen, far better than Cadfael across the river could hope to see, whatever manner of trophy the impudent invader from the Foregate had discovered in the shallows. He let out an indignant cry, and came running down the grass to snatch at the cupped hand. Something dropped, briefly glinting, into the turf, and Griffin fell upon it like a hawk swooping and caught it up jealously. The other boy, startled, leaped to his feet and made to grab at it in his turn, but gave back before a taller challenger. He was not greatly disturbed at losing his toy. There was some exchange, light-hearted on his side, slow and sober on Griffin's. The two youthful voices floated light, excited sounds across the water. The Foregate urchin shrilled some parting insult, dancing backwards towards the river, jumped in with a deliberate splash, and struck out for his home waters, sudden and silvery as a trout.

Cadfael moved alertly to where the child must come ashore, but kept one eye on the slope opposite also, and saw how Griffin, instead of plunging in after his repulsed rival, went back to lay his trophy carefully in the folds of the shirt he had discarded by the bushes. Then he slid down the bank and waded out into the water, and lay face-down upon the current in so expert and easy a fashion that it was plain he had been a swimmer from infancy. He was rolling and playing in the eddies when the other boy hauled himself ashore into the grass of Cadfael's bank, shedding water and glowing from his play, and began to caper and clap his arms about his slender body in the sunny air. Grown men would hardly be trying that water for a month or so yet, but the young have energy enough to keep them warm, and as old men tend to say tolerantly, where there's no sense there's no feeling.

'Well, troutling,' said Cadfael, knowing this imp as soon as he drew close, 'what was that you fished out of the mud over yonder? I saw you take to the land. Not many yards ahead of the vengeance, either! You picked the wrong haven.'

The boy had aimed expertly for the place where he had left his clothes. He darted for his cotte, and slung it round his nakedness, grinning. 'I'm not afeared of all the town hobbledehoys. Nor of that big booby of the locksmith's, neither, but he's welcome to his bit of trumpery. Knew it for his master's, he said! Just a little round piece, with a man's head on it with a beard and a pointed hat. Nothing to fall out over.'

'Besides that Griffin is bigger than you,' said Cadfael innocently.

The imp made a scornful face, and having scrubbed his feet and ankles through the soft grass, and slapped his thighs dry, set to work to wriggle into his hose. 'But slow, and hasn't all his wits. What was the thing doing drifted under the gravel in the water there, if there was any good in it? He can have it for me!'

And he was off at an energetic run to rejoin his friends, leaving Cadfael very thoughtful. A coin silted into the gravel under the bank there, where the river made a shallow cove, and clawed up in the fist of a scrambling urchin who happened to sprawl on his face there in evading pursuit. Nothing so very strange in that. All manner of things might turn up in the waters of Severn, queerer things than a lost coin. All that made it notable was that this one should turn up in that particular place. Too many cobweb threads were tangling around the Aurifaber burgage, nothing that occurred there could any longer be taken as ordinary or happening by chance. And what to make of all these unrelated strands was more than Cadfael could yet see.

He went back to his seedlings, which at least were innocent of any mystery, and worked out the rest of the afternoon until it drew near the time to return for Vespers; but there was still a good half-hour in hand when he was hailed from the river, and looked round to see Madog rowing upstream, and crossing the main current to come to shore where Cadfael was standing. He had abandoned his coracle for a light skiff, quite capable, as Cadfael reflected with a sudden inspiration, of ferrying an inquisitive brother across to take a look for himself at that placid inlet where the boy had dredged up the coin of which he thought so poorly.

Madog brought his boat alongside, and held it by an oar dug into the soft turf of the bank. 'Well, Brother Cadfael, I hear the old dame's gone, then. Trouble broods round that house. They tell me you were there to see her set out.'

Cadfael owned it. 'After fourscore years I wonder if death should be accounted troublous. But yes, she's gone. Before midnight she left them.' Whether with a blessing or a curse, or only a grim assertion of her dominance over them and defence of them, loved or unloved, was something he had been debating in his own mind. For she could have spoken, but had said only what she thought fit to say, nothing to the point. The disputes of the day, surely relevant, she had put clean away. They were her people. Whatever needed judgement and penance among them was her business, no concern of the world outside. And yet those few enigmatic words she had deliberately let him hear. Him, her opponent, physician and — was friend too strong a word? To her priest she had responded only with the suggested movements of her eyelids saying yea and nay, confessing to frailties, agreeing to penitence, desiring absolution. But no words.

'Left them at odds,' said Madog shrewdly, his seamed oak face breaking into a wry smile. 'When have they been anything else? Avarice is a destroying thing, Cadfael, and she bred them all in her own shape, all get and precious little give.'

'I bred them all,' she had said, as though she admitted a guilt to which her eyelids had said neither yea nor nay for the priest.

'Madog,' said Cadfael, 'row me over to the bank under their garden, and as we go I'll tell you why. They hold the strip outside the wall down to the waterside. I'd be glad to have a look there.'

'Willingly!' Madog drew the skiff close. 'For I've been up and down this river from the water-gate, where Peche kept his boat, trying to find any man who can give me word of seeing it or him after the morning of last Monday, and never a glimpse anywhere. And I doubt Hugh Beringar has done better enquiring in the town after every fellow who knew the locksmith, and every tavern he ever entered. Come inboard, then, and sit yourself down steady, she rides a bit deeper and clumsier with two aboard.'

Cadfael slid down the overhanging slope of grass, stepped nimbly upon the thwart, and sat. Madog thrust off and turned into the current. 'Tell, then! What is there over there to draw you?'

Cadfael told him what he had witnessed, and in the telling it did not seem much. But Madog listened attentively enough, one eye on the surface eddies of the river, running bland and playful now, the other, as it seemed, on some inward vision of the Aurifaber household from old matriarch to new bride.

'So that's what's caught your fancy! Well, whatever it may mean, here's the place. That Foregate lad left his marks, look where he hauled his toes up after him, and the turf so moist and tender.'

A quiet and almost private place it was, once the skiff was drawn in until its shallow draught gravelled. A little inlet where the water lay placid, clean speckled gravel under it, and even in that clear bottom the boy's clutching hands had left small indentations. Out of one of those hollows — the right hand, Cadfael recalled — the small coin had come, and he had brought it ashore with him to examine at leisure. Withies of both willow and alder grew out from the very edge of the water on either side of the plane of grass which opened out above into a broad green slope, steep enough to drain readily, smooth enough to provide an airy cushion for bleaching linen. Only from across the river could this ground be viewed, on this town shore it was screened both ways by the bushes. Clean, washed, white pebbles, some of considerable size, had been piled inshore of the bushes for weighting down the linens spread here to dry on washing days when the weather was favourable. Cadfael eyed them and noted the one larger stone, certainly fallen from the town wall, which had not their water-smoothed polish, but showed sharp corners and clots of mortar still adhering. Left here as it had rolled from the crest, perhaps used sometimes for tying up boats in the shallows.

'D'you see ought of use to you?' asked Madog, holding his skiff motionless with an oar braced into the gravel. The boy Griffin had long since enjoyed his bathe, dried and clothed himself, and carried away his reclaimed coin to the locksmith's shop where John Boneth now presided. He had known John for a long time as second only to his master; for him John was now his master in succession.

'All too much!' said Cadfael.

There were the boy's traces, clutching hands under the clear water, scrabbling toes above in the grass. Down here he had found his trophy, above he had sat to burnish and examine it, and had it snatched from him by Griffin. Who knew it as his master's, and was honest as only the simple can be. Here all round the boat the withies crowded, there above in the sward lay the pile of heavy pebbles and the fallen stone. Here swaying alongside danced the little rafts of water-crowfoot, under the leaning alders. And most ominous of all, here in the sloping grass verge, within reach of his hand, not one, but three small heads of reddish purple blossoms stood up bravely in the grass, the fox-stones for which they had hunted in vain downstream.

The piled pebbles and the one rough stone meant nothing as yet to Madog, but the little spires of purple blossoms certainly held his eyes. He looked from them to Cadfael's face, and back to the sparkling shallow where a man could not well drown, if he was in his senses.

'Is *this* the place?'

The fragile, shivering white rafts of crowfoot danced under the alders, delicately anchored. The little grooves left by the boy's fingers very gradually shifted and filled, the motes of sand and gravel sliding down in the quiver of water to fill them. 'Here at the foot of their own land?' said Madog, shaking his head. 'Is it certain? I've found no other place where this third witness joins the other two.'

'Under the certainty of Heaven,' said Cadfael soberly, 'nothing is ever quite certain, but this is as near as a man can aim. Had he stolen and been found out? Or had he found out too much about the one who *had* stolen, and was fool enough to let it be known what he knew? God sort all! Ferry me back now, Madog, I must hurry back to Vespers.'

Madog took him, unquestioning, except that he kept his deep-browed and sharp-sighted old eyes fixed on Cadfael's face all the way across to the Gaye.

'You're going now to render account to Hugh Beringar at the castle?' asked Cadfael.

'At his own house, rather. Though I doubt if he'll be there yet to expect me.'

'Tell him all that we have seen there,' said Cadfael very earnestly. 'Let him look for himself, and make what he can of it. Tell him of the coin — for so I am sure it was — that was dredged up out of the cove there, and how Griffin claimed it for his master's property. Let Hugh question him on that.'

'I'll tell him all,' said Madog, 'and more than I understand.'

'Or I, either, as yet. But ask him, if his time serves for it, to come down and speak with me, when he has made what he may of all this coil. For I shall be worrying from this moment at the same tangle and may, who knows? — God aiding! — may arrive at some understanding before night.'

Hugh came late home from his dogged enquiries round the town which had brought him no new knowledge, unless their cumulative effect turned probability into certainty, and it could now be called knowledge that no one, in his familiar haunts or out of them, had set eyes on Baldwin Peche since

Monday noon. News of Dame Juliana's death added nothing, she being so old, and yet there was always the uncomfortable feeling that misfortune could not of itself have concentrated such a volley of malice against one household. What Madog had to tell him powerfully augmented this prevading unease.

'There within call of his own shop? Is it possible? And all present, the alders, the crowfoot, the purple flower . . . Everything comes back, everything comes home, to that burgage. Begin wherever we may, we end there.'

'That is truth,' said Madog. 'And Brother Cadfael is cudgelling his wits over the same tangle, and would be glad to consider it along with you, my lord, if you can spare him the needed hour tonight, however late.'

'I'll do that thankfully,' said Hugh, 'for God knows it wants more cunning that I have alone, and sharper vision, to see through this murk. Do you go home and get your rest, Madog, for you've done well by us. And I'll go knock up Peche's lad, and have out of him whatever he can tell us about this coin he claims for his master's.'

By this same hour Brother Cadfael had eased his own mind by imparting, after supper, all that he had discovered to Abbot Radulfus, who received it with thoughtful gravity.

'And you have sent word already to Hugh Beringar? You think he may wish to take counsel with you further in the matter?' He was well aware that there was a particular understanding between them, originating in events before he himself took office at Shrewsbury. 'You may take whatever time you need if he comes tonight. Certainly this affair must be concluded as soon as possible, and it does increasingly appear that our guest in sanctuary may have very little to do with any of these offences. He is within here, but the evil continues without. If he is innocent of all, in justice that must be shown to the world.'

Cadfael left the abbot's lodging with time still for hard thought, and the twilight just falling. He went faithfully to

Compline and then, turning his back on the dortoir, went out to the porch where Liliwin spread his blankets and made his bed. The young man was still wide awake, sitting with his knees drawn up and his back braced comfortably into the corner of the stone bench, a small, hunched shadow in the darkness, singing over to himself the air of a song he was making and had not yet completed to his satisfaction. He broke off when Cadfael appeared, and made room beside him on his blankets.

'A good tune, that,' said Cadfael, settling himself with a sigh. 'Yours? You'd best keep it to yourself, or Anselm will be stealing it for the ground of a Mass.'

'It is not ready yet,' said Liliwin. 'There lacks a proper soft fall for the ending. It is a love song for Rannilt.' He turned his head to look his companion earnestly in the eyes. 'I *do* love her. I'll brave it out here and hang rather than go elsewhere without her.'

'She would hardly be grateful to you for that,' said Cadfael. 'But God willing you shall not have to make any such choice.' The boy himself, though he still went in suspense and some fear, was well aware that every day now cast further doubt upon the case against him. 'Things move there without, if in impenetrable ways. To tell truth, the law is coming round very sensibly to my opinion of you.'

'Well, maybe . . . But what if they found that I did leave here that night? They wouldn't believe my story as you did . . .' He cast a doubtful glance at Brother Cadfael, and saw something in the bland stare that met him that caused him to demand in alarm: 'You haven't told the sheriff's deputy? You promised . . . for Rannilt's sake . . .'

'Never fret, Rannilt's good name is as safe with Hugh Beringar as with me. He has not even called on her as a witness for you, nor will not unless the affair goes to the length of trial. Tell him? Well, so I did, but only after he had made it plain he guessed the half. His nose for a reluctant liar is at least as keen as mine, he never believed that "No" he wrung out of you. So the rest of it he wrung out of me. He

172

found you more convincing telling truth than lying. And then there is always Rannilt, if ever you need her witness, and the watchmen who saw you pass in and out. No need to trouble too much about *your* doings that night. I wish I knew as much about everyone else's.' He pondered, conscious of Liliwin's intent and trusting regard. 'There's nothing more you've recalled? The smallest detail concerning that house may be of help.'

Hesitantly Liliwin cast his mind back, and told over again the brief story of his connection with the goldsmith's house. The host at a tavern where he had played and sung for his supper had told him of the marriage to be celebrated next day, he had gone there hopefully, and been engaged for the occasion, he had done his best to earn his money and been cast out, and hunted as a thief and murderer here into the church. All of it known already.

'How much of that burgage did you ever see? For you went first in daylight.'

'I went to the shop and they sent me in through the passage to the hall door, to the women. It was they who hired me, the old woman and the young one.'

'And in the evening?'

'Why, as soon as I came there they sent me to eat with Rannilt in the kitchen, and I was there with her until they sent out for me to come and play and sing while they feasted, and afterwards I played for dancing, and did my acrobatics, and juggled — and you know how it ended.'

'So you never saw more than the passage and the yard. You never were down the length of the garden, or through the town wall there to the waterside?'

Liliwin shook his head firmly. 'I didn't even know it went beyond the wall until the day Rannilt came here. I could see as far as the wall when I went through to the hall in the morning, but I thought it ended there. It was Rannilt told me the drying-ground was beyond there. It was their washing day, you see, she'd done all the scrubbing and rinsing, and had it all ready to go out by mid-morning. But usually she has the dinner to prepare as well, and watches the weather, and fetches the clothes in before evening. But that day Mistress Susanna had said she would see to everything, and let Rannilt come here to visit me. That was truly kind!'

Strange how sitting here listening to the boy's recollections brought up clearly the picture of that drying-ground he had never seen but through Rannilt's eyes, the slope of grass, the pebbles for anchors, the alders screening the riverside, the town wall shielding the sward from the north and leaving it open to the south . . .

'And I remember she said Mistress Susanna had her shoes and the hems of her skirts wet when she came in from putting out the washing and found Rannilt crying. But still she took note first for my girl being so sad . . . Never mind my wet feet, she said, what of your wet eyes? Rannilt told me so!'

All ready to go out by mid-morning . . . As Baldwin Peche had gone out in mid-morning for the last time. The fish rising . . . Cadfael, away pursuing his own thoughts, suddenly baulked, realising, belatedly, what he had heard.

'What was that you said? She had her feet and skirts wet?'

'The river was a little high then,' explained Liliwin, undisturbed. 'She'd slipped on the smooth grass into the shallows. Hanging out a shirt on the alders . . .'

And she came in calmly, and sent the maidservant away so that none other but herself should go to bring in the linen. What other reason would any have for passing through the wicket in the wall? And only yesterday Rannilt had been sitting in the doorway to have the light on her work, mending a rent in the skirt of a gown. And the brown at the hem had been mottled and faded, leaving a tide-mark of dark colour round the pallor . . .

'Brother Cadfael,' called the porter softly from the archway into the cloister, 'Hugh Beringar is here for you. He said you would be expecting him.'

'I am expecting him,' said Cadfael, recalling himself with

an effort from the Aurifaber hall. 'Bid him come through here. I think we have word for each other.'

It was not quite dark, the sky being so clear, and Hugh knew his way everywhere within these walls. He came briskly, made no objection to Liliwin's presence, and sat down at once in the porch to show the silver coin in his palm.

'I've already viewed it in a better light. It's a silver penny of the sainted Edward, king before the Normans came, a beautiful piece minted in this town. The moneyer was one Godesbrond, there are a few of his pieces to be found, but few indeed in the town where they were struck. Aurifaber's inventory listed three such. And this was stuck between the boards of the bucket in their well the morning after the theft. A scrap of coarse blue cloth, the lad says, was caught in with it, but he thought nothing of that. But it seems to me that whoever emptied Aurifaber's coffer tipped all into a blue cloth bag and dropped it into that bucket — the work of a mere few moments — to be retrieved later at leisure in the dark hours, before the earliest riser went to draw water.'

'And whoever hoisted it out again,' said Cadfael, 'snagged a corner of the bag on a splinter . . . a small tear, just enough to let through one of the smaller coins. It could be so. And Peche's boy had found this?'

'He *was* the earliest riser. He went to draw water and lit on this. He took it to his master, and was rewarded, and told not to let it out to any other ears that the locksmith possessed any such. A great value, Peche said, he set on this.'

So he well might, if it meant to him that someone there in that very household must be the thief, and could be milked of the half of his gains in return for silence. The fish were rising! Now Cadfael began gradually to comprehend all that had happened. He forgot the young man hugging his knees and stretching his amazed ears in the corner of the bench close to them. Hugh had hardly given the boy a thought, so silent and so still he was.

'I think,' said Cadfael, picking his way without too much

175

haste, for there might yet be pitfalls, 'that when he saw this he knew, or could divine with very fair certainty, which of that household must be the robber. He foresaw good pickings. What would he ask? A half-share in the booty? But it would not have made any difference had he been far more modest than that, for the one he approached had the force and the passion and the ruthlessness to act at once and waste no time on parley. Listen to me, Hugh, and remember that night. They sought Master Walter, found him stunned in his shop, and carried him up to his bed. And then someone — no one seems certain who — cried that it must be the jongleur who had done this, and sent the whole mob haring out after him, as we here witnessed. Who, then, was left there to tend the stricken man, and the old woman threatened by her fit?'

'The women,' said Hugh.

'The women. Of whom the bride was left to care for the victims upstairs in their own chambers. It was Susanna who ran for the physican. Very well, so she did. But did she run for him at once, or take but a few moments to run first to the well and place what she found there in safer hiding?'

In a brief and awed silence they sat staring at each other.

'Is it possible?' said Hugh marvelling. *'His daughter?'*

'Among humankind all things are possible. Consider! This locksmith had the key to the mystery put into his hands. If he had been honest he would have gone straight to Walter or to Daniel and showed it, and told what he knew. He did not, for he was not honest. He meant to gain by what he had found out. If he did not approach the one he believed guilty until the Monday, it was because he had no chance until then of doing so in private. He was as able as we to remember how all the menfolk had gone baying after Liliwin here, and to reason that it was a woman who reclaimed the treasury from the well and put it safely away until all the hue and cry should be over, and a stray lad, with luck, hanged for the deed. And who kept the keys of the house and had the best command over all its hiding-places? He chose Susanna. And on Monday his time came, when she took her basket of linen and went down through the wall to spread it out in the drying-ground. About mid-morning Baldwin Peche was last seen in his shop, and went off with some remark about the fish rising. No one saw him, living, ever again.'

Liliwin, hitherto mute in his corner, leaned forward with a soft, protesting cry: 'You can't mean it! She . . . But she was the only one, the only one who showed Rannilt some kindness. She let her come to me for her comfort . . . She did not truly believe that *I* . . .' He saw in time where he was headed, and halted with a great groan.

'She had good reason to *know* that you never harmed her father's person or stole his goods. The best! And a sound reason, also, for sending Rannilt away out of the house so that she herself, and none but she, should fetch in the washing, or have any other occasion to go down to the riverside, where she had left the extortioner dead.'

'I cannot believe,' whispered Liliwin, shaking, 'that she could, even if she would, do such a thing. A woman . . . kill?'

'You underrate Susanna,' said Cadfael grimly. 'So did all her kin. And women have killed, many a time.'

'Granted, then, that he followed her down to the river,' said Hugh. 'You had better go on. Tell us what you believe happened there, and how this thing came about.'

'I think he came down after her to the brink, showed her the coin, and demanded a share in her gains to pay for his silence. I think he, of all people, had worst underestimated her. A mere woman! He expected prevarication, lies, delay, perhaps pleading, some labour to convince her he knew what he knew and meant what he said. He had greatly mistaken her. He had not bargained for a woman who could accept danger instantly, with no outcry, make up her mind, and act, stamping out the threat as soon as it arose. I think she spoke him fair while she went on laying out the washing, and as he stood by the water's edge with the coin in his hand she so arranged that she passed behind him with a

177

stone in her hand, reaching to a corner of linen, and struck him down.'

'Go on,' said Hugh, 'you cannot leave it there. There was more done than that.'

'I think you already know. Whether the blow quite stunned him or not, it flung him face-down into the shallow water. I think she did not wait to give him time to recover his wits and try to rise, but went on acting instantly. Her skirt and shoes were wet! I have only just learned it. And remember the bruises on his back. I think she stepped upon him in the water, almost as he fell, and held him down until he was dead.'

Hugh sat silent. It was Liliwin who uttered a small whimper of horror at hearing it, and shook as if the night had turned cold.

'And then considered calmly the possibility that the river might find force enough to float him away, and took steps to pin him down where he was, under the alders, under the water, until he could be conveyed away by night, to be discovered elsewhere, a drowned man. Do you recall the pitted bruise on his shoulders? There is a jagged stone fallen from the town wall, beside the pebbles there. As for the coin, it was under his body, she did not try to recover it.'

Hugh drew deep breath. 'It could be so! But it was *not* she who followed her father to his shop and struck him down, for she is one person who *is* vouched for fully, all that time that he was gone, until she went to look for him. And then she cried out at once for help. There was no time at all when she could have struck the blow or made off with the booty. She may have removed it from the well later, she certainly did not put it there. You are arguing, I take it, that there were two who planned this between them?'

'Two are implied. One to strike and steal and hide, the other to retrieve the goods by night and secrete them in a safer place. One to destroy the extortioner as soon as he declared himself, and the other to take away the body and dispose of it by night. Yes, surely two.'

'Then who is the second? Certainly brother and sister who suffered from such parsimonious elders might compound together to get their hands on what was withheld from them, and certainly Daniel was abroad that night and furtive about it. And for all his tale of a married woman's bed rings likely enough, I have still had an eye on him. Even shallow men can learn to lie.'

'I have not forgotten Daniel. But you may, for of all men living, her brother is the least likely to have had any part in Susanna's plans.' Cadfael was recalling, as in a storm-flash of illumination, small, unremarkable, unremarked things, Rannilt repeating the words she had overheard, Juliana's improbable praise of her granddaughter's excellent housewifery, in preserving her oatmeal crock half-full past Easter, and Susanna's bitter taunt: 'Had you still a place prepared for me? A nunnery, perhaps?' And then the old woman shrieked and fell down . . .

No, wait! There was more to it, he saw it now. The old woman at the head of the stairs, the only light that of the little lamp she carried, a falling light, pricking Susanna's form and features into sharpest light and shade, every curve or hollow magnified . . . Yes! She saw what she saw, she shrieked and clutched her breast, and then fell, letting fall the revealing lamp from her hand. Somehow she had known the half of it, and come forth by night to confront her only, her best antagonist. She, too, must have seen the torn skirt, the stained hem, and made her own connections. And she had still, she had said, a use for those concealed keys of hers before she surrendered them at last. Yes, and the last words she ever spoke: 'For all that, I should have liked to hold my great-grandchild . . .' Words better understood now than when first he had heard them.

'No, now I see! Nothing now could have held her back. The man who compounded with her to steal was no kinsman, nor one they would ever have admitted as kin. They made their plans perforce, those two, to vanish from here together at the first favourable time, and make a life somewhere far away from this town. Her father grudged her a dowry, she has taken it for her herself. Whatever his name may be, this man, we know now *what* he is. He is her lover. More, he is the man who has got her with child.'

# Twelve

HUGH WAS ON HIS FEET BEFORE THE LAST WORDS WERE SPOken. 'If you're right, after what has happened they won't wait for a better time. They've left it late as it is and so, by God, have I.'

'You're going there now? I am coming with you.' Cadfael was not quite easy about Rannilt. In all innocence she had spoken out things that meant nothing evil to her, but might uncover much evil to those who listened. Far better to have her away before she could further threaten Susanna's purposes. And it seemed that the same fear had fallen upon Liliwin, for he scrambled hastily out of the shadows to catch at Hugh's arm before they could leave the cloister.

'Sir, am I free now? I need not hide here any longer? Then take me with you! I want to fetch my girl away out of that house. I want her with me. How if they take fright at her too much knowledge? How if they do her harm? I'm coming to bring her away, whether or no it's safe for me!'

Hugh clapped him heartily on the shoulder. 'Come, and welcome. Free as a bird, and I'll ensure my men shall know it and hold you safe enough. Tomorrow the town shall know it, too.'

There were no lights in the Aurifaber house when Hugh's sergeant hammered at the hall door. The household was already abed, and it took some time to rouse any of the family. No doubt Dame Juliana, by this time, was shrouded and ready for her coffin.

It was Margery who at last came down to enquire quaveringly through the closed door who was without, and what was the matter at this time of night. At Hugh's order she opened and let them in, herself surprised and vexed that Susanna, who slept downstairs, had not saved her the trouble. But it soon became clear that Susanna was not there to hear any knocking. Her room was empty, the bed undisturbed, the chest that had held her clothes now contained only a few discarded and well-worn garments.

The arrival of the sheriff's deputy and others, with several officers of the law, very soon brought out all the inhabitants, Walter coming down blear-eyed and suspicious, Daniel hurrying solicitously to his wife's side, the boy Griffin peering uncertainly from the other side of the yard. A curiously shrunken and unimpressive gathering, without its two dominant members, and every one of these few who remained utterly at a loss, staring about and at one another in consternation, as though somewhere among the shadows of the hall they might still discover Susanna.

'My daughter?' croaked Walter, looking about him helplessly. 'But is she not here? She must be . . . she was here as always, she put out the lights as she always does, the last to her bed. Not an hour since! She cannot be gone!'

But she was gone. And so, as Cadfael found when he took a lantern and slipped away by the outdoor stairs at the rear of the house and into the undercroft, was Iestyn. Iestyn the Welshman, without money or family or standing, who would never for a moment have been considered as fit for his master's daughter, even now she had ceased to be necessary to the running of his master's house, and was of no further value.

The undercroft ran under stone-vaulted ceilings the length of the house. On impulse Cadfael left the cold, abandoned bed, and lit himself through to the front, where a narrow stair ran up to a door into the shop. Directly opposite to him, as he opened it, stood the pillaged coffer where Walter had kept his wealth. There had been no shadow that night, no sound, only the candle had flickered as the door was silently opened.

A few yards away, when Cadfael retraced his steps and again climbed the outdoor stair, lay the well. And on his right hand, the door into Susanna's chamber, by which she could pass quickly between hall and kitchen, and a young man from below-stairs could as well enter when all was dark.

They were gone, as they had surely planned to go one night earlier and been detained by death. Acting on another thought, Cadfael went in by Susanna's door, and asked Margery to open for him the locked door of the store. The big stone crock in which Susanna had kept her stock of oatmeal stood in one corner. Cadfael lifted the lid, and held his lantern over it. There was still a respectable quantity of grain left in the bottom of it, enough to hide quite a large bundle, suitably disposed, but bereft of that padding it showed much less than a quarter full. Juliana with her keys had been before him, and left what she found there, intending, as always, to manage the fortunes of her own clan with no interference from any other. She had known, and she had held her peace when she could have spoken. And that stark girl, her nearest kin, all desperation and all iron calm, had tended her scrupulously, and waited to learn her fate without fear or complaint. The one as strong as the other, for good or for evil, neither giving nor asking quarter.

Cadfael replaced the lid, went out and relocked the door. In the hall they were fluttering and bleating, anxious to insist on their own innocence and respectability at all costs, distracted at the thought that a kinswoman should be suspect of such an enormity as robbing her own family. Walter stammered out his answers, aghast at such treachery, almost incoherent with grief for his lost money, lost to his own child. Hugh turned rather to Daniel.

'If she intended a long journey tonight, to take her out of our writ, or at least out of our hold, where would she run? They would need horses. Have you horses they may have taken?'

'Not here in the town,' said Daniel, pale-faced and tousled from bed, his comeliness looking almost idiot at this pass, 'but over the river we have a pasture and a stable. Father keeps two horses there.'

'Which way? In Frankwell?'

'Through Frankwell and along the westward road.'

'And the westward road may well be our road,' said Cadfael, coming in from the store, 'for there's a Welshman missing from under here, and what little he had gone with him, and once well into Wales he can thumb his nose at the sheriff of Shropshire. Whatever he may have taken with him.'

He had barely got it out, to indignant and disbelieving protests from Walter, outraged at the mere suggestion of such a depraved alliance, when Liliwin came bursting in from the rear quarters, his small person stiff and quivering with alarm.

'I've been to the kitchen — Rannilt is not there. Her bed's cold, she's left her things just as they are, nothing taken . . .' How little she must have to take, but he knew the value, to one with virtually nothing, of the poor possessions she had left behind. 'They've taken her with them — they're afraid of what she knows and may tell. That woman has taken her,' he cried, challenging the household, the law and all, 'and she has killed and will kill again if she sees need. Where will they have gone? For I am going after them!'

'So are we all,' said Hugh, and turned on Walter Aurifaber. Let the father sweat for his own, as the lover did for his love. For his own by blood or by greed. 'You, sir, come with us. You say she had but an hour's start of us and on foot. Come, then, let's be after them mounted. I sent for horses from the castle, they'll be in the lane by now. You best know the way to your own stable, bring us there fast.'

The night was dark, clear and still young, so that light lingered in unexpected places, won from a smooth plane of the river, a house-front of pale stone, a flowering bush, or scattered stars of windflowers under the trees. The two women had passed through the Welsh gate and over the bridge without question. Owain Gwynedd, the formidable lord of much of Wales, withheld his hand courteously from interfering in England's fratricidal war, and very cannily looked after his own interests, host to whoever fled his enemy, friend to whoever brought him useful information. The borders of Shrewsbury he did not threaten. He had far more to gain by holding aloof. But his own firm border he maintained with every severity. It was a good night, and a good time of night, for fugitives to ride to the west, if their tribal references were good.

Through the dark streets of the suburb of Frankwell they passed like shadows, and Susanna turned westward, keeping the river still in view, along a path between fields. The smaller bundle, but the heavier, Susanna carried. The large and unwieldy one that held all her good clothes they carried between them. It would have been too clumsy for one to manage alone. If I had not your help, she had said, I must have left half my belongings behind, and I shall have need of them.

'Shall you get far tonight?' wondered Rannilt, hesitant but anxious for assurance.

'Out of this land, I hope. Iestyn, who is nobody here, has a kinship of his own, and a place of his own, in his own country. There we shall be safe enough together. After tonight, if we make good speed, we cannot be pursued. You are not afraid, Rannilt, coming all this way with me in the dark?'

'No,' said Rannilt sturdily, 'I'm not afraid. I wish you well, I wish you happy, I'm glad to carry your goods for you, and to know that you don't go unprovided.'

'No,' agreed Susanna, with a curious twist to her voice that suggested laughter, 'not quite penniless. I have earned my future, have I not? Look back now,' she said, 'over your left shoulder, at that mole-hill of the town.' It showed as a hunched shadow in the shadowy night, stray flickers of light cast up the pale stone of the wall from the silver of the river in between. 'A last glimpse,' said Susanna, 'for we have not far now to go. Has the load been heavy? You shall soon lay it down.'

'Not heavy at all,' said Rannilt. 'I would do more for you if I could.'

The track along the headlands was rough and rutted, but Susanna knew it well, and stepped securely. On their right the ground rose, its darkness furred and fragrant with trees. On their left the smooth green meadows swept down to the lambent, murmuring Severn. Ahead, a roof heaved dimly out of the night, bushes banked about it, rough ground sheltering it to northwards, the pasture opening serenely to the south.

'We are there,' said Susanna, and hastened her step, so that Rannilt hurried to keep up with her and balance their burden.

Not a large building, this one that loomed out of the night, but stout in its timbers, and tall enough to show that above the stable it had a loft for hay and fodder. There was a double door set wide upon deep darkness, out of which the scent of horseflesh and hay and grainy, dusty warmth came to meet them. A man emerged, a dark shape, tensed to listen for any approaching foot. Susanna's step he knew at once and he came with spread arms; she dropped her end of the bundle and opened her arms to him. Not a word, not a sound had passed between them. Rannilt stood clutching her end of the load, and shook as though the earth had trembled under her, as they came together in that silent, exultant embrace, laced arms straining. Once at least, if never again, she had experienced a small spark of this devouring flame. She closed her eyes, and stood quivering.

Their breaking apart was as abrupt and silent as their coming together. Iestyn looked over Susanna's shoulder, and fixed his black glance on Rannilt. 'Why did you bring the girl? What do we want with her?'

'Come within,' said Susanna, 'and I'll tell you. Have you saddled up? We should get away quickly.'

'I was about it when I heard you.' He picked up the roll of clothing, and drew her with him into the warm darkness of the stable and Rannilt followed timidly, only too aware how little need they now had of her. Iestyn closed the doors, but did not fasten them. 'Who knows, there may still be some soul awake along the river, no need to let them see any movement here until we're away.'

She heard and felt them embrace again in the dark, even in this brief contact becoming one by passionate consent. She knew then that they had lain together as she and Liliwin had lain, but many times and with no better hope. She remembered the rear door of Susanna's chamber and the stair to the undercroft not many yards distant. Every temptation lavishly offered, and all countenance denied.

'This child here,' said Iestyn softly, 'what's your intent with her? Why did you bring her all this way?'

'She sees too clear and notices too much,' said Susanna shortly. 'She has said to me, poor fool innocent, things she had better not have said, and had better not say to any other, for if they understood more than she by it, they might yet be the death of us. So I brought her. She can go with us — a part of the way.'

Iestyn demanded, after a brief, deep silence: 'What do you mean by that?'

'What do you suppose? There are woods enough and wild places your side the border. Who's to look for her? A kinless kitchen slave.' The voice was so calmly and reasonably Susanna's voice that Rannilt could not take in what it was saying, and stood utterly lost and feeling herself forgotten, even while they spoke of her.

A horse stamped and shifted in the dark, the warmth of its big body tempering the night air. Shapes began to emerge faintly, shadow separating itself from shadow, while Iestyn breathed long and deeply, and suddenly shuddered. Rannilt felt him quake, and still did not understand.

'No!' he said in a muted cry just below his breath. 'No, that we cannot, that I will not. Good God, what harm has she ever done us, a poor soul even less happy than we?'

'You need not,' said Susanna simply. 'I can! There is nothing now I cannot do to have you mine, to belong to you, to go by your side through this world. After what I've done already, what is there I dare not do?'

'No, not this! Not this offence, not if you love me. The other was forced on you, what loss was he, as mean as your kin! But not this child! I will not let you! Nor's there no need,' he said, turning from ordering to persuading. 'Here are we, well out of the town, leave her here and go, you and I together, what else matters here? Let her make her way back by daylight. Where shall we be? Far past pursuit, over the border into Welsh land, safe. What harm can she do us, who has never done any yet, nor ever willed any?'

'They *will* pursue! If ever my father gets to know . . . You know him! He would not stir a step for me, but for this — this . . .' She spurned with her foot the bundle she had brought with her, and it rang faintly in the dark. 'There could be barriers on the way into Wales, accidents, delays . . . Far better be sure.'

'No, no, no! You shall not so despoil my love, I will not have you so changed. I want you as you are now . . .'

The horses shifted and blew, uneasy at having disturbing company at this hour, yet wakeful and ready. Then there was a silence, brief and fathoms deep, and ending in a long-drawn sigh.

'My heart, my love,' Susanna said in a melting whisper, 'as you will, as you order . . . Have it your way, then . . . Yes, let her be! What if we are hunted? There's nothing I can refuse you — not my life . . .'

And whatever it had been between them, and concerning her, it was over. Rannilt stood helpless in the corner of the stable, trying to understand, willing them away, westward into Wales, where Iestyn was a man and a kinsman instead of a menial, and Susanna might be an honourable wife, who had been hitherto a household servant, baulked of her rights, grudged her dowry, a discard woman.

Iestyn plucked up the clothing roll, and by the stirring and trampling of one of the horses, he was busy strapping it into balance behind the saddle. The other bundle, the heavy one, gave forth again its soft, metallic sound as Susanna hoisted it, to be stowed behind the second mount. They were still barely visible, those horses. An occasional splinter of light glanced from their coats and was lost again; their warmth breathed on the air with every movement.

A hand swung wide the half of the double door, and a sector of sky peered in, lighter than the darkness, bluer than the blackness, growing luminous with the rising of a half-moon. One of the horses stirred into motion, led towards that paler interstice.

There was a short, sharp cry, so soft and desolate that the air ached with it. The opened half-door slammed to again, and Rannilt heard hasty hands fumbling with heavy bars, hoisting and dropping them into solid sockets. Two such beams guarding the door had the force and assurance of a fortress.

'What is it?' Susanna's voice pealed sharply out of the dusk within. She was holding the bridle, the abrupt halt made the horse stamp and snort.

'Men, a good number, coming down from the headland! There are horses, led behind! They're coming here — they know!'

'They cannot know!' she cried.

'They do know. They're spreading, to ring us round, I saw the ranks part. Get up the ladder! Take her with you. She may be worth all to us yet. What else,' he cried, suddenly raging, 'have we between ourselves and the judgement?'

Rannilt, bewildered and frightened, stood trembling in the darkness, stunned by the confusing turmoil of hooves stamping round her, and bodies in violent, blind motion, warm stable smells eddying on the air and pricking her nostrils as the stirrings of terror prickled her skin. The doors were barred, and Iestyn between her and that way out, even if she could have lifted the beams. And still she could not believe, could not take in what was happening to her, or relate these two desperate people with the Susanna and the Iestyn she had known. When a hand gripped her wrist and tugged her towards the rear corner of the stable, she went helplessly with the urgent compulsion. What else could she do? Her ankle struck against the lowest rung of a ladder, the hand dragged her upwards. Fumbling and panting, she went where she was hauled, and was tossed face-down into a pile of hay that enveloped her in dust and dry sweetness. Dimly she was aware of punctures of sky shining through the hay, distinguishably paler in the timber darkness before her, where whoever built this stable and loft had placed a ventilation lattice to air his store.

Somewhere behind her, at the door end of the loft, a larger square of sky looked in, the hatch by which the hay harvest was forked in here for storage, high above the barred doors below. She heard the rungs of the ladder creak at Iestyn's weight as he climbed in haste, and ran to fling himself on his knees beside that outlet, to watch his enemies close about his refuge. She heard, and suddenly was able to comprehend what she heard. The thud of fists hammering on the barred doors, the challenge of the law without.

'Open and come forth, or we'll hack you out with axes. We know you there within and know what you have to answer for!'

Not a voice she knew, for an eager sergeant had outrun his lord and his fellows when he heard the bars slam home, and had come well first to the doors. But she knew the import of what he bellowed to the night, and understood fully at last into what peril she had been brought.

'Stand back!' Iestyn's voice rang loud and hard. 'Or answer to God for a life, you also! Well away from those doors, and don't venture back, for I see you clearly. And I'll speak no more with you, underling, but only with your master. Tell him I have a girl here between my hands, and a knife at my belt, and so sure as axe strikes at these timbers, my knife slits her throat. Now bring me here someone with whom I can parley.'

There was a sharp command without and then silence. Rannilt drew herself back as far as she dared into the remaining store of hay, towards the faint pattern of stars. Between here and the head of the ladder by which she had climbed there was a silent, motionless presence which she knew for Susanna, on guard over her lover's only weapon.

'What did I ever do to you?' said Rannilt, without rancour or hope.

'You fell foul,' said Susanna, with unblaming bitterness. 'Your misfortune and ours.'

'And will you truly kill me?' She asked it in pure wonder, even her terror momentarily forgotten.

'If we must.'

'But dead,' said Rannilt, in a moment of desperately clear vision putting her finger on the one disastrous weakness in the holding of hostages, 'I am of no more use to you. It's only *living* that I can get you what you want. If you kill me you've lost everything. And you don't *want* to kill me, what pleasure would that be to you? Why, *I'm no use to you at all!*'

'If I must pull the roof down upon myself,' said Susanna with cold ferocity, 'I'll pull it down also upon as many of the innocent as I can contrive to crush with me and not go alone into the ark.'

# Thirteen

*Friday night to Saturday morning*

HUGH HAD HALTED HIS MEN INSTANTLY AT IESTYN'S CHAL-
lenge, drawn back those who had reached the stable doors,
and enjoined silence, which is more unnerving than violent
assault or loud outcry. Moving men could be detected, stillness made them only dubiously visible. The rising ground to
the headland bore several small clumps of trees and a hedge
of bushes, cover enough for men to make their way halfway
round the stable, and the rest of the circle they closed at a
greater distance, completing a ring all round the building.
The sergeant came back from his survey, shadowy from tree
to tree down the slope to the meadow, to report the stable
surrounded.

'There's no other way out, unless he has the means to hew
a way through a wall, and small good that would do him.
And if he boasts of a knife, I take it he has no other weapon.
What would a common workman carry but his knife for all
purposes?'

'And we have archers,' mused Hugh, 'if they have no
light to show them a target as yet. Wait — nothing in haste!

If we have them securely, it's we who can afford to wait, not they. No need to drive them to madness.'

'But they have Rannilt in there — they're threatening her life,' whispered Liliwin, quivering at Brother Cadfael's shoulder.

'They're offering to spend her for their own ends,' said Hugh, 'therefore all the more they'll keep her safe to bargain with, short of the last despair, and I'll take good care not to drive them over the edge. Keep still a while, and let's see if we can tire them out or talk them out. But you, Alcher, find yourself the best place in cover to command that hatch above the doors, and keep it in your eye and a shaft always ready, in case of the worst. I'll try to hold the fellow there in the frame for you.' The loading door where Iestyn kneeled to watch them was no more than a faint shape darker still in the dark timber wall and the deep-blue light, but like the doors it faced due east, and the first pre-dawn light, however many hours away yet, would find it early. 'No shooting unless I bid. Let's see what patience can do.'

He went forward alone, fixing the square of darkness with intent eyes, and stood some twenty paces distant from the stable. Behind him in the bushes Liliwin held his breath, and Brother Cadfael felt the boy's slight body quivering and taut, like a leashed hound, and laid a cautioning hand on his arm in case he slipped his leash and went baying after his quarry. But he need not have feared. Liliwin turned a white face and nodded him stiff reassurance. 'I know. I trust him, I must. He knows his business.'

At their backs, unable to be still, Walter Aurifaber sidled and writhed about the tree that sheltered him, biting his nails and agonising over his losses, and saying never a word to any but himself, and that in a soft, whining undertone that was half malediction and half prayer. At least all was not yet lost. The malefactors had not escaped, and could not and must not break loose now and run for it westward.

'Iestyn!' called Hugh, gazing steadily upward. 'Here am

I, Hugh Beringar, the sheriff's deputy. You know me, you know why I am here, you best know I am about what it is my duty to do. My men are all round you, you have no way of escape. Be wise, come down from there and give yourself — yourselves — into my hands, without more damage and worse offence, and look for what mercy such good sense can buy you. It's your best course. You must know it and take heed.'

'No!' said Iestyn's voice harshly. 'We have not come so far to go tamely to judgement now. I tell you, we have the girl, Rannilt, here within. If any man of yours comes too near these doors, I swear I will kill her. Bid them keep back. That's my first word.'

'Do you see any man but myself moving within fifty paces of your doors?' Hugh's voice was calm, equable and clear. 'You have, then, a girl at your mercy. What then? With her you have no quarrel. What can you gain by harming her but a hotter place in hell? If you could reach my throat, I grant you it might possibly avail you, but it can neither help you nor give you satisfaction to slit hers. Nor does it suit with what has been known of you heretofore. You have no blood-guilt on your hands thus far, why soil them now?'

'You may talk sweet reason from where you stand,' cried Iestyn bitterly, 'but we have all to lose, and see no let to making use of what weapons we have. And I tell you, if you press me, I will kill her, and if then you break in here after me by force, I will kill and kill as many as I can before the end. But if you mean such soft, wise talk, yes, you may have the girl, safe and sound — at a price!'

'Name your price,' said Hugh.

'A life for a life is fair. Rannilt's life for my woman's. Let my woman go free from here, with her horse and goods and gear and all that is hers, unpursued, and I will send out the girl to you unharmed.'

'And you would take my word there should be no pursuit?' Hugh pressed, angling after at least a small advantage.

'You're known for a man of your word.'

Two voices had let out sharp gasps at the mention of such terms, and two voices cried out: 'No!' in the same breath. Walter, frantic for his gold and silver, darted out a few steps towards where Hugh stood, until Cadfael caught him by the arm and plucked him back. He wriggled and babbled indignantly: 'No, no such infamous bargain! *Her* goods and gear? Mine, not hers, stolen from me. You cannot strike such a bargain. Is the slut to make off into Wales with her ill-gotten gains? Never! I won't have it!'

There was a shadowy flurry of movement in the hatch above, and Susanna's voice pealed sharply: 'What, have you my loving father there? He wants his money, and my neck wrung, like that of any other who dared lay hands on his money. Poor judgement in you, if you expected *him* to be willing to pay out a penny to save a servant-girl's life, or a daughter's either. Never fear, my fond father, I say no just as loudly as you. I will not accept such a bargain. Even in peril of death I would not go one step away from my man here. You hear that? My man, my lover, the father of my child! But on terms I'll part from him, yes! Let Iestyn take the horse, and go back unmolested into his own country, and I'll go freely, to my death or my wretched life, whichever falls on me. *I* am the one you want. Not he. I *have* killed, I tell you so open . . .'

'She's lying,' cried Iestyn hoarsely. 'I am the guilty man. Whatever she did she did only for me . . .'

'Hush, love, they know better! They know which of us two planned and acted. Me they may do as they like with — you they shall not have!'

'Oh, fool girl, my dearest, do you think I would leave you? Not for all the world's treasures . . .'

Those below were forgotten in this wild contention above. Nothing was to be seen but the agitated tremor of certain pallors within the dark frame, that might have been faces and hands, faces pressed despairingly cheek to cheek, hands embracing and caressing. Next moment Iestyn's voice lifted sharply: 'Stop her! Quickly, stir! Mind your fawn!' And the shadowy embrace broke apart, and a faint, frustrated cry from deep within made Liliwin shiver and start against Cadfael's arm.

'That was Rannilt. Oh, God, if I could but reach her . . .' But he spoke only in a whisper, aware of a tension that ought not to be broken, that was spun out here like the threatened thread of Rannilt's young life, and his own hope of happiness. His desperation and pain was something he must bear, and keep silent.

'Since she cries out,' whispered Cadfael firmly into his ear, 'she is alive. Since she made a bid to slip away out of reach while they were beset, she is unharmed and unbound. Keep that in mind.'

'Yes, true! And they don't, they can't hate her or want to harm her . . .' But still he heard the extreme anger and pain of those two voices crying defiance, and knew, as Cadfael knew, that two so driven might do terrible things even against their own natures. More, he understood their suffering, and was wrung with it as though it matched his own.

'No comfort for you,' shouted Iestyn from his lair. 'We have her still. Now I offer you another choice. Take back the girl and the gold and silver, give us the two horses and this night free of pursuit, together.'

Walter Aurifaber broke free with a whimper of half-eager, half-doubtful hope and approval, and darted some yards into the open. 'My lord! My lord, that might be acceptable. If they restore my treasury . . .' Even his lawful revenge did not count for much by comparison.

'There is a life they cannot restore,' said Hugh curtly, and motioned him back so sternly that the goldsmith recoiled, chastened.

'Are you listening, Iestyn?' called Hugh, raising his eyes once again to the dark hatch. 'You mistake my office. I stand here for the king's law. I am willing to stand here all night long. Take thought again, and better, and come down with unbloodied hands. There is no better thing you can do.'

'I am here. I am listening. I have not changed,' Iestyn responded grimly from above. 'If you want my woman and me, come and fetch us forth, and fetch away first this little carcase — *your* prey, not ours.'

'Have I raised a hand?' said Hugh reasonably. 'Or loosened my sword in the scabbard? You see me, clearer than I can see you. We have the night before us. Whenever you have ought to say, speak up, I shall be here.'

The night dragged with fearful slowness over besiegers and besieged, for the most part in mourn silence, though if silence continued too long Hugh would deliberately break it, to test whether Iestyn remained awake and watchful, though with care not to alarm him, for fear he should be driven to panic action in expectation of an attack. There was no remedy but to outwait and outendure the enemy. In all likelihood they had very little food or water with them. They could as easily be deprived of rest. Even in such tactics there was the danger of sudden and utter despair, which might bring on a massacre, but if all was done very gradually and softly that might yet be avoided. Weariness has sometimes broken down spirits braced implacably to defy torture, and inaction sucked away all the resolution armed for action.

'Try if you can do better,' said Hugh softly to Cadfael, some time well past midnight. 'They cannot know you're here, not yet, you may find a chink in their mail that's proof against me.'

In those small hours when the heart is low, the least surprise may prick home as it could not do by day, in the noon of the body's vigour. Cadfael's very voice, deeper and rougher than Hugh's, startled Iestyn into leaning out from his watch-tower for one incautious stare at this new visitant.

'Who's that? What trick are you playing now?'

'No trick, Iestyn. I am Brother Cadfael of the abbey, who

came sometimes to the house with medicines. You know me, I dare not say well enough to trust me. Let me speak with Susanna, who knows me better.'

He had thought that she might refuse either to speak or to hear him. When she had set her mind upon one course, she might well be stone to any who sought to divert her or stand in her way. But she did come to the hatch, and she did listen. At least that was a further respite. Those two lovers changed places in the loft. Cadfael felt them pass, and now they passed without touching or caressing, for there was no need. They were two halves of one whole, living or dead. One of them, it was clear from the earlier outcry, must keep an eye on their prisoner. They could not bind her, then, or else they had not thought it needful. Perhaps they had not the means. They were trapped in the instant of flight. Was it unpardonable to wish they had ridden away half an hour earlier?

'Susanna, it is not too late to make restitution. I know your wrongs, my voice shall speak for you. But murder is murder. Never think there is any escape. Though you elude the judgement here, there is another you cannot avoid. Better far to make what amends can be made and be at peace.'

'What peace?' she said, bitter and chill. 'There is none for me. I am a stunted tree, denied the ground to grow, and now, when I am in fruit, in despite of this world, do you think I will abate one particle of my hate or love? Leave me be, Brother Cadfael,' she said more gently. 'Your concern is with my soul, mine is all with my body, the only heaven I've ever known or ever hope to know.'

'Come down and bring Iestyn with you,' said Cadfael simply, 'and I take it upon myself to promise you, as I must answer to God, that your child and his shall be born and cared for as befits every human soul brought innocent into the world. I will invoke the lord abbot to ensure it.'

She laughed. It was a fresh, wild and yet desolate sound. 'This is not Holy Church's child, Brother Cadfael. It belongs to me, and to Iestyn my man, and there is none other shall ever cradle or care for it. Yet I do thank you for your good will to my son. And after all,' she said, with bitter derision in her voice, 'how do we know the creature would ever be brought forth living and whole? I am old, Brother Cadfael, old for childbirth. The thing may be dead before me.'

'Make the assay,' said Cadfael stoutly. 'He is not wholly yours, he is his own, your maybe child. Do him justice! Why should he pay for your sins? It was not he trampled Baldwin Peche into the gravel of Severn.'

She made a dreadful, muted sound, as if she had choked upon her own rage and grief, and then she was calm and resolved again, and immovable. 'Three are here together and made one,' she said, 'the only trinity I acknowledge now. No fourth has any part in us. What do we owe to any man living?'

'You forget there is a fourth,' said Cadfael strongly, 'and you are making shameful use of her. One who is none of yours and has never done you wrong. She also loves — I think you know it. Why destroy another pair as little blessed as you?'

'Why not?' said Susanna. 'I am all destruction. What else is left to me now?'

Cadfael persisted, but after a while, talking away doggedly there past the mid of the night, he knew that she had risen and left him, unconvinced, unreconciled, and that it was Iestyn who now leaned in the hatch. He waited a considering while, and then took up his pleading for this perhaps more vulnerable ear. A Welshman, less aggrieved than the woman, for all his hardships; and all Welsh are kin, even if they slit one another's throats now and then, and manure their sparse and stony fields with fratricidal dead in tribal wars. But he knew he had little hope. He had already spoken with the domina of that pair. There was no appeal to this one now that she could not wipe out with a gesture of her hand.

He was eased, if not verily glad, when Hugh came back to relieve him of his watch.

He sat slack and discouraged in the spring grass under the hedge of bushes, and Liliwin came plucking softly but urgently at his sleeve. 'Brother Cadfael, come with me! Come!' The whisper was excited and hopeful, where hope was in no very lavish supply.

'What is it? Come with you where?'

'He said there's no other way out,' whispered Liliwin, tugging at the sleeve he held, 'and by that token none in, but there is . . . there could be. Come and see!'

Cadfael went where he was led, up through the bushes on the headland, and along the slope in cover, just below the level of the stable roof and at no great distance from it, to the western end of the building. The timbers of the roof projected above the low gable, the fellow to the eastern one in which Iestyn crouched on watch. 'See there — the starlight shows dappling. They let in a lattice there for air.'

Peering narrowly, Cadfael could just discern a square shape that might well be what Liliwin described, but measured barely the span of hand and forearm either way, as close as he could estimate. The interstices between the slats, which the straining eye could either discern or imagine for a moment, only to lose them again, were surely too small even to admit a fist. Nor was there any way of reaching them, short of a ladder or the light weight and claws of a cat, even though the timbers of the wall below were rough and uneven.

'That?' breathed Cadfael, aghast. 'Child, a spider might get up there and get in, but scarcely a man.'

'Ah, but I've been down there, I know. There are toe-holds enough. And I think one of the slats is hanging loose already, and there'll be others ready to give way. If a man could get in there, while you hold them busy at the other end . . . She is up there, I know it! You heard, when they ran to hold her, how far it was to run.'

It was true. Moreover, if she had any choice she would be huddled as far away from her captors as she could get.

'But, boy, even if you stripped away two or three of the boards — could you do more, unheard? I doubt it! There's not a man among us could get through that keyhole to her. No, not if you had time to strip the whole square.'

'Yes, *I can!* You forget,' whispered Liliwin eagerly, 'I'm small and light and I'm an acrobat, bred to it from three or four years old. It's my craft. I *can* reach her. Where a cat can go I can go. And she's even smaller than I, though she may not be trained as a tumbler. If I had a rope, I could make it fast there, and take my time opening up the way for her. Oh, surely, surely it's worth the attempt! We've no other way. And I *can* do it, and I *will!*'

'Wait!' said Cadfael. 'Sit you here in cover, and I'll go broach it to Hugh Beringar and get you your rope, and make ready to hold them fast in talk, as far as may be away from you. Not a word, not a movement until I come back.'

'No madder than whatever else we may do to break this dam,' said Hugh when he had listened and considered. 'If you put some trust in it, I'll go with you. Can he really creep in there, do you think? Is it possible?'

'I've seen him tie himself in a knot a serpent might be proud of,' said Cadfael, 'and if he says there's room enough there for him to pass, I say he's the better judge of that than I. It's his profession, he takes pride in it. Yes, I put my trust in him.'

'We'll send to fetch him his rope, and a chisel, too, to pry loose the slats, but he must wait for them. We'll make good certain they stay wakeful and watchful at this end, and try a feint or two, if need be, short of driving them to panic. And let him take his time, for I think we might be advised to wait for the first light, to give Alcher a clear view of that hatch and whatever body fills it, and a shaft fitted and aimed in case of need. If we must let a decent poor lad risk his life, at least we'll stand ready with all the cover we can give him.'

'I had rather,' said Cadfael sadly, 'there should be no killing at all.'

'So would I,' agreed Hugh grimly, 'but if there must be, rather the guilty than the innocent.'

The dawn was still more than an hour and a half away when they brought the rope Liliwin needed, but already the eastern sky had changed, turned from deepest blue to paler blue-green, and a faint line of green paler still outlined the curves of the fields behind them, and the towered hill of the town.

'Rather round my waist than my neck,' whispered Liliwin hardily, as Cadfael fastened the rope about him among the bushes.

'There, I see you have the true spirit in you. God keep you, the pair of you! But can she come down the rope, even if you reach her? Girls are not such acrobats as you.'

'I can guide her. She's so light and small, she can hold by the rope and walk backwards down the wall . . . Only keep them busy there at the far end.'

'But go slowly and quietly, no haste,' cautioned Cadfael, anxious as for a son going into battle. 'I shall be running messenger between. And daylight will be on our side, not on theirs.'

Liliwin kicked off his shoes. He had holes in the toes of both feet of his hose, Cadfael saw. Perhaps none the worse for this enterprise, but when he came to be sent out into the world — God so willing, as surely God must — he must go better provided.

The boy slid silently down from the headland to the foot of the stable wall, felt with stretched arms above his head, found grips a heavier man would never have considered, set a toe to a first hold, and drew himself up like a squirrel on to the timbers.

Cadfael waited and watched until he had seen the rope slipped through the firmest boards of the lattice and made fast, and the first rotten slat prised free, slowly and carefully, and let fall silently at arm's-length into the thick grass below. More than half an hour had passed by then. From time to time he caught the sound of voices in weary but alert exchanges to eastward. The criss-cross of boards at the air-vent showed perceptibly now. The removal of one board had uncovered a space big enough to let a cat in and out, but surely nothing larger or less agile. The vault of the sky lightened very gradually before there was any visible source of light.

Liliwin worked with a bight of the tethered rope fast round him, and half-naked toes braced into the timbers of the wall. He had begun patiently prising loose the second slat, when Cadfael made his way back in cover to report what he knew.

'God knows it looks impossible, but the lad knows his business, and if he is sure he can pass, as a cat knows by its whiskers, then I take his word for it. But for God's sake keep this parley alive.'

'Take it over for me,' said Hugh, drawing back with eyes still fixed on the hatch. 'Only some few moments . . . A fresh voice causes them to prick their ears afresh.'

Cadfael took up the vain pleas he had used before. The voice that answered him was hoarse with weariness, but still defiant.

'We shall not go from here,' said Cadfael, roused out of his own weariness by a double anxiety, 'until all these troubled here, body and soul, have freedom and quiet, whether in this world or another. And who so prevents to the last, on him the judgement fall! Nevertheless, God's mercy is infinite to those who seek it, however late, how ever feebly.'

'The light will not be long,' Hugh was saying at that same moment to Alcher, who was the finest marksman in the castle garrison, and had long since chosen his ground with the dawn in view, and found no reason to change it. 'Be ready, the instant I shall call, to put an arrow clean into that hatch, and through whoever lurks there. But no shooting unless I do call. And pray God I am not forced to it.'

'That's understood,' said Alcher, nursing his strung bow

and fitted shaft, and never shifting his eyes from their aim, dead-centre of the dark opening, now growing clearly visible above the stable doors.

When Cadfael again made his way along the headland, the lattice was a lattice no longer, but a small square opening under the eaves, and the dislodged slats lay cushioned in the thick grass below. Liliwin had one arm stretched within, to ease aside the hay cautiously, with as little sound as possible, and make room to creep within. Now if only Rannilt could keep from starting or crying out when she found herself approached thus from behind! It was high time to make as much and as menacing ado before the stable doors as possible. Yet Cadfael could not help standing with held breath to watch, until Liliwin slid head and shoulders through the space that seemed barely passable even for his slenderness, and drew the rest of himself after in one coiling, rapid movement, vanishing in a smooth somersault, and without a sound.

Cadfael made his way back in haste to a point still out of sight from the hatch, and signalled urgently to Hugh that the time of greatest danger was come. Alcher saw the waving arm before Hugh did, and drew his bow halfway to the ear, narrowing his eyes upon the moving blurs of drab brown coat and paler face that showed as his target. Behind him the sun was just showing a rim over the horizon, and its first ray gleamed along the ridge of the roof. In a quarter of an hour it would be high enough for the light to reach the hatch, and the shot would be an easy matter.

'Iestyn,' called Hugh sharply, mustering those of his men nearest him into plain sight, though not too near to the doors, 'you have had a night's grace to consider, now show decent sense, and come forth of your own will, for you see you cannot escape us, and you are mortal like others, and must eat to live. You are not in sanctuary there, there are no forty days of respite for you.'

'There's nothing but a halter for us,' shouted Iestyn savagely, 'and well we know it. But if that's our end, I swear to

204

you the girl shall go before us, and her blood be on your head.'

'So you say, big talk from a small man! Your woman may not be so ready either to kill or to die. Have you asked her? Or have you the only voice in the matter? Here, master gold-smith,' called Hugh, beckoning, 'come and speak to your daughter. However late in the day, she may still listen to you.'

He was bidding to sting her, to bring them both flying to the hatch to spit their joint defiance and leave their prisoner unwatched. But oh, not too fast, not too fast, prayed Cad-fael, gnawing his knuckles on the headland. The boy needs a few more minutes yet . . .

Liliwin tunnelled stealthily through the stored hay, as much in terror of sneezing, as the odorous dust tickled his nostrils, as he was of making too audible a rustling and betraying himself all too soon. Somewhere before him, very close now, he could hear the faint stirrings Rannilt made in her nest, and prayed that they would cover whatever sound he was making. After a while, pausing to peer through the thinning screen, he caught the shape of her shrinking shoul-ders and head against the dim morning light. Carefully he enlarged the passage he had hollowed out, so that he might have room to draw to one side of her, and have her creep past him, to come first to the frame of the lattice. Iestyn was leaning out at the far end of the loft, shouting angry curses now at those without, threatening still but not looking this way.

There was a woman to fear, for wherever she was now, she was silent. But surely if those without were pressing, half at least of her care must be with her lover. And here in the loft it was still blessedly dark.

His hand, probing delicately ahead, found and touched Rannilt's bare forearm. She flinched sharply, but made no sound at all, and in a moment he slid his hand down to find hers, and clung. Then she knew. All he heard was a faint, long sigh, and her fingers closed on his. He drew her gently, and by slow inches she shifted and drew nearer, into the cavity he opened for her. She was beside him, the fragile screen of hay hiding him and already half shielding her, and still no outcry. He urged her on past him with the pressure of his hand, to come first to the lattice and the rope as he covered her going. Outside the stable doors the circling voices were raised and peremptory, and Iestyn, wild with weariness and anger, roared back at them incoherent defiance. Then, blessedly, Susanna's voice, surely close there at her lover's shoulder, soared above the clamour:

'Fools, do you think there's any power can separate us now? I hold as Iestyn holds, I despise your promises and your threats as he does. Bring my father to plead with me, would you? Let him hear, then, what I owe him, and what I wish him. Of all men on earth, I hate him! As he has made me of no worth, so I set no value on him. Dare he say I am no longer his daughter? He is no longer my father, he never was a father to me. May he be fed molten gold in hell until belly and throat burn to furnace ashes . . .'

Under the fury of that raging voice, clear and steely as a sword, Liliwin hustled Rannilt past him and thrust her bodily through his dusty tunnel towards the lattice and the rope, all caution cast to the winds, for if this moment escaped them, there might be no other.

It was Iestyn's quick ear that caught, even through Susanna's malediction, the sudden frenzied rustling of hay. He swung round with a great cry of rage at what he saw, and lunged away to prevent it. The first ray of light entering caught the flash of the naked knife.

Hugh was quick to understand and act. 'Shoot!' he cried, and Alcher, who had that first finger of sunlight now bright on Iestyn's body, loosed his shaft. Meant for the breast, it would have been no less mortal in the back, if Susanna, for all her bitter passion, had not taken in all these signs in one breath. She uttered a shriek rather of rage than fear, and flung herself into the opening of the hatch, arms spread and braced to ward off her lover's death.

At the first cry Liliwin had thrust Rannilt towards the way of escape, and sprung erect out of the hay to put his own slight body between her and harm. Iestyn bore down on him, the brandished dagger caught the levelled ray of sun and sent splinters of light dancing about the roof. The blade hung over Liliwin's heart when Susanna's shriek caused Iestyn to baulk and shudder where he stood, straining backwards like a horse suddenly reined in, and the point of the knife slid wildly down, slicing along the boy's parrying forearm, and drawing a fine spray of blood into the hay.

She was melting, she was dissolving into herself, as a man of snow folds into himself gradually when the thaw comes. The impact of the arrow, striking full into her left breast, had spun her round, she sank slowly with her hands clutching the shaft where it had pierced her, and her eyes fixed, huge and clouded, upon Iestyn, for whom the death had been intended. Liliwin, dazedly watching as the man sprang back to clasp her, said afterwards that she was smiling. But his recollections were confused and wild, what he chiefly recalled was a terrible howl of grief and despair that filled and echoed through the loft. The knife was flung aside, and struck quivering in the boards of the floor. Iestyn embraced his love, moaning, and sank with her in his arms. Round the fearful barrier of the arrow she essayed to lift her failing arms to clasp him. Their kiss was a contortion the trained contortionist in Liliwin remembered lifelong with pity and pain.

Liliwin came to himself soon, because he must. He drew Rannilt up by the hand, away from the lattice of which they had no more need, and coaxed her after him down the ladder to the stable floor where the loaded horses stamped and shifted uneasily after all these nightlong alarms. He hoisted the heavy bars that held the doors, and it took all the strength he had left to lift them. The eastern light reached his face but no lower, as he pushed open both heavy doors, and led Rannilt out into the green meadow.

They were aware of men flowing in as they came gladly

out. Their part was done. Brother Cadfael, breathing prayers of gratitude, took them both in his arms, and swept them aside to a grassy knoll at the foot of the headland, where they dropped together thankfully into the spring turf, and drew in the May air and the morning light, and gradually turned and stared and smiled, like creatures in a dream, waking to be glad of each other.

Hugh was first up the ladder and into the loft, the sergeant hard on his heels. In the shaft of sunlight, bolder and broader now, and blindingly bright above the lingering dimness of the hay-strewn floor, Iestyn knelt with Susanna in his arms, tenderly holding her up from the boards, for the shaft had pierced clean through her, and jutted at her shoulder. Her eyes were already filmed over as though with sleep, but still kept their fixed regard upon her lover's face, a mask of grief and despair. When the sergeant made to lay a hand on Iestyn's shoulder, Hugh waved him away.

'Let him alone,' he said quietly, 'he will not run.' There was no future left to run for, nowhere to run to, no one to run with. Everything he cared for was in his arms, and would not be with him long.

Her blood was on his hands, on the lips and cheek that had caressed her frantically for a moment, as though caresses could make all whole again. He had given over that now, he only crouched and clasped her, and watched her lips trying to form words to take all upon herself, and deliver him, but making no sound, and presently ceasing to attempt it. He saw the light go out behind the glassy grey of her eyes.

Not until then did Hugh touch him. 'She is gone, Iestyn. Lay her down now and come with us. I promise you she shall be brought home decently.'

Iestyn laid her in the piled hay, and got to his feet slowly. The climbing sun fingered the knotted binding of the one bundle they had brought up here with them. His dulled eyes fell upon it, and flamed. He plucked it from the floor, and hurled it out through the hatch, to burst asunder in the grass of the meadow, scattering its contents in a shower of sparks as the level beams crept across the pasture.

A great howl of desolation and loss welled up out of Iestyn's throat to bay at the cloudless and untroubled sky:

'And I would have taken her barefoot in her shift!'

Outside in the pasture another aggrieved wail arose like an echo, as Walter Aurifaber grovelled in the grass on his hands and knees, frantically clawing up from among the tussocks his despised gold and silver.

# Fourteen

*Afterwards*

THEY TOOK BACK THE LIVING AND THE DEAD ALIKE INTO
Shrewsbury in the radiant, slanting light of morning. Iestyn,
mute now and indifferent to his fate, to a lodging in the castle; Susanna, safe from any penalty in this world, to the de-
peopled household from which three generations together
would shortly be carried to the grave. Walter Aurifaber followed dazedly, hugging his recovered wealth, and regarding
his daughter's body with a faint frown of bewilderment, as
though, tugged between his loss and his gain, he could not
yet determine what he should be feeling. For after all, she
had robbed him and vilified him at the end, and if he had
been deprived of a competent housekeeper, that was his sole
serious loss, and there was another woman at home now to
take her place. And with Daniel surely maturing and taking
a pride in his own craftsmanship, he might very well manage without having to pay a journeyman. Whatever conflict
disrupted Walter would soon be resolved in favour of satisfaction.

As for the two delivered lovers, bereft of words, unable to
unlock eyes or hands, Cadfael took them in charge and,

mindful of the proprieties, of Prior Robert's chaste disapproval and Abbot Radulfus' shrewd regard for the ordered peace of the rule, thought well to speak a word in Hugh's ear and enlist the ready sympathy of Hugh's lady. Aline welcomed Rannilt into her care with delight, and undertook to provide and instruct her in everything a bride should possess and know, to feed her plump and rosy, and coax into full light those beauties in her which hitherto had gone veiled and unregarded.

'For if you intend to take her away with you,' said Cadfael, propelling the half-reluctant Liliwin back over the bridge towards the abbey gatehouse, 'you'd best marry her here, where there'll be shame-faced folk enough anxious to set you up with small favours, to pay for their misuse of you earlier. No need to despise the gifts of this world when they come honestly. And you'll be doing the givers a kindness, they'll have made their peace with their consciences. You come back to us, and don't grudge a week's waiting to make ready for your marriage. You could hardly bring your girl back to share your bed in the porch.' Or behind an altar, he thought but did not say. 'She'll be safe there with Hugh's lady, and come to you with every man's good will.'

Cadfael was right. Shrewsbury had a bad conscience about Liliwin, as soon as word of the scandalous truth was being passed round over market-stalls and shop counters and traded along the streets. All those who had been too hasty in hunting him took care to proffer small favours by way of redress. The provost, who had taken no part, noted the sad state of the young man's only pair of shoes, and set an example by making him a fine new pair in which to resume his travels. Other members of the guild merchant took the hint. The tailors combined to clothe him decently. He bade fair to emerge better provided than ever before in his life.

But the best gift of all came from Brother Anselm.

'Well, since you won't stay and be celibate here among us,' said the precentor cheerfully, 'here is your own rebec ready for playing, and a good leather bag to carry it in. I'm pleased with my work, it came out better than I dared hope, and you'll find it still has a very sweet voice, after all its misadventures.' And he added sternly, while Liliwin embraced his recovered treasure with a joy far more profound than if it had been gold and silver: 'Now bear in mind what you've learned here concerning the reading and writing of music. Never lose your skills. Let me not be ashamed of my pupil when you come this way and visit us again.'

And Liliwin poured out fervent thanks, and promises he might never be able to keep, though he meant them with all his heart.

They were married at the parish altar, where Liliwin had first taken refuge, by Father Adam, priest of the Foregate parish, in the presence of Hugh and Aline Beringar, Brother Cadfael, Brother Oswin, Brother Anselm, and several more of the brothers who felt a sympathetic interest in their departing guest. Abbot Radulfus himself gave them his blessing.

Afterwards, when they had packed up their wedding clothes and put on the everyday homespun in which they meant to set out together, they sought out Hugh Beringar, who was sitting with Brother Cadfael in the ante-chamber of the guest-hall.

'We should be off soon,' said Liliwin, speaking for both, 'to get the best of the day on the road to Lichfield. But we wanted to ask, before we go . . . His trial must be weeks away, we might never hear. He won't hang, will he?'

So little they had, those two, even if it was more than ever they had possessed before, and yet they had so much that they could afford pity. 'You don't want him to hang?' said Hugh. 'He would have killed you, Rannilt. Or do you not believe that, now it's all past?'

'Yes,' she said simply, 'I do believe it. I think he would have done it. I know she would. But I don't want his death. I never wanted hers. He won't hang, will he?'

'Not if my voice is heard. Whatever he may have done, he did not kill, and all that he stole has been restored. Whatever he did was done at her wish. I think you may set out with quiet minds,' said Hugh gently. 'He'll live. He's younger than she. He may yet take another, even if it must be a second-best.'

For whatever else might be called in question about those two unhappy sinners, Rannilt had been a witness to the devoted and desperate love between them.

'He may end as a decent craftsman, settled with wife and children,' said Hugh. Children who would be born in peace, not buried still in the womb, like Susanna's child. Three months gone, was the physician's estimate. Even if she had not seized the opportunity of her brother's wedding feast, she would have had to make her bid for freedom very soon.

'He would have given himself up for her sake,' said Liliwin seriously, 'and so would she for him. And she did die for him. I saw. We both saw. She knew what she did. Surely that must count?'

So it might, and so, surely, must the pity and prayers of two young creatures so misused and so magnanimous. Who should more certainly prevail?

'Come,' said Brother Cadfael, 'we'll bring you through the gate and see you on your way. And God go with you!'

And forth they went, hopefully and happily, the new leather bag slung proudly on Liliwin's shoulder. To a life that could never be less than hard and insecure, he the wandering entertainer at fairs and markets and small manors, she, no doubt, soon just as adept with that pure, small voice of hers, and a dance or two to her husband's playing. In all weathers, at all seasons, but with luck finding a decent patron for the winter, and a good fire. And at the very worst, together.

'Do you truly believe,' asked Cadfael, when the two little figures had vanished along the Foregate, 'that Iestyn also may have a life before him?'

'If he can make the effort. No one is going to press for his death. He is coming back to life, not willingly, but because he must. There is a vigour in him he can't shift all on to the past. It will be a minor love, but he'll marry and breed yet.'

'And forget her?'

'Have I said so?' said Hugh, and smiled.

'Whatever she did of worst,' said Cadfael soberly, 'came of that in her that might have been best, if it had not been maimed. She was much wronged.'

'Old friend,' said Hugh, shaking his head with rueful affection, 'I doubt if even you can get Susanna into the fold among the lambs. She chose her way, and it's taken her far out of reach of man's mercy, if ever she'd lived to face trial. And now, I suppose,' he said, seeing his friend's face still thoughtful and undismayed, 'you will tell me roundly that God's reach is longer than man's.'

'It had better be,' said Brother Cadfael very solemnly, 'otherwise we are all lost.'

## About the Author

Ellis Peters is a pseudonym for Edith Pargeter, author of many books under her own name. The recipient of the C.W.A. Silver Dagger Award, she is also well known as a translator of poetry and prose from the Czech. Miss Pargeter makes her home in Shropshire, England.